# A MURDER ON THE MOUNTAIN

ELLIE ALEXANDER

Storm
PUBLISHING

This is a work of fiction. Names, characters, businesses, places, events and incidents are either the products of the author's imagination or used in a fictitious manner. Any resemblance to actual persons, living or dead, or actual events is purely coincidental.



Previously published in 2014 as *Scene of the Climb* by Kate Dyer-Seeley by Kensington Publishing Corp.



Ebook ISBN: 978-1-83700-144-6
Paperback ISBN: 978-1-83700-146-0

Cover design: Dawn Adams
Cover images: Dawn Adams

Published by Storm Publishing.
For further information, visit:
www.stormpublishing.co

## ALSO BY ELLIE ALEXANDER

**Meg Reed Investigates**

*A Slaying at the Ski Lodge*

*A Body at the Beach*

*A Body at Boot Camp*

*Revenge on the Rocks*

**A Secret Bookcase Mystery**

*The Body in the Bookstore*

*A Murder at the Movies*

*Death at the Dinner Party*

*A Holiday Homicide*

*A Victim at Valentine's*

*A Body at the Book Fair*

*A Cozy Kind of Christmas*

*Clued in to Love*

*To the OG Meg readers! This one is for you.*

# ONE

## ANGEL'S REST SUMMIT, OREGON

My fingernails dug into the soggy dirt as my body lurched closer to the sheer cliff face. I desperately jabbed deeper into the ground for traction. It didn't work.

I kicked frantically into a boulder on my right, trying to slow my momentum. The trail was disappearing. Fast. A few more feet and I would launch over a ledge, straight down the side of the rock face.

That's when I heard the scream. It took a minute to work out whether the sound was coming from my lungs or somewhere ahead. Definitely ahead.

I skidded over slick, jagged rocks. They jammed into my exposed skin and snagged my paper-thin T-shirt.

Damn, not the shirt.

I'd spent a wad of cash I didn't have on the shirt. When I spotted it on the rack with its pale pink ivy vine design and the words LIVE. LOVE on the front, it spoke to me, as Gam liked to say. It was the perfect blend of Northwest chic—equal parts hippie and hipster.

At that moment I looked up to see a man's body plummet over the ledge.

I should have been concerned that I was losing ground and about to fly off after him. Instead, all I could think about was that I never should have taken that umbrella.

Yep, an umbrella. It all started four months ago with a lousy umbrella.

The winter had been particularly wet. So wet, in fact, that I almost considered following my mom's nagging advice. "Mary Margaret Reed, you need to invest in an umbrella." My mom would never be caught without her Burberry checkered print model.

I, on the other hand, had held a firm belief since childhood that no one should ever use an umbrella. We lived in Portland, Oregon, where it rained 256 days a year. Umbrellas were for tourists and people who lived in the Pearl, the pretentious upscale neighborhood where I'd been crashing on my best friend Jill's couch.

Don't get me wrong; my bestie, Jill Pettygrove, wasn't the least bit pretentious. Her neighborhood was. There was a lengthy waiting list for a coveted spot in Jill's building, with its swanky lofts and shared rooftop garden where they hosted nightly cocktails. Of course, most of these amenities were completely lost on Jill. She much preferred cozy nights in, on her couch with Miss Marple and munchies. Her apartment was furnished with upcycled pieces and eclectic art.

Crashing on her couch wasn't exactly how I planned to launch into the working world after graduating from college last summer, but I didn't have any other options.

Well, that's not entirely true. My dad had offered me the option of moving back to the family farmhouse to keep him company, but the thought of my Pepto-Bismol pink bedroom and Pops's collection of old newspapers stacked in every corner of the dilapidated farmhouse made me pass—a decision I'd regretted daily in the last year. He died in a freak accident not long afterward. I hadn't been back since. The thought of being in the space he so boldly occupied was too much to bear. I was grossly underprepared for his death and still not dealing with it well—if I was even dealing with it at all. Which, frankly, I wasn't. It was better to stuff away the pain and ignore the permanent tightness in my chest that refused to loosen its hold.

Gam, my mystic healer grandmother, had provided me with a soft place to land in the days following his accident and even offered me her spare room. For the record, she most certainly was not the umbrella type. I appreciated the gesture, but I knew if I moved in with her, I'd cramp her style and encroach on her limited space. She'd have to box up her drums, crystals, gems, candles for smudging, and essential oils. Not that she would care. She would have gladly welcomed me with open arms and baked me batches of homemade cookies and banana bread, but staying with Gam would have forced my grief to the surface. There was no hiding from her kind, wise eyes and I wasn't ready for that—not yet.

Jill came to my rescue. She always did. Back in second grade we'd hit it off instantly. We're both only children and quickly bonded over that and found we shared so many common interests—like reading, art, books, and slumber parties in our PJs where we would make up our own choreography and pretend we were starring in music videos.

Alas, I graduated with a degree in journalism, which I quickly realized was not the wisest career choice in today's changing media environment. Since before I could ride a bike, I'd dreamed about writing for *The O*—Oregon's Pulitzer Prize-winning paper. Journalism school prepped us for the harsh reality of today's job market as reporters. I think my advisor's exact words were "Newspapers are dinosaurs."

But somehow I hoped I'd be immune. I loved newspapers and thought I was in with a shot. The investigative work I'd done for our student newspaper had led to an editorship my senior year. Getting a job at *The O* should have been a cakewalk, especially because Pops had been their lead investigative reporter for twenty years. But let's just say he wasn't on the best terms with the editor in chief before he died. That's another story.

Call it an unkind twist of fate or plain crummy luck, my degree arrived crisp in my hand on the same day *The O* announced they were laying off forty reporters. It wasn't just *The O*. Every indie paper in town shuttered its doors. Magazines weren't much better. None were hiring. Most were scaling staff to refocus their efforts on digital media.

No one wanted to hire a recent college grad with no real-world experience.

So I piecemealed together a few freelancing gigs to pay for my meager meals of grilled cheese and tomato soup and thanked Jill daily for her rent-free couch. I perused job postings daily for any glimmer of a writing position. My searches yielded requests for Chinese and Russian translators. Nope and nope. Why hadn't I studied a foreign language in college? My two terms of conversational French weren't any help in the job hunt.

After five gloomy months, I'd given up hope. I plastered my résumé at coffee shops and dive bars. Nothing. If I couldn't find a job (any job) soon, even grilled cheese would be off the menu.

It was an especially soggy January morning when I threw on a pair of pink yoga pants, a long-sleeved T-shirt, my pink and black polka-dotted rain boots, and my coral Columbia rain jacket, and trudged through biting wind and sloppy sidewalks to the coffee shop two blocks from Jill's place.

The windows sweated with steam. Punk music played overhead. A bearded barista in black wire-framed glasses didn't make eye contact as I snuck a look around before placing my order.

"Double mocha. Extra hot," I said, my voice barely more than a whisper. In a town where pour-overs and strong, bitter espressos were king, my creamy, chocolatey order might raise a few eyebrows, but truth be told, I'd order it with extra sprinkles, too, if that were an option.

"Milk?" The barista kept his head down, leafing through an alternative rock magazine.

"Whole." I tried to cough the word out under my breath. "Oh, and extra whip, please."

He raised his eyebrows. "It's your stomach."

I inched my way through the crowd waiting at the other end of the bar for their drinks. Rain leaked from my coat. My yoga pants were plastered to my thighs. Another barista shouted out my drink order. "Mocha with extra whip is up."

Scanning the room to make sure I didn't know anyone, I tried to slink casually to grab my drink. The tile floor was slick and my boots skidded through a wet puddle. I landed on my ass, soaking the only dry area remaining on my body, and nearly knocking over the customer in front of me who had retrieved her drink. A quad-shot Americano, I might add. She shot me a nasty look as her high heels clicked over the wet floor. Before I had a chance to haul myself up, a rough hand reached down and pulled me to my feet.

"You okay?" The voice came from a lanky, impeccably scruffy man. His chestnut hair fell in waves over his right eye and his muscular chest was easily visible in his one-size-too-tight mud marathon T-shirt. He held a dripping salmon-pink umbrella in his left hand.

"Uh, yeah. Thanks," I said, brushing water off my yoga pants.

"I believe this is yours?" the stranger said.

A white paper cup with a mound of whipping cream overflowing from the top sat on the counter. He stretched his free arm out and handed me the cup.

"You might want to lick that before it melts," he chuckled.

I smiled uncomfortably, wishing I had bothered to brush my hair or teeth before leaving Jill's. Then I winked awkwardly, holding the cup in a toast. "Ah, the life of an unemployed writer—sometimes it calls for small pleasures."

I took a taste of the cream and could feel some stick to my nose. Reaching to grab a lid from the counter, I quickly wiped it off and tried squeezing the lid over the top. Whipped cream oozed down the sides of the cup. Even with a staggeringly gorgeous man in front of me (was his skin naturally olive or did he have an actual tan in January?), I couldn't resist licking the melting whipped cream off my index finger.

Pulling my jacket hood over my head, I said, "Well, I'm out. Thanks again." I squeezed around tiny bistro tables as I made my way to the front door. A gust of icy air greeted me outside. I tried to balance my coffee in one hand as I zipped my coat and cinched my hood tighter.

Someone tapped my shoulder.

"You didn't let me finish. I was saying I think this belongs to you," the stranger repeated, thrusting the salmon-pink umbrella at me. A car zoomed by on the street, spraying dirty water in our direction. The stranger stepped backward to avoid the splatter. I stood there dumbfounded.

"Nope. That's definitely not mine." I shook my head.

"But it's pink and"—he paused, eyeing me from head to toe and waving his hand from my hood to my boots—"you're pink."

"Today I am, but I don't own an umbrella. I don't believe in umbrellas."

"How can you not believe in umbrellas?"

What happened next was what Gam attributed to universal karma. The coffee shop door burst open and a man in a business suit exited, brushing past us, struggling to open his ginormous golf umbrella against the wind. The moment it popped open, it caught a gust and instantly blew backward, bending the metal frame and soaking the man.

I smiled and pointed at the businessman making his way down the street with a mangled umbrella. "That's how!"

"Touché." He offered his free hand. "I'm Greg. Nice to meet you, anti-umbrella woman."

"Meg," I replied, shaking it. "Nice to meet you and your pink umbrella."

He moved toward the entrance of the coffee shop and pushed open the door. "Why don't you finish your drink inside with me, where it's warmer?"

Uh, okay. It wasn't every day that an attractive man asked me for a drink.

Greg reminded me of Don Draper from my favorite show, *Mad Men*. He was probably about the same age and his body moved with the same easy swagger. If only I could have transplanted myself back in time. I'd definitely have landed in the *Mad Men* era. I hesitated for a moment before following him into the coffee shop.

Greg pulled another chair to an iron bistro table next to the window and we sat down.

My short blonde hair needed a blow-dry and serious product to make it appear funky and fun. Wet hair was not becoming on me. I could only imagine that it was probably matted to my head and an ugly shade of dishwater brown. Usually I was more put together than this. Why, today of all days, had I left the loft without lip gloss or mascara?

Greg leaned in. "You're a writer?"

I could feel heat rising in my cheeks. "Uh, yeah. I mean, not exactly. Jobs are scarce, you know, but I've been getting by with freelancing."

Greg rested his hand on his chin and paused, staring intently as if considering me. I fidgeted in my seat, breathing in the aroma of fresh-baked banana muffins warming in the oven. God, I'd do anything for a muffin right now.

"What do you write?"

I tugged my wet coat off, wishing I had a lengthy list of publications I could rattle off to impress him. "Nonfiction," I said, wrapping my arms around my chest. "I was the editor of the student newspaper at the University of Oregon. My writing's been published in a few national magazines and a bunch of blogs."

"Hmm." Greg nodded. "So your degree's in what? English? Journalism?"

"Journalism. It's kind of in my blood." I paused for a second before blurting out, "My dad wrote for *The O*."

"Would I know him?"

"Maybe." I swirled my coffee in my cup. "His name was Charlie Reed."

Greg let out a whistle. "The Charlie Reed? As in the Charlie Reed who blew open the meth investigation?"

"Yep."

"Okay, so that tells me you can probably write." He fingered the stubble on his cheeks and watched me swirl my drink. "Sorry to hear about his accident. That must have been rough."

I nodded. I didn't trust myself to respond, as my ribs grew tight, restricting my breath.

He looked at me curiously and then said, "I might be able to help. It happens I'm looking for a junior writer."

He slid a business card across the table. My fingers were sticky from the whipping cream and adhered to the card as I picked it up. The card was grainy, made of recycled paper, and had a silhouette of a man scaling a rock wall. It read, GREG DIXON. EDITOR IN CHIEF, *NORTHWEST EXTREME*.

Damn, he was as lovely in print as in person.

"I'm looking for someone who can write, help with layout,

cover regional climbs and races, that kind of thing. Do you climb or hike much?"

I took a sip of my coffee. The honest answer was no, but this sounded too good an opportunity to turn down. "Well, I mean not lately, but I grew up practically living in the forest with my dad. He loved the outdoors. I swear he knew every square inch of green space within a hundred miles of the city."

"Do you do any extreme sports?"

"I'm a huge fan of windsurfing and skiing." I bit my lip. That wasn't a lie. I am a *fan*. "Have you seen that new blog *Summit to Surf*? I'm totally addicted, especially their YouTube channel."

"No, I don't know it. But that's good. I'm really trying to push our media online. That's stuff you can do?"

"Oh yeah, for sure," I said, sloshing my coffee cup. "I managed the online media for our student newspaper."

"Charlie Reed's daughter or not, I'll need to see a writing sample, and I have to forewarn you the pay is terrible. Basic benefits. Two weeks of vacation, but on the flip side, you'll get travel expenses. We have a very flexible working schedule, and I strongly encourage my staff to exercise and get outside. We're all a bunch of adrenaline junkies."

"Great! No problem. I have a portfolio of clips—I can show you," I said too eagerly as I reached for my phone.

Greg stood and returned the chair to its normal position. "Email's fine." He picked up the pink umbrella and rested it on the table. "You keep it."

He turned and sauntered toward the door. Pausing, he looked over his shoulder and said, "By the way, you have whipped cream on your nose."

My hand flew to my nose. I scraped the dried whipped cream off, grinning from ear to ear. Then I raced back to Jill's apartment, not noticing the pounding wind or caring that I was completely soaked again.

# TWO

When I arrived at Jill's, the lights and heat were off. I dropped my newly acquired umbrella by the door and flew around the echoing room with its concrete floors and extensive windows, flipping on lights.

I tried to avoid looking out of the loft's windows. They made me dizzy.

Jill kept blown-glass bowls filled with Skittles, M&M's, and jellybeans on the island countertop. Her addiction to candy was legendary. I snatched a handful of candy and dug my laptop out of my bag. I tapped nervously on the granite countertop as my machine hummed to life. *Come on, come on.*

I googled Greg Dixon. A hefty list of links popped up. Apparently in addition to managing *Northwest Extreme*, he was a world-class rock climber. And ridiculously gorgeous. I found myself clicking on every photo and expanding them to full screen.

Next, I looked over the *Northwest Extreme* website, where I discovered the job posting.

Do you love adventure? Are you an intrepid pioneer with a pen and penchant for travel? *Northwest Extreme* seeks an entry-level reporter with reckless abandon to cover everything from motocross to snowboarding. Degree in journalism, editorial and layout experience, and a lust for physical challenges required. Send salary, résumé, and three published clips.

I met all the necessary requirements, minus the tiny detail of being an outdoor adventurer. Rather than listening to the nagging voice in my head telling me this was not the job for me, I texted Matt and Jill. The three of us had been besties since our third year in college.

Matt Parker was the nicest guy I knew, and sometimes I wondered if we were star-crossed lovers. There was an undeniable spark—a zappy undercurrent to our friendship, but neither of us had ever acted on it. Anytime it felt like our relationship was about to shift, an obstacle would appear, blocking any hope of igniting that spark. Maybe it was better that way.

I texted him first:

OMG! Job Alert! Think I just landed a legit writing gig. fill you in soon. XX

Then I checked in with Jill.

Emergency!!! Might have a job. Lunch in 30?

Yay! For sure. Raindrop?

Thirty minutes later, while waiting at the Raindrop, a swanky cocktail bar, I scanned my phone for my best clips. Once I picked my top three, I attached them to an email. The waitress came by twice to see if I'd prefer a glass of chardonnay or something other than water. She glared when I flashed her a grin and said, "Nope, water's great."

I could tell Jill had arrived before she made her way to the table. The energy in the room shifted. Men sat taller in their seats. Heads turned in the direction of the door. Jill breezed in, wearing a silky caramel-colored raincoat. Water beaded and rolled off with ease. She glided over to me, completely unaware that half the restaurant was undressing her with their eyes.

"Meg, what's up?" Jill settled herself in the empty chair across from me and squeezed my hand. Her fingernails were cut short and painted with a translucent polish that made them shimmer. She pressed one to her lip and frowned. "Why are you wet?"

"I ran all the way here," I said, pointing to my sopping raincoat on the back of the chair and leaning in so the table adjacent to us wouldn't hear our conversation. I spilled all the juicy details of my fateful coffee with Greg.

The waitress returned to take our order.

"I'll have a cup of coconut curry soup," I said.

The waitress looked unimpressed as I declined a side salad or entrée. Raindrop prices were absolutely not in my budget.

Jill ordered the salmon without a second glance at the price. Her mahogany locks fell in artistically cut layers to her shoulders and her fine bone structure could have hailed from aristocratic lineage.

I leaned over the table. "Listen, here's the deal. I met an editor, who happens to be super cute, although I think he's over thirty."

Jill laughed. "You make it sound like thirty's old."

"Well, it kind of is. Anyway, he might have a job for me."

"What's the job?"

I strummed my fingers on my lips before answering, "Writing for *Northwest Extreme* magazine."

"Oh, my God, Meg. That's perfect. How many hours have you binged adventure races in the last six months?"

"You don't even want to know. Um, maybe a few, like ten or fifteen." I smirked.

"I think you need to bump that number up." Jill raised her thumb.

"Come on, give me a break. I haven't had much to do lately. But in all seriousness, I feel terrible. I told him my dad was Charlie Reed. I can't believe I did that. It just kind of came out."

Jill put her fork with a piece of salmon stuck on the end on her plate. "That's good, Meg. You should tell him. Charlie's someone to be proud of."

"I know. It's not that. It's more that it feels weird to use him to get a job."

"You're not using him. If he were here, he'd be knocking down every door to get you hired."

I tasted my soup and sighed. "You're probably right. But there's another little problem. Greg, the editor, asked a bunch of questions about my climbing and outdoor skills. When I read the job description it sounds like they want someone with extreme sports experience. I need some ideas. Where'd you go rock climbing last month?"

Jill shook her head and poked at her salad, barely drizzling any dressing over the top. "Listen, Meg. You know I'll totally help, but you're not really thinking of claiming to be adventurer for this gig, are you? I don't think it's a good idea."

"What's the worst that can happen?"

"Where should I start? You could die! I mean seriously. Don't these kinds of reporters typically have to do the actual sports they're sent to cover?"

I slurped my soup. "Probably, but I can fake it. Plus, you know how badly I need a job. And I know how badly you want me off your couch."

Jill patted my hand. "You can stay on my couch as long as you need. I like the company." She laughed as she continued. "I get it. I'll help, but please promise me you'll be careful."

"I heart you," I squealed, and scrambled for my laptop bag

under the table so I could take copious notes on Jill's outdoor pursuits.

In college she'd competed on both the ski team and cross-country team. From an early age, Jill's doctor parents carted her along on trekking vacations and sailboat races. They invited me on a ski trip once. I spent the entire weekend sliding the slopes on my derrière and sneaking into the lodge for hot chocolate. The last time I went sailing with Jill, I slipped climbing onto the boat and sprained my ankle.

I was a hopeless case. Mom blamed it on Pops's genes, claiming I came out with his Reed family klutz. My only saving grace was my quick wit and fast fingers on a keyboard.

"Let me get this," Jill said as the waitress handed us the bill.

"No way. I'll get my own."

Jill tucked her credit card into the black sleeve. "You sure?"

I recovered a damp, crumpled bill from my raincoat pocket and slapped it in the receipt holder. "I'm sure."

Jill gave me a pleading look but didn't say more.

After she left to go back to work, I whipped out an email highlighting my (okay, well, Jill's) many globetrotting ventures, reviewed my work, and hit send. What did I have to lose?

# THREE

Two weeks later, I found myself employed. Sure, it wasn't *The O*, and I wasn't likely to be in a line for a Pulitzer anytime soon, but hey, a job's a job. And I had one. A bona fide writing job at that. I could officially call myself "a writer."

The converted warehouse where *Northwest Extreme* was based was a rustic space that felt suitably writerly with its earthy exposed brick walls. As I met my new colleagues and got settled in the office, I didn't care that I was the youngest person on staff. I did care, however, that my coworkers were die-hard adventure enthusiasts—snowboarders, climbers, parasailers, and windsurfers.

As a kid, Pops took me hiking so I knew enough to get by. The problem was, I was far from a hard body. Nature walks were more my speed. All too soon I would come to regret the stretching of the truth that had landed me the position. But that thought was nowhere in my mind when I'd skipped into headquarters on my first day.

I did what any legitimate journalist would do and studied up. I read everything I could on extreme climbing culture, versed myself in the lingo, studied the history of the sport, and, most importantly, asked a lot of questions.

I think I endeared myself to my coworkers in my first few weeks on the job. It helped that I was willing to make coffee and line-edit copy, a task that everyone else seemed to loathe.

It also helped that the entire office was consumed with preparing for the arrival of the *Race the States* contestants.

*Race the States* was the first-ever adventure race filming in Oregon. Ten participants had signed on for the race of a lifetime. Starting in New York City, they competed in extreme outdoor events across the country. At each stop one contestant was eliminated. The finale was set to take place here in Oregon in late April, with the final three contestants battling it out for a million-dollar prize. Greg partnered with *Race the States* as an exclusive sponsor. We'd be allowed full access, interviews, and on-air mentions when the race was broadcast nationwide in the fall.

After a couple months of writing junk filler, speccing ad space, and managing social media, I was surprised when Greg summoned me into his office on a sunny afternoon in April.

I hadn't seen much of him during my first months on the job. He'd been traveling to watch the earlier legs of the race. Getting called in for a one-on-one made me want to make a beeline for the front door.

"Have a seat," he said, pointing to the cushy wingback chair in front of his desk as I poked my head into his office.

The walls were littered with photos, magazine covers, and feature stories of him scaling cliffs and swinging into canyons. My stomach lurched as I settled into the chair. I wasn't sure if it was in reaction to this overload of imagery of him looking buff, or because every time I was around him, I seemed to stumble over my words.

Maybe I was trying too hard to act the part of adventure-lover. I didn't want him to discover that my outdoor skills weren't quite as honed as those of everyone else on staff. Gam would say I wasn't living authentically and the Universe was simply bringing that fact to the surface.

"How are you liking it here?" he asked, pushing his chair back and propping his feet on the desk.

I couldn't help but stare at his bulging muscles as he leaned back, linking his fingers together behind his head.

"Great! Really great. Yeah, everyone's been great." *God, I'm such an idiot. Could I string together an intelligible sentence not containing the word "great" in it, please?*

Greg hid a smile. "I've heard talk around the office about you."

Blood rushed to my head. I could hear my heartbeat pounding in my ears.

I'd been found out. I must not have fooled my coworkers after all.

Greg sat up and pulled a file folder from a stack on his desk. He leafed through it while bile rose in my throat. I couldn't manufacture a story fast enough. I'd have to come clean and beg for mercy. After all, times were rough. I wasn't the only starving writer who might have fudged her qualifications in favor of a paycheck.

I gulped. "I can explain—"

Greg looked at me funny and cut me off. "I took a risk with you, Meg."

Tears started to brim in my eyes. *Not now*, I willed myself, pursing my lips and nodding solemnly.

Closing the file, Greg held it in his hand, shaking it toward me. "There were staffers who didn't think you were ready, but I had a feeling about you." He paused, staring hard at me. "And not just because of your dad."

I blinked tears back and mumbled, "Allergies."

Holding the file, he said, "This is good. Consistently good. I knew you had it in you."

"Huh?" I wiped water from underneath my eyelids.

"Impressive writing," he said as he leafed through hard copies of the filler and sidebars I'd been tasked with. "Today is your lucky day, Meg. You probably heard that Mitch took a nasty fall off Smith Rock?"

I nodded. Mitch was *Northwest Extreme*'s most seasoned writer. No one would question his athletic prowess. He'd scaled every peak on the planet, many times over. Last week a belay line snapped when he was climbing Smith Rock. He fell thirty feet, breaking his leg and dislocating his shoulder. It was the talk of the office.

"How's he doing?" I asked Greg.

"He'll be okay, but he's laid up for the moment. That's where you come in. I'm short-staffed and there's no one else to take Mitch's assignment."

Could this really be happening? I fiddled with a button on my dress while waiting for him to continue.

"It's a big one. As you know, we're sponsoring *Race the States*. This is going to be huge for the magazine. I'm putting my trust in you." He shoved a file in my hand.

I looked at it wide-eyed and managed to stammer out thanks.

An assignment. A real assignment. He was giving me an assignment.

Poor Mitch, but yay me.

Bending over, he pulled a large box from under his desk. "We had a good laugh when these came in. I knew right away you were going to have to write this review."

He chuckled as he removed the cutest pair of hiking boots I'd ever seen.

They were a deep pinkish/purple shade with raspberry sherbet laces and midsoles. "These are for me?" I asked, examining the boots.

"If they fit."

"Huh?"

"You know how critical fit is when it comes to shoes. If these aren't the right size, expense a new pair."

"Right. Yeah. Thanks."

He waved me off. "I want a five-hundred-word sidebar on them. I need to jump on a call. Details on travel and expenses will be in your email. Good luck."

Trying to steady the paper quivering in my hand, I got to my feet and gushed another round of thanks for the assignment and the hiking boots. As I put my hand on the knob of his office door, he called out, "Meg, by the way, you have something under your eye."

I wiped my finger under my eyes. My mascara had bled. Great. I probably looked like a deranged football player. What was it with looking and acting like a fool anytime I saw Greg? He seemed to bring out the twelve-year-old girl in me.

Despite my Greg blunder, I floated to my desk. What luck. I thought I was about to get the boot, and instead scored a pair of new boots? The day couldn't get any better. Well, maybe it could. I looked around at my coworkers, and suddenly felt like I might be in over my head.

It would have been instantly obvious to anyone who walked into the converted warehouse that housed *Northwest Extreme* that I was the newbie. The shirtwaist dress I was wearing with its green vertical stripes, sleeves that turned up, and a tidy collar wasn't exactly in line with my coworkers' attire. Most were hearty Northwest types—lots of flannel and khaki. No pink. Climbing boots were standard issue. Writing copy from my desk hadn't warranted special attire. Going out in the field meant I needed to gear up my wardrobe, like now.

The folder Greg gave me outlined the details of my assignment. My mouth dropped open as I scanned the file. I'd be covering the final leg of *Race the States*. What an opportunity.

Thanks, Mitch! I'd have to shoot him a get-well email and promise to try to do justice to the feature.

Now, time to get to work. The three remaining contestants would be arriving from Arizona (the previous leg of the race) tomorrow. I'd be introduced to the racers and film crew at a meet-and-greet tomorrow night, followed by a hike at Angel's Rest to film B-roll footage and a welcome barbecue at our office the next day. The week was packed with climbs and press junkets all leading to the finale. I shuddered. This was the real deal.

I wondered what the three contestants would be like. They'd been competing against each other for the last two months for a shot at a million dollars. The race had taken them from New York to Kentucky and Texas to Utah, with multiple stops between. Along the way, the bulk of the contestants had been eliminated. These top three contenders must be ultra-athletes. How was I going to keep pace with them?

I pushed aside used coffee cups, gum, reference guides, and red Sharpie pens on my desk. Time to focus. I clicked on Greg's email. My first stop would be the library. I had some serious studying-up to do. The *Race the States* contestants would be climbing Angel's Rest, Beacon Rock, Table Mountain, and zip-lining off the Bridge of the Gods. I needed to be well-versed in the history of each location.

As I scanned the document for more details, I let out a little gasp. Under the category labeled billable expenses, one line stuck out: equipment and supply costs. Did that mean I could expense hiking gear? At least that way I'd look the part.

In hindsight, I should have forgone the boots, ditched the pink umbrella (which was sitting next to my desk at *Northwest Extreme*), and heeded Jill's advice. I could hear her voice in my head when I asked her what the worst thing that could happen would be if I took the job. "You might die!" She wasn't kidding.

# FOUR

A heap of clothes surrounded me as I glanced at the minimalistic orange clock mounted on Jill's concrete wall. Ugh. As always, I was running late. I was due to meet the cast and crew of *Race the States* at a kickoff dinner at Shared Table. The restaurant had received accolades from all of Portland's foodies and most recently a write-up in the *New York Times*.

I was going to have to throw something on, and fast. The last thing I wanted to do on my first assignment was start with a bad impression. Settling for a flared, knee-length black skirt, black tights, a maroon turtleneck, and a silver scarf, I pinched my cheeks, grabbed a pinstriped raincoat, and raced out the door. Although it was technically spring, April weather in the Pacific Northwest was like a teenager—a volatile mess of hormones one minute and serene the next. Today fell in the latter category, for which I was thankful.

Dusk was starting to usher itself in. The sky faded into periwinkle, and tiny cherry blossom buds peeked out along the river walk. I knew the rough vicinity of where Shared Table was located but kicked myself for not looking up the address.

I hustled between theater-goers in suits and sleek dresses,

panhandlers begging for change, and hipsters in knit hats. My first assignment and I was going to be late. I had no excuse. I left the office with plenty of time to change. But I'd whittled away my time trying to figure out what to wear and what to do with my hair. Typically I wore my short pixie cut in a shag style. It made for fast mornings—throw in mousse and blow-dry upside down—and ta-da, I was good to go. This occasion called for something more upscale. After curling, flat-ironing, and flipping, I finally opted to tuck my bangs behind my ear with an antique silver barrette Gam gave me years ago. The effect wasn't half bad.

A block ahead I could see the Shared Table sign, an intentionally weathered brown sign with simple lettering. I picked up the pace, not bothering to wait for the red hand flashing in the crosswalk. Portlanders didn't obey street signs. Nor did we honk.

The restaurant was darkly lit. The only light came from votive candles lining twelve-foot tables throughout one large room. Exposed wood beams stretched across the ceiling, and the last remains of daylight filtered in through paned windows. Shared Table started a family-style dining craze in Portland. Privacy was not on the menu. Diners were seated together and food was served family-style. It smelled of fresh thyme, sweet honey, and simmering wine sauce.

I felt a hand on the small of my back and turned to see Greg gazing down at me with his ebony eyes.

He let out a low whistle. "You're looking good, Meg." Thankfully it was too dark for him to notice me blush.

"I didn't know you were coming." My heart skipped a beat as his hand guided me to the farthest table from the door.

"Have to schmooze, you know." He caught the eye of a weathered gray-bearded gentleman. "Dave, how are you, friend?"

Dave rose to greet him in a huge hug, followed by a slap on

the back. He wore an Australian outback hat with a mesh string wrapped under his chin. It looked like the hat had seen plenty of time on the trail. "Hey, mate! Good to see you." His jovial Australian accent reverberated through the room. Noticing me, he continued, "And who's this babe?"

Babe? I grimaced internally, but forced a smile.

"Dave Shepard, may I introduce Meg Reed, our newest team member. She's going to be covering the race. Meg, Dave is the executive producer of *Race the States* and has quite the reputation for extreme sports himself."

I stepped forward to shake Dave's hand. He grabbed mine firmly, pumping it rapidly. "Lovely to meet you, Meggie."

I didn't bother to correct him. The way he stretched the "e" in "Meggie" had a nice ring. Plus, he reminded me of a grizzly, athletic version of Santa Claus.

Dropping my hand, he waved at the other two people sitting at the table. "Uh, we're a bit short on our mates tonight. A couple of our racers needed a rest."

I noticed the petite woman seated next to him shoot him a look. He shrugged it off and offered introductions. "This here's Krissy Miles, my production assistant and right-hand lassie."

She flashed a subtle smile and nodded to both Greg and me. Her gaze rested on Greg, who spoke in a hushed tone to Dave. I caught her eye, and she winked.

Greg returned his attention to me as an odd expression crossed Dave's face. Gathering himself, he introduced his camera guy, Andrew, a shaggy, sweaty guy in his early thirties, who stood to shake our hands. His grasp was clammy.

"Sorry about that," he said as he wiped his hands on his cargo shorts. "It's roasting in here—eh?"

"Are you filming tonight?" I asked, pointing to the earpiece looped over his ear and the professional film camera on his shoulder.

"Nope." He scratched his chocolate-colored goatee. Patting the camera, he said, "This baby doesn't leave my side."

I pegged him as Canadian with his signature "Eh."

Dave steered me to the open seat next to Krissy. Greg took the chair to Andrew's right. I watched him appraise Krissy and give her an appreciative nod.

"He's your boss?" Krissy's high-pitched whisper matched her tiny body. I thought I caught a whiff of cigarette smoke when she leaned closer. She didn't strike me as a smoker, more like a librarian with platinum hair curling in soft waves around her sharp face and thin black wire-rimmed glasses.

"Yeah, not too shabby, huh?" I said, drooling as I read the evening's fare. The menu was fixed: duck confit spring rolls, fingerling potatoes with Gorgonzola and fresh herbs, crab bisque, prosciutto-and-rosemary-wrapped cod with lemon and greens, and a caramel fig tart with vanilla bean sauce.

*Oh, my God, please let someone else pay the bill*, I thought in a momentary flash of panic. My bank account didn't have enough to cover the appetizers. I'd spent most of my meager pay from *Northwest Extreme* on reference materials. The rest went into savings. My goal was to be off Jill's couch by summer.

"Is he taken?" Krissy asked, moving her eyes in Greg's direction and circling her finger on an empty wineglass. "No ring."

"Not as far as I know, but I haven't asked."

"You should. But you're a bit young for him anyway." She elbowed me with a chuckle.

Bottles of Spanish red wine arrived at the table. The entire restaurant erupted in applause as waitstaff delivered wooden trays with cheeses, marinated olives, and spiced nuts to the tables and the head chef emerged from the kitchen. He rambled on about the evening's menu and how the food had been sourced from local organic farmers. No one at our table seemed interested.

"None of the contestants are coming tonight?" Greg asked, filling our wineglasses.

Krissy started to say something, but Dave jumped in. "No worries. I think Lenny's coming, and we'll see everyone at the hike and barbie tomorrow."

He raised his wineglass. "Cheers, mates! It's going to be a fight to the finish."

I tried not to grimace as I took a sip of the strong, tart wine. If only I could order a beer.

Greg and Dave discussed how much access we'd have for individual contestant interviews, while Andrew and Krissy gave me a rundown of the taping and production schedule. Appetizers were passed around the table. I bit into a delicate duck confit spring roll bursting with flavor and juice. It splattered on my chin and dribbled onto my scarf. I grabbed my napkin and inconspicuously tried to rub it.

While I was chiding myself for being so clumsy, a commotion broke out at the bar where the head chef was still rattling on. A man with badly bleached blond hair and a fake tan was yelling at the bartender. His gold-chained jewelry glinted in the candlelight. I could hear his brash East Coast accent spewing a trail of profanity.

Dave sighed heavily, pushed his chair out, and jumped to his feet. "That guy. Be right back." He ran to the bar, clapped his hand on the man's shoulder, and said something in a low tone to the bartender.

"Who's that guy?" I asked Krissy.

"Lenny Ray. He thinks he's a mobster, but he's really from the suburbs in Hoboken, New Jersey. A word of advice: Steer clear of him. He's got a reputation as being quite the womanizer."

"How does Dave know him?" She didn't need to warn me. I could already tell Lenny was the type of guy I'd go out of my way to avoid.

The scene appeared to be under control at the bar. I saw Dave hand his credit card to the bartender, who poured a round of drinks.

"Lenny is a contestant." Krissy sighed. "As much as I hate to admit it, a good one. The man is an athlete and his personality is going to make for great television. Viewers are going to love to hate him."

The hate part seemed like an easy sell from my vantage point, but loving him? That was a stretch. Greg must have caught the nervous grimace on my face.

"Don't sweat it, Meg." He popped an olive in his mouth. "I know these types. A lot of bark. No bite!"

Dave steered Lenny toward our table. Lenny kept shooting his head in the direction of the bartender, I assumed in an attempt to intimidate him.

"Meggie, let me introduce you to one of our finalists, Lenny Ray." Dave's tone was smooth and upbeat, as if the entire restaurant weren't staring at our table.

Lenny jeered and flexed his pec muscles under his tight black T-shirt. "Hey, babe," he said to me. He tried to fist bump with Greg, who didn't catch on quickly enough. Lenny ended up hitting Greg's palm into the air and laughing.

The only empty seat left at the table was to my right. Lenny pounced on it and scooted his chair a quarter inch away from mine. I tugged on my skirt to pull it over my knees. The scent of his spicy cologne was overpowering. It reminded me of the pine tree air freshener Mom kept in her car. His breath reeked of stale alcohol and his words had a slight slur to them.

"You're a magazine girl, huh? Means you're coming along for the ride with Len the Con."

Who was this guy? He couldn't be for real. I shifted in my seat and inched closer to Krissy. "Uh, yeah, well, I'm hoping to be one. This is my first assignment."

Damn. Why did I say that?

"Don't worry, sweetheart. I'll give you full private access to this," he said, massaging his chest.

*Ugh. Gross.* I scooted away from him.

Greg cleared his throat. "Meg will be coordinating interview times with Krissy. Otherwise, I'm sure you'll want to focus on your training efforts for the finale." Greg held his body steady, his firm gaze resting on Lenny. "This may be her first assignment, but I know from her résumé alone that Meg is a skilled outdoorswoman."

I choked on my wine a little.

"Are you okay?" Greg questioned before he continued. "She and I will be on site for the upcoming challenges."

This was news to me. I had no idea Greg was planning to attend the events with me. It made sense. He didn't want to send a rookie out alone on an assignment this important, but one look at me trying to scale a mountain and he'd be on to my lie.

Lenny turned his attention to Andrew, the camera operator, sitting across the table from us. "Am I getting actual airtime in this segment, man?"

Andrew twisted his napkin in his hand. Sweat beaded on his round, red face. "I'm not doing this here. How many times have I told you all contestants get the same amount of airtime?"

Lenny pounded his fist on the table, making my wine slosh in the glass. "Bullshit! Stop busting my balls. That tree-hugger Leaf is getting more time than me."

I could see sweat rings under the arms of Andrew's black *Race the States* T-shirt. He looked pleadingly at Dave, whose amicable face was lined with anger.

He gave a little shake and turned to Lenny with a forced smile. "Come on, mate, we'll work this out. See if we can't get you a couple extra minutes. Right, Andrew?"

Andrew shook his head and looked away.

A new bottle of wine was delivered to the table. Greg

sniffed the cork and moved his glass in a circular motion, tasting the blackberry-colored liquid. He nodded his approval to the waiter. The wine probably cost a small fortune, but it was totally lost on me.

I tried to swallow another taste of the wine. "This is really good," I said to Greg.

"The vintner's a friend of mine. I'll introduce you some time," he said. Then he leaned over the table and launched into an intimate discussion about Oregon wines with Krissy. She giggled and bit her bottom lip.

Dinner arrived. We tucked into flaky cod and greens tossed in a lemon-butter sauce. After dessert and another round of drinks, my head was swimming from the wine. Dave paid the bill with fanfare and a final toast.

I needed sleep. I needed Jill.

Tomorrow we would meet at Angel's Rest in the Columbia River Gorge, where Andrew could shoot B-roll of the contestants and landscape. It was a short two-and-a-half-mile hike one way—a warm-up for the endurance athletes competing in the race. But I hadn't hiked in years. And now Greg would be there. How was I going to get myself out of this? I was in way over my head.

Greg escorted me to the door. "You sure you're ready for this?"

"Of course! No worries, mate." I winked and socked him playfully on the arm, his firm, ripped arm.

He laughed. "You familiar with Angel's Rest?"

"Sure, I've done it dozens of times." Good God, what was wrong with me? "Remind me, how high is it again?"

"It's nothing. Maybe 1,500 feet of elevation gain."

A wave of nausea swept over my body. Trying to act casual, I scoffed and said, "1,500—no problem."

"See you tomorrow." He leaned as if he were going to kiss my cheek. I backed up. But instead he grabbed his jacket from the coat rack behind me and gave me a funny look. Throwing the jacket over his shoulder, he thrust the door open for me. "Better get some sleep."

I held my hand in a half-wave that he didn't see.

I needed to get it together. Crushing on Greg was not a wise idea, I thought as I watched his athletic legs in stone chinos stroll down the street. His perfectly cut Oxford baby-blue shirt was neatly tucked in. I tried not to stare at his ass. My stomach flopped again. Sleep? Unlikely. Tomorrow held the promise of an encounter with my unnervingly hot boss and the extreme likelihood I would die of fright, embarrassment, or both. Oh yeah, and lose my job.

# FIVE

I was late. Again. There was no time to spare. I was due at Angel's Rest in less than an hour.

I rubbed my eyes and threw on my new hiking gear. It wasn't my fault I was late; I'd been up half the night scouring hiking message boards for insight into Angel's Rest and slept through my alarm. Probably because it was nicknamed "the quad killer." What had I gotten myself into?

Plus my dreams had been muddled with Greg's rock-hard body morphing into a rock face.

Maybe I could claim car trouble and just not show? No, I had to go. I had a job to do. There was no talking myself out of this one.

At least my feet looked the part. I laced the hiking boots Greg gave me, grabbed my new pack, and hurried to my car.

My GPS reported that I-84, the interstate connecting Portland to Angel's Rest in the Columbia River Gorge, was closed due to an early-morning rollover accident. That meant I'd have to take the meandering Historic Columbia River Highway.

Pops loved the picturesque highway. On weekends when I was a kid, we'd drive the old road and Pops would tell me all about the engineering feat it took to cut a road through the Gorge. It was constructed in the early 1920s as part of an initiative with the National Parks Service to create more accessibility for tourists within the park system. It cuts seamlessly through the landscape and runs parallel to the Columbia River.

This morning the road was slick with rain. I swerved around a corner to avoid hitting the rust-colored mossy guardrail. Glancing at the clock on the dashboard that read 11:45 A.M., I pushed my foot on the gas pedal. fifteen minutes to get to the trailhead.

Have I mentioned I was terrified of heights? People used the word "terrified" too casually. Forget miniscule fears about spiders or dirt. Spiders could be squashed. Dirt could be washed. Heights equaled death. Period.

Mom tried to arrange gymnastics classes for me when I was in grade school. I wasn't an idiot. I saw those girls in their pink leotards steady themselves with arms outstretched on the balance beam six feet in the air. It didn't matter that the beam they started me on was five inches off the floor.

"Mary Margaret Reed"—Mom gave me the look—"don't be silly. The beam is on the ground. You have nowhere to fall."

Despite my mom's nagging to "get over my silly little fear," I never did. And, I might add, I'd been successful at avoiding situations that put me near the top of skyscrapers or mountain summits for the past twenty-three years. Until now.

The tips of my fingers were numb from clutching the steering wheel. I wiggled them and tried concentrating on the mantra I'd written for myself:

*I am safe. Climbing is safe. The Universe surrounds and protects me.*

Gam hooked me on positive mantras as a kid. Mom thought they were ridiculous. They were the source of many an argument between the two of them, but Gam won, buying me tarot decks and rose quartz crystals. I slept with the rose crystal under my pillow last night. I loved Gam and her positive attitude, but had to admit, though, that neither that nor the mantra seemed to be working.

The Gorge was a true geological wonder and the only sea-level passage through the Cascade Mountains. Its towering plateaus on both sides of the massive Columbia River looked as if they'd been chiseled with a carving knife. I continued east past waterfalls and under a canopy of evergreen trees. The air held a slight hint of spring. An assault of beautiful colors hit my eyes—lush greens, churning blues, and budding pinks.

The morning rain left leaves shimmering as the noontime sunlight emerged through the clouds. I slowed to read the trailhead markers lining the side of the road. A brown sign shot up with bullet holes showed Angel's Rest a mile ahead. That's where I needed to meet the crew.

In my research, I learned that Angel's Rest connected to Devil's Rest. At some point, they branched apart to take hikers onto backcountry trails connecting above Multnomah Falls, the largest and most popular falls in the Gorge. There was something sinister about a trail named after devils and angels. Gam would have told me to simply call in the angels to help abate my fear. I usually bought into her quirky theories, but I couldn't squelch my worry about the hike.

The good news was that, thanks to my expense account, I was outfitted to play the part of adventurer. Jill and I scoured the outlets for the latest high-fashion outdoor gear. My favorite score was my pale pink Lucy top. Jill told me I had to break in the hiking boots, but I ran out of time. I stuck Band-Aids into my CamelBak backpack in case they rubbed. I bit my lip and hoped that a blister or two would be the extent of my worries.

I spotted the crew in the parking lot across the street from the Angel's Rest trail marker. It was midweek in April; not many hikers were around. A sunny spring weekend would bring out day-trippers and families with babies in backpacks, but it was too early in the season and too soggy for anyone other than serious climbers.

It took every ounce of courage to steer the car into the parking lot. The small gravel lot sat empty on the river side of the highway. A bank of trees and wildflowers marked the entrance to Angel's Rest across the road.

Dave and Andrew were testing camera equipment. Krissy leaned against a rented white van, studying a clipboard in her hand. Two new faces chatted near the van. There was no sign of Lenny, the thug. Maybe he was passed out back at the hotel. I scanned the parking lot, looking for Greg, but he hadn't arrived. Surprising, given I just made it. The clock read 11:59.

I yanked my pack from the trunk. The pack made me feel like a true hiker. I could do this. I was a professional journalist, right?

It was an effort to lug it over my shoulder. I think I may have overpacked. Something would have to go.

I threw an assortment of guidebooks, sunscreen, and bug repellant in the back of my car. Then I repacked my notepads, granola bars, Band-Aids, Gatorade, and first-aid kit. My pack was considerably lighter but still hard to lift with one hand. I was going to break a sweat before we left the parking lot.

Was I really going to do this?

Fortunately, I had a secret weapon stashed in the trunk—trekking poles. I'd discovered them on display under a sign claiming they were "the best carbon poles ever tested." The sales clerk assured me their folding design was cutting-edge, and all the endurance runners and fast-packers raved about them. At a price of a hundred and fifty bucks, they had to be cutting-edge, right?

With my lightweight poles tucked into the sides of my pack, I slung it on my back. Staggering from the weight, I wobbled a little, trying to regain my balance. I cinched the straps and straightened my back, taking a timid step forward toward the van.

A magnetic decal the size of a prize-winning pumpkin was plastered to the side of the van with the *Race the States* logo—a cutout of the United States with the silhouette of a hiker zip-lining from New York to Oregon.

Krissy looked up from the clipboard she was holding. "That's quite a pack, Meg." Her suicide-blond curls were tied in a tight knot, making her angular face appear sharper.

"It's all my stuff—for interviews, you know." I scraped my hand through my hair, feeling my nerves tick up.

"What are those?" she asked, pointing to the trekking poles.

"Black Diamonds. The best on the market." Why was she looking at me with that smirk? I squared my shoulders, trying to stand taller.

"But what are they?"

"Trekking poles," I retorted, as heat crept into my cheeks. Maybe the poles were too much.

"Never heard of them." She shrugged, twisting her lips and frowning.

"Really? All the climbers around here use them." I felt the lie tumble out of my mouth before I could stop it. What was wrong with me?

"Hmm, interesting. I'm not much of a climber myself." She called over to the two contestants, "Alicia! Leaf! Come meet Meg."

I raised my hand in a half-wave as the two made their way in our direction.

"Meg, meet two of our top contestants—Leaf Green and Alicia Abbott," Krissy said, pushing her glasses up on her nose.

"Heeey." Leaf greeted me in a long, low voice, stretching out the greeting. Definitely stoner speak. His russet-colored hair twisted in matted dreadlocks on his shoulders. He looked to be in his mid- to late thirties, but it was hard to tell behind all his mangy facial hair. He stretched out his hand. I recoiled slightly from the smell—a combination of stale pot, sweat, and patchouli. That's when I noticed his feet were bare. Caked in dirt, pocked with calluses and who knows what else.

*This guy's a top competitor?* Alicia Abbott was the yin to Leaf's yang. She fit the image I'd conceived in my head of an adventure racer. Her black hair pulled in a tight ponytail reminded me of a raven. Sunglasses shielded her eyes. There wasn't a hint of makeup on her face. She wore a navy-blue and lime-green sports bra.

She pulled a package of strawberry energy gels from her pocket, stuck one in her mouth, and offered the bag to Krissy and me. "Want one?"

We both declined. Alicia shrugged, stuck the gel in her pocket, and stretched her quads. "When are we taking off?" she asked Krissy. As she bent over, she ripped a brittle yellow spine off a shrub.

"What are you doing!?" Leaf yanked it from her hand. Alicia looked at him in disbelief.

"This is Devil's Club," Leaf said as he gently stroked the woody leaves of the shrub. "It's one of the most sensitive plants we have in these forests. You can't touch it, let alone rip it. It's a living, breathing thing. Takes forever to grow."

"Sorry," Alicia snarled. "I didn't know."

"Stop killing the forest. This show is such a joke when it comes to being green." Leaf cradled the Devil's Club in his hand.

"Take it up with Dave," Alicia said, glaring at him.

"A little help?" Leaf asked Krissy.

Krissy ignored Leaf's request and examined her toggled platinum watch. Obviously, she didn't intend to make the trek to the summit. I knew enough to recognize her pencil skirt and ballet flats weren't going to lend themselves to hiking.

"It's time. Will you two knock it off and wake Lenny?" To

me, she sighed, "No one seems to realize that we're producing what's going to be an Emmy-winning show here."

"Do you think it'll win an Emmy?" I asked.

"That's the plan. If I have anything to do about it." She made a final note on her clipboard and scurried off.

"Have you met Lenny?" Alicia asked, raising her unwaxed eyebrows over her sunglasses.

"Last night," I said with a nod.

"Lucky you." She elbowed Leaf. "You go get him."

Leaf reached his arms over his head and brought his hands together in front of his chest in a gratitude pose. He gave us a warning not to touch any plants and turned on his bare feet toward the van.

"Is he going to hike like that?" I asked Alicia.

"Yep. He doesn't believe in shoes." She shrugged and pulled off her sunglasses to assess me. "You look top-heavy. What's with the pack?"

"I like to be prepared," I said, shifting my weight, and rubbed the back of my neck. "Never know what I might need for an interview. I sort of have an addiction to paper. Plus, notebooks are much easier to lug around than laptops."

"I wouldn't say that to Leaf if I were you." Alicia whispered, "He did jail time last year for trying to plow down a couple of loggers. He gets pretty worked up. Got in a wicked fight with one of the earlier contestants about making the show greener. It's his thing. He thinks he's on some kind of nature quest, not competing for a million bucks."

She paused and looked over her shoulder before continuing. "Anyway, it got pretty violent. Dave almost kicked him off the show. In fact, I'm not sure why he didn't..." She trailed off as the sound of Lenny's brash Jersey accent whizzed across the parking lot.

"Knock it off. Give me five minutes."

Leaf casually made his way to us, ignoring Lenny's rant. His tattered Greenpeace T-shirt, shredded cutoff shorts, and lackadaisical attitude didn't seem to fit the violent anarchist picture Alicia painted of him. Gam would have told me to tap into my intuition to learn more. My intuition wasn't talking. I'd have to keep my eye on him. He could make for an interesting blurb to accompany my story.

Ten minutes later, Lenny emerged from the back of the van. He staggered and swayed toward us. Was he still drunk? Catching my eye, he puffed his shoulders and strutted my way. I tried to duck as he tossed an arm around my shoulder. My pack threw me off balance. I nearly fell, face-first, on the gravel. Lenny's beefy arm grabbed my pack and pulled me to standing in one swoop.

"Easy there, girlie."

Last night's alcohol radiated from his every pore. Obviously, he never made it into a shower. I shook myself free from his grasp. The weight of my pack dug into my shoulders. We'd been waiting maybe ten minutes. How was I ever going to drag myself up the side of a cliff with thirty extra pounds weighing me down?

"You're hiking in that, Lenny?" Alicia drew our attention to the collection of gold chains around Lenny's neck. Talk about weighing someone down.

"There's plenty more where that came from, baby," Lenny said in a slur.

"You are such a Neanderthal." Alicia threw up her hands in disgust.

Lenny ignored her and preened himself, slicking his peroxide-colored hair by licking his hand with his tongue. His V-neck white T-shirt left nothing to the imagination. We all had an eyeful of his pecs and chest hair.

"Okay, mates." Dave called everyone to the middle of the parking lot, where he, Andrew, and Krissy had been talking.

The sun hid behind a sturdy wall of blowing clouds overhead. Uh-oh, it looked like the rain might return. I noticed Alicia didn't bother to remove her sunglasses. Instead, she pulled a dandelion from the gravel and twisted it around her finger.

"We'll scramble up the side of this little cliff. It should be a quickie. Keep you in tip-top shape until the next challenge." He motioned to Andrew, who was untwisting a jumble of cables. "Andrew here will be shooting footage of our gorgeous location. And Meggie here may stop you along the way to get your first-hand account of the trek. Any questions?"

"You're timing us, right?" Lenny asked from behind hitman sunglasses.

"Didn't plan to." Dave paused and turned to Krissy. "What do you think?"

"Fine by me. I've got all your stats here anyway," she said, holding her clipboard.

She turned to me and said, "Meg, in case you're not up to speed, the plan for today is the contestants will run to the top of the summit. Mainly we want Andrew to shoot footage we'll use for promos. This isn't an official leg of the race."

Andrew held a clear plastic camera the size of a plum in his palm. "I've positioned twelve of these along the route."

"Those are cameras?" I asked.

"GoPros. Most amazing camera on the market." Andrew beamed. He pulled a remote not much bigger than his thumb from his pack. "Best part is, they're Wi-fi enabled." He clicked the remote. "One button and I can activate any camera on the trail."

"All right, we'll clock you. Anything else?" Dave asked.

Lenny flexed his arms and puffed his chest. "You get me airtime, got it?" he snarled at Andrew.

Andrew threw his free hand in the air. "I can't work like this," he said to Dave. "Tell this jackass to shut it or I'm out." He stormed over to the van.

"What? You're going to rage quit?" Lenny shouted after him.

Raising her hand, Alicia asked, "Do we have a time set for the next challenge?"

Dave patted Krissy's shoulder. "Krissy here will work on the permits and final details while we all go climb this little peak." He adjusted his Australian hat to shade the sun from his eyes.

Krissy cleared her throat and flipped through the paper on her clipboard. "We're at the mercy of the county at the moment. I'm going to push them hard. We can't start building the zip-line until we get approval. Hopefully, I'll have good news and a firm date when you get down."

"What the hell are we supposed to do in Oregon while we wait?" Lenny asked.

Krissy threw Dave a concerned look. "I'm working on that. I should have an updated itinerary ready later today. I'm working around the clock to get this production wrapped. We've got hours of film to start editing."

Dave brushed her off. "No worries. Plenty of time."

It didn't look like Krissy agreed. She folded her arms over the clipboard and stared at Dave.

Andrew returned to glaring at Lenny as he repositioned Alicia's GoPro camera. All the contestants were required to wear the indestructible cameras that Andrew mounted on their packs. He'd equipped the cameras with flexible poles extending from their packs around their shoulders to get forward-facing shots.

Andrew whispered something in Alicia's ear as he made an adjustment to her camera mount. She flicked the dandelion she'd been playing with at him. Andrew appeared wounded. With sagging shoulders, he headed across the historic highway, loaded down with camera equipment. What was that all about?

Dave turned to me. "Greg had another meeting come up. He told me to tell you he'll catch up. If not, he'll see you at the barbie later. You want do anything with the crew before we head up?"

My mind went blank. In my panic about the hike, I suddenly forgot how to form words.

*Focus, Meg. You prepared for this.*

I looked at the motley crew of contestants in front of me. There was Lenny, the gold-chained gangster; Leaf, the hotheaded hippie; and Alicia, the fitness femme fatale. Yes, I'm a fan of alliteration, and obviously, that opening line needed work. I shrugged my pack off. It felt like I was a million pounds lighter. I riffled through it for my journal, pen, and phone.

"Okay, squeeze together," I said, holding my phone.

While the magazine staffed an in-house photographer, most of the photos Greg used were from freelancers. He'd told me to take as many candids as I could. Once the final challenge was set up, he'd send a professional photographer out with me. But for now, I could use the candids to jog my memory while writing the feature. Plus, Greg put me in charge of social media. He wanted me live-streaming race coverage. We'd use video promos and teasers to build excitement.

Dave stepped to the right to get out of the picture. "No, you too, Dave," I said, waving him in. "This article is going to be about the entire crew—not just the contestants."

I spent a good twenty minutes making them pose. I had no clue what I was going to do with all these photos, but I figured more was better. That was a cardinal rule I'd learned in journalism school. Overprepare for every story.

"One question before you go: How do you feel about being in Oregon for the finale of *Race the States*?" Okay, I know it's a totally lame question, but I had to start somewhere.

Dave piped up first. "Oregon, she's a real beauty. My production assistant, Krissy, chose this spot for the finale because of its untamed, rugged scenery. She was right—I'm ready to see more."

I took notes frantically as he spoke, and my pen flew over the page. This was what I was trained to do.

"Yeah, the Oregon ladies aren't so bad to look at either," Lenny said, his gaze resting on me for more than a minute too long. "I thought you all would be hairy like Leaf."

Leaf tugged on one of his dreads. "That's right, Lenny. I'm a hairy Oregonian and proud of it. You've seen the bumper stickers by now, the 'Keep Oregon Weird' ones? That's exactly what I love about Oregon and can't stand about megacities filled with megalomaniacs like you."

"Knock it off," Krissy said. "She's trying to get a story. Listen, Meg, can we finish this later? At the summit?"

"Totally," I said, shutting the journal and packing it into my bag.

"Totally?" Alicia rolled her eyes with a heavy sigh.

"Yeah. Something wrong with that?" I bit the side of my lip, wishing I could fit in with this crowd. Obviously, they were seeing right through me.

She curled her upper lip. "Are you twelve?"

What had I done to irritate her? I'd have to find a way to win her over. As one of the three finalists, she'd be a prominent piece of my feature.

Krissy clicked on a stopwatch. "Ready, everyone?" They all nodded. "It's approximately two and a half miles. An easy five miles round-trip. On my count, ready, set, go!"

Alicia, Lenny, and Leaf bolted across the highway and disappeared into the forest.

"Need a hand there, Meggie?" Dave asked, picking up my pack and guiding it onto my back effortlessly. "Think we can catch them?"

I laughed nervously, trying to look casual. "Uh, yeah, I may be slower because I'll need to stop and take photos and notes along the way. If you want to go ahead, it's cool. Maybe have everyone wait for me at the top. I'll do interviews and take a few more shots?"

"I'll tell you what," Dave said, smiling at me with twinkling eyes. "It's a deal."

I had pegged him correctly as a fit Santa—emphasis on "fit." He sprinted with ease after the contestants, leaving me and Krissy in the parking lot.

"Good luck, Meg," she called as she turned to head to the van. "I overheard a hiker say that the trail's really slick this morning."

I swallowed hard, forced my feet forward, and said a silent prayer to the Universe.

# SIX

## ANGEL'S REST TRAILHEAD

The Universe didn't answer my prayer.

There was no reprieve. The trail began right at the base of the pavement. A narrow path, packed tight with gravel, headed straight into heavily forested woods. I looked ahead to see if I could spot any of the contestants. Nope. The forest was eerily quiet.

Why had I gone blank on interview questions? When Greg told me I was taking over Mitch's story, I'd studied his notes and pored over contestant bios. I'd spent endless hours preparing for this, but in the moment, I drew a blank. What a rookie mistake.

"Well, it's now or never, Meg," I said aloud, knowing there was no one close enough to hear.

I gave a wistful glance across the street to the parking lot.

*One clunky step at a time*, I told myself. *One step at a time.*

The trail twisted through a jungle of ferns and quickly ascended into a dark cover of pine, spruce, and hemlock trees. Sunlight filtered through the canopy, casting shadows and flickering light along the path.

The first hill made my knees weak.

My boots struggled to make traction. Loose rocks shifted under my feet. I slid backward. This was going to be a long day.

After two hundred feet, the trail curved to the right and revealed a massive uphill climb. Gravel slowly transitioned into a mud-covered mess. Tree roots, loose rock, a sprinkling of pine needles, and muddy footprints lay ahead. I hugged the right side of the trail.

I sucked in air. My cheeks burned with heat. At this rate, I'd be lucky to make it to the summit before sunset.

I needed a rest. I stopped, pulled my phone from my pack, and took a number of photos. Once I regained my breath, I stuck my phone back in my pack and continued on.

A typical April east wind kicked in hard. The spindly deciduous trees around me swayed from side to side. I kept catching glances of movement out of the corner of my eye. A slow and steady howling sound followed—surely it was the wind and not a cougar. According to the experts, cougars were prolific in these parts. While human and cougar encounters were rare, cougars had been known to stalk hikers in silence. I didn't want to find out.

*Keep it moving, Meg.*

The bushes moved with the wind, rustling ominously. A section of new-growth trees looked like knob-kneed teenagers with bare legs.

I heard water as I rounded the next bend. A spontaneous waterfall sprouted from the side of the cliff. Lime-green lichen surrounded the falls. The path was washed out. Water pooled at my feet and gushed beneath the trail as it continued off the other side and meandered its way to the Columbia River far below.

I'd have to jump.

I leaped across the giant puddle and landed with a splat right in the middle.

Mud splattered on my calves. So much for the new boots.

As I sloshed through the murky water, my entire body gave an involuntary shudder. I could feel the cold from the piercing mountain runoff creeping into my skin. *This should make the rest of the climb fabulous*, I thought, turning to sarcasm, which, as Mom likes to remind me, is not my best trait.

Feeling vulnerable, I thought of Pops. *He would love this.* He would have egged me on—told me to splash my way through the puddles. The ache of missing him crept in like the mud in my socks.

*Not now, Meg. You have to concentrate.*

Something electronic sounded in the trees. I turned my head in the direction of the sound. One of Andrew's cameras swiveled on a spruce tree. Crap. I forgot about the cameras. Was Andrew watching me falter? He said he could activate any camera on the trail with his remote.

*Move it, Meg.*

As I pushed on, the tree cover became so thick I could barely see the sky. Evergreens draped with heavy moss waved at me in the wind. Something moved ahead. I halted midstride.

"Hello? Is anyone there?" I called.

Where was everyone? Had they already summited? This was stupid. I should have stuck with the group.

I hurried along. The trees disappeared and an enormous basalt rock garden appeared in front of me. I edged as close as I could to the far side of the narrow trail and stood frozen in fear. One misstep here and I'd tumble hundreds of feet over the jagged rocks.

I snuck a peek downward. Big mistake.

My entire body felt as if it were on a Tilt-A-Whirl. I shuddered again, not sure if it was from the cold or the impending feeling of doom growing larger by the moment.

My throat tightened in a knot as I turned my back to the cliff and shuffled one foot at a time over the narrow trail. A baseball-sized rock slipped under my foot—crashing its way over the rocky cliff and sending a smattering of other rocks in an avalanche with it. It sounded like the entire side of the mountain would give way.

I clutched the slick, wet cliff behind me, trying to dig my nails in for traction. There wasn't anything to grab. My backpack scraped along the rock. One of the trekking poles grated in the side pocket, making a sound like nails on a chalkboard. I tiptoed carefully, wanting to sprint and stay frozen at the same time. finally, my foot landed on solid, syrupy mud. I'd made it to the other side.

Relief washed over me, followed by a new thought—this was the only way down. Last night I read that climbers who summited Everest often died on the descent. Not a comforting thought. It made me feel even worse for Mitch. This was the kind of assignment he lived for.

The landscape shifted again. This section of the trail had burned in a forest fire. Snags, partly dead trees still standing, and burned trees littered the side of the cliff. It gave me an eerie feeling, like walking through a tree cemetery. I quickened my pace and scurried along the wider trail.

Around the next bend, I heard voices. fighting voices? Was someone coming? I stood absolutely still. Nothing.

*Maybe it was the wind*, I thought, slogging along. *Or maybe I'm paranoid.*

I could feel my heels rubbing against my wet socks. They were raw, and I had a sinking feeling they were bleeding. I thought about stopping to adhere Band-Aids, but it was doubtful they'd do much good with wet socks. I should have thought about packing extra socks.

No wonder I never hiked. This was miserable and creepy. I'd never been alone in a forest without Pops. The quiet was making it impossible to stop thinking about him.

Out of the corner of my eye, I saw movement and the flash of bright red. A deer trail darted off from the main trail, winding its way deeper into the forest. I peered into the woods and saw what looked like a person in a red jacket crouched in a dugout.

"Hey! Who's out there?" I shouted. Someone or something bolted in the woods. "Hello?"

I grabbed my phone and tried to zoom in. I couldn't see anything. I took a couple pics anyway.

Maybe my eyes were playing tricks on me? I rubbed them and checked again. Whoever or whatever it was, it was gone. Why would someone hide in a dugout? There was no way I was venturing any deeper into the woods to find out.

I panted my way up switchback after switchback, stopping every ten minutes to catch my breath and slug water. The trail opened onto another rocky ledge of slate and basalt. I heard voices again. But this time I recognized the voices.

I'd made it.

*Whew!*

A sweeping view of the Columbia River Gorge made my head spin. Both Oregon and Washington were visible from this vantage point. The brilliant blue waters of the Columbia River cut between the two states, weaving past an island in the middle and continuing west toward the ocean. Boulders scattered in various shapes and sizes up to the tree line.

From there, trees dropped away—straight down to the river. A collection of backpacks, water bottles, and gear was strewn about. The sun appeared from behind the cloud cover, heating the rocks. Alicia, Dave, Lenny, and Leaf all lounged on the sizzling rocks. My body felt like strawberries dumped into a blender—pulsing and swirling together.

Dave noticed me first. "Hey there, Meggie. We were wondering where you got to." He was precariously perched on the top of a huge overhang—a slab of rock that protruded over the side of the cliff. His feet stuck off the edge. I tried to look away from the crumbly rocks below.

"Yeah, I stopped a bunch to take photos and notes," I lied.

"Didn't happen to see my hat by chance, did you?" Dave patted his silver hair. He looked bald without the hat.

"No. Did you lose it?"

"Must have fallen off. It'll turn up. No worries."

Alicia looked like she was asleep on a cluster of smaller rocks at the base of the trail. Her head rested on her backpack and her stomach was exposed to the sun. Leaf stood upon my arrival, stretching and bowing to the sun. Lenny gave me a leering look, and jumped to his feet.

"Let's roll!"

I couldn't tell if Alicia opened her eyes behind her sunglasses. Her body betrayed no movement as she said, "What's the plan, Dave? That was hardly a warm-up."

Dave sat straight on his ledge and pulled a map from his pocket. "Want to head to Multnomah Falls? It looks like it's a quick eight or nine. I can call Krissy and tell her to pick us up there. What do you say, Meggie?"

A quick eight or nine more miles? No way!

I found a solid-looking rock at the top of the trail, as far away from the edge as possible, and parked myself on it. "You go ahead. I'm going to go through my notes and get more pictures from the summit here."

"Summit?" Leaf asked. His bare feet were caked in mud. I wondered if they hurt.

"Yeah, I think it'll be important to have a photo and write-up from here."

"This isn't the summit," Leaf said, twirling a dreadlock.

"Huh?" I gulped. My mouth felt dry and sandy. This wasn't the summit.

"That's the summit," he said, pointing to a collection of car-sized boulders above us that looked as if they'd been tossed in the sky by a giant.

*No. Oh, no. No.*

"Oh, yeah. I know. I just meant this might be a better spot for photos."

"Right, Meggie. That's why we waited for you. Thought you might want to see them all scramble to the top," Dave said, grinning and getting to his feet.

My heart pounded so fast, I was sure they could see it pumping through my shirt. Andrew came around the corner with a red sweatshirt tied around his waist and a camera over his shoulder. His backpack looked as if it had exploded. Cords and cables were twisted together and spilled from the sides.

"Hiya!" he greeted me, and to Dave he said, "Got it! Good footage from that angle. Took a little spill, though. I need to get this all sorted out."

"Were you on a deer trail?" I asked him.

"Deer trail?" he asked as he untangled a mess of black cables longer than me.

"You know those side trails carved by deer going through the woods."

"Hell, no! You won't get me off the main path without bonus pay. There are probably all kinds of spiders in there." He mopped his forehead with the sleeve of his sweatshirt.

"Won't get you much of anywhere, Tubby." Lenny leered at Andrew. "Maybe if Dave hired a real professional instead of a fatty, we'd be getting somewhere with this show."

"Knock it off. We're way past the era of body shaming, man," Andrew said, glaring at Lenny. He rummaged through a hard black case of gear.

"You get me my airtime, or I'll knock you off." Lenny flexed his pecs.

"This is the most unprofessional production I've ever seen. Can you say 'imploding'?" Andrew said, stalking over to the rocks near me. He adjusted his earpiece and tapped at the microphone mounted in front of his mouth.

Leaf stopped stretching and said to Lenny, "Dude, stop with the airtime thing. We're all getting equal time. It's in the contract. What we should be concerned about is the lack of sustainability. An eco-show and look at this." He motioned to a granola-bar wrapper and Gatorade bottle on the rocks. "No one's green."

"What are you smoking, hippie? This show ain't green and I'm not sharing my airtime with you and your pot-smoking following," Lenny said. "I'm here for the million bucks. This show's making me a TV star."

Leaf looked like he was about to say something when Dave clapped his hands. "Enough!"

He flitted over the rocks to Lenny and put an arm around his shoulder. "We'll get you airtime, mate. No worries. All right! Let's get Andrew here up the cliff first. He can shoot from there. Let's race."

Alicia yawned and slowly sat up. Leaf gathered his pack, keeping an eye on Lenny the entire time. Andrew did a check of each contestant's camera and the microphones.

"I need to switch your audio settings. They're not working," he said, sitting next to Alicia.

She fiddled with a piece of grass, wrapping it around her finger.

Once he finished checking her microphone, he looked like he was trying to talk to her about something. She kept her gaze forward toward the river.

Andrew gave up, slung his camera over his shoulder, and started the dangerous ascent up the side of the rocks toward the summit.

I needed to stall. They had to go ahead of me.

*Think, Meg, think.*

"Hey, do you think I could do a quick interview with each of you before you head out again?"

"Here?" Alicia asked with a doubtful expression on her

face. She pushed her sunglasses up on her brow with her middle finger.

"Sure. You know, I'd love to hear your first impressions of the climb and the Gorge," I said, pointing out toward the river below us.

"Great idea, Meggie!" Dave said. "Go ahead and do a quick interview. I'm going to catch up with Andrew."

Before I could blink, he was halfway up the cliff. I watched him expertly maneuver over the rocks. He grabbed the camera from Andrew and disappeared.

I turned to the remaining three contestants. "Who wants to go first?" I asked, grabbing my notebook and pen.

# SEVEN

Alicia glared at me. "Seriously? How long is this going to take?"

I intended to cement myself to the rock formation at the base of the summit for as long as possible, but Alicia didn't need to know that. "Oh, a couple minutes at most," I said breezily.

She got to her feet and leaped over a cluster of rocks to reach me.

"I'm stretching while we do this." She pulled her ankle behind her back.

"Fine. Yeah, not a problem," I said as I snapped a photo of her in a swanlike pose with the rugged landscape behind her. I got the vibe she didn't like me, but why? "Tell me, how did this first climb here in our great state of Oregon feel?"

She looked at me as if I must be joking. "Are you for real?"

I nodded and motioned with my hands for her to continue.

Shrugging, she said, "That wasn't a hike." She gestured to the top. "Ask me again when we do this next leg. I've heard Multnomah Falls is impressive. Plus, since Dave made us wait for you, my heart rate's barely up. I'm ready to pick up the pace."

She bounced on her feet and turned her head toward the

river. "Must say, though, this view is pretty spectacular. Never seen anything like it."

"What about your fellow contestants—can you tell me what it's like to be the only woman left in the race?"

"Unlike those two jackasses, I'm serious about this show. I want the million dollars. It's going to pay for my training and let me ski full-time."

"Yeah, tell me more about skiing. I read in your bio that you're hoping to make the Olympic team. I think our readers will really love to learn about what it's like to train at your level." I felt like I was finally starting to get in a groove.

Alicia's eyes traveled in the direction of Lenny and Leaf. They looked an odd match—a hippie and thug who looked like they were sparring on the side of a mountain. I couldn't hear what they were saying but could tell from their rigid body language they weren't swapping trail secrets.

Alicia leaned toward me and spoke quietly. "You want a story? Do a little research into those two. There's shady stuff going on. This show is going to blow up."

What did she mean? Before I could ask her, she stopped abruptly and shouted to Lenny and Leaf, "I'm out of here! See if you can catch me, boys." With that she jumped over the rocks and was gone.

Odd response. What were Leaf and Lenny arguing about?

Although Lenny outweighed Leaf by at least fifty pounds, Leaf didn't appear to be backing down. In fact, Gam would have said he was holding the space between them. His body was poised in a hardened yoga stance.

Whatever he said to Lenny made Lenny's chest muscles deflate. If only I could hear what they were saying. Drama made for the best stories.

I scrawled a couple of sentences in my notebook and called Leaf over.

"Tell me about your impressions of this first hike. I know

you're an Oregon native, but how does it compare to other climbs you've done?"

Leaf looked at me with lazy eyes. "Not really a climb, is it? But hey, it's cool because this is what it's all about—communing with nature, becoming a breathing part of the ecosystem."

He paused, closed his eyes and inhaled deeply. "You know, this is where I live. I'm part of this."

I tried not to stare at his feet, but couldn't help myself. His calluses reminded me of stale chicken nuggets. Gross.

Leaf caught me staring and lifted a foot in the air. "It's taken me years to build these."

"Does it hurt? What about rocks and prickly vines?"

"A knife couldn't cut through this." He stuck a dirty fingernail into his heel to prove his point.

"Would it be safe to say you're happy to be able to share this experience and your home—Oregon—with everyone who'll watch the show?"

Leaf's body stiffened. "I didn't say that."

"Oh, uh, I guess I assumed you would."

"You assumed wrong."

"Well, what I'm trying to get at is, obviously, you're really in touch with nature. Aren't you excited a national television program is going to showcase that?"

Glancing over at Lenny, who was sunning himself on a rock, Leaf shook his head with disgust. "No. I'm bummed to see where the show's going. Dave promised me it would be the first eco-show in the U.S. I'm looking into some other options to make that happen."

I looked at him with surprise and whispered, "Really? Like what?"

Before he could answer, we heard Alicia shouting from the summit, "Come on! Get up here. I want to go."

Leaf's lanky body disappeared over the rocks and Lenny took his cue. He squeezed his beefy body next to mine on the rock. I scooted to the edge. It was sharp and dug into my thigh.

"Saved the best for last, yeah?" He put his hand on my knee.

Oh God, why had I left him last? This was a big mistake. I was stuck on the ledge with a wannabe Jersey mafia member.

"Uh, okay. So, Lenny," I said, removing his hand from my knee. "How does this experience compare to other locations you've seen?"

"The ladies are hot as shit?" He ogled me.

I laughed uncomfortably, scooting away from him. "Anything else?"

"Not really my thing—no nightlife here, no action."

"But what about the race? Haven't the legs of the race been filmed outdoors?"

"Yeah. Still not my thing. I mean, I'm obviously the best competitor here"—he flexed his arm muscles—"but I don't need all this nature shit. Gimme a brewski, a couple of hotties, and I'm good to go."

Was this guy for real? He was like something out of a bad movie. How did he end up on an extreme adventure race? I studied my notebook, trying to think of anything to ask him that wouldn't lead to him regaling me with a laundry list of his exploits.

"How do you feel about your competitors?" I asked, keeping my eyes on my journal.

Lenny pointed at himself with a double hang-loose sign. "Please, look at me. There's no competition. Alicia's all hot 'n' shit, but she's too uptight for me, and that hippie scum can't beat me. I got this one in the bag. The cash is mine."

Wow, the words flew out of him. I'd have great material to work with later. Little did he know none of it would be flattering.

The farther I traveled with this ragtag team, the more unbelievable it seemed that the production was legit. Something tugged at my intuition. I didn't know much about producing a television show, but this couldn't be typical. Maybe there was a Pulitzer in my future after all. Once I dragged myself off this rock face, I was going to have to brush up on my investigative skills and get to the bottom of the real story behind *Race the States*. That should impress Greg.

Lenny reached over and gave my knee another hard squeeze. He smelled like stale rum and pomade. "Catch ya later." His tight torso and bulky calves flexed with each step he took. I couldn't tell if he walked that way naturally or was trying to impress me. Either way it wasn't working.

Now the question was, how to get down?

But first, a little snack to help fortify my thoughts. I pulled a bag of chocolate almond trail mix and a bottle of lemon Gatorade from my backpack. I gulped Gatorade without breathing and chomped on the salty-sweet mix.

Questions swarmed in my mind. Should I ask Greg what he knew about the race? He was a key sponsor, after all. How much research had he done before partnering with Dave? And where was he?

I glanced at my watch; it was after 1:00. Greg should have been here by now.

Who were the contestants and how were they chosen for the show? Was Alicia right that Leaf thought he was participating in some sort of eco-challenge? Had he really gotten in a physical fight over it? And what did he mean when he said he was looking into other options for the show? The whole thing seemed odder by the minute.

While I ruminated on the many questions surrounding *Race the States*, I heard Dave's voice shouting from above, "Hey, Meggie! Come up here!"

When could a girl catch a break? I thought they were going ahead without me.

*Might as well get on with it.* I sighed and stuffed the trail mix, Gatorade, and my notes into my pack. The pack didn't feel any lighter when I slung it over my shoulders. Nor did my feet. Sitting had made them worse.

I treaded carefully, feeling the skin on my ankles rubbing off onto my soggy socks.

The basalt formation comprising the summit was a gnarly collection of giant boulders with jagged edges. No wonder the guidebooks said this hike was not kid-friendly. I took another tentative step forward. Smaller rocks slipped below my feet. My entire body lurched forward.

*Don't look down. DO NOT look down!*

Was any job worth this? Maybe Jill's couch wasn't so bad after all.

I willed myself forward one baby step at a time. Hobbling at a snail's pace, I'd gotten about a quarter of the way.

Dave's voice echoed from above. "Keep it up, Meggie! You're close."

Our ideas of close weren't exactly in alignment. The summit looked insurmountable from my vantage point. I felt more exposed than ever with the wind whipping over my head. The sun disappeared behind a patch of granite clouds. A rumbling sound erupted. I prayed it wasn't an avalanche of rock debris heading my way. Instead, it was an airplane making its descent into the Portland airport. It was flying so low it looked as if I could reach out and swipe the underbelly of the fuselage. The plane's wings tilted and tipped with the wind. Not a flight I'd want to be on. I could only imagine the nervous passengers who were likely gripping armrests and clenching their teeth tightly on the bumpy descent.

The rumbling quieted as the plane bounced its way above the Columbia River, dipping beneath my line of sight. Something sleety and wet landed on my head. A rain shower burst out of the clouds, impaling the rocks and me with fat drops.

The rain made the going more difficult. The trail was like a sheet of ice. Within minutes, I was soaked to my underwear. Water pooled in the crevices of my pack and streamed down the back of my legs. Rain trickled down my sweat-stained face, leaving the taste of salt in my mouth.

I laughed out loud. Otherwise, I would have cried. What else could go wrong today?

Slogging my way to the crest, I realized the path was carved between basalt boulders. On either side, a sheer cliff dropped into rock graveyards. I was done. No way was I going any farther. That's when I heard Greg's voice below.

"Hey! Meg, is that you?"

Very carefully, I turned around and glanced down. I thought I was going to vomit. Greg's angular body waved at me from the exposed bluff below.

I raised my hand in a half wave and gulped.

"Greg! You made it, mate!" Dave's scruffy body emerged past the rock cliffs on a solid wooded trail maybe fifty yards ahead of me. He waved energetically at Greg and caught my frozen eye. "Coming, Meggie?"

I grimaced and pretended to adjust the straps on my backpack. "Yeah, one sec."

Greg on my heels, Dave in plain sight, I froze and, for the briefest moment, considered faking a fall. That would be a sure way to get out of this.

But instead, I did what any self-respecting journalist would do—I mustered up every ounce of courage and continued onward.

However, in a strange twist of fate, my foot slipped as it made contact with the ground. Suddenly I was airborne.

*Oh no!*

I flailed my arms and let out a little scream as I landed with a hard thud. My hands hit the wet rubble first. My skin burned as I slid along the gravelly slab. Half of my body dangled on the slick rock protruding over the edge. I dug my hands into the loose tangle of pebbles, desperately trying to slow my momentum.

How ironic, or maybe more like instant karma. That's the last time I'd ever think about faking a fall. Was I actually about to sail over the side of the cliff?

Something opaque flashed in front of my eye. The earth under my knees stalled. I heard a deep guttural scream. I looked up in time to see Lenny's body flying backward from the top of a craggy rock about three feet above me.

# EIGHT

"Oh, my God!" I heard my voice wailing, but it didn't sound like me. It took a moment to get my bearings. Was I really flat on the ledge of the summit? Had I really seen Lenny fall? Could this all be a terrible dream?

I refused to move my body for fear of launching myself over the side of the cliff. Taking an internal inventory, I tried wiggling my fingers and toes. Nothing broken.

I pushed up to my hands and knees. There was a gash on my right thigh, and blood was oozing onto my khaki shorts. My left elbow throbbed. Everything else, aside from scrapes and bruises, felt okay.

Slowly, I crawled forward. I had to know if my eyes were playing tricks on me.

Had I seen Lenny fly past me? Rock fragments were cemented in my dirty hands, but I had to know if what I'd seen was legit.

I crawled so my entire body was back on the trail. I craned my neck to see over the side of the cliff. Large boulders blocked my view. There was the sound of yelling ahead and behind me, but in my muddled state, I couldn't make out who or what was being said.

Dave's strong hands shook me back to reality. He pulled me to my feet in one swoop. "Meggie, are you all right? You took a nasty fall."

How did he get to me that quickly?

Dave caught me as I swayed. "Easy there."

Uncontrollable shaking overcame my entire body. "Le—Le—Lenny," I managed to squeak out.

Dave rubbed my arms vigorously and pulled my pack off. "You're in shock. Let's get you over here to sit down." He gently kicked my pack to the side of the trail and eased me along the path toward the group of boulders that Lenny had fallen from.

I clawed his arm with my nails and stood frozen and shaking. "I can't."

"Come on, lassie, it's okay, I've got you," Dave said as he maneuvered behind me and wrapped his tanned arms around my body. He guided me with a firm grasp on both my shoulders. Something cracked under his feet. He reached down and picked up one of Andrew's waterproof cameras. "Wonder how that got here," he said, examining the plastic camera in the air and tucking it in his pocket.

He lowered me onto a rock. Behind me on the spiny summit was an expansive view of Beacon Rock and Silver Star Mountain. I whipped my head around.

"Meg!" Greg cried as he sprinted over the slick path to where I was sitting. "I saw you disappear and heard a scream." He looked at Dave crouched next to me, still rubbing my arms to generate heat. "You're a mess!"

Dave got to his feet, put his hand on Greg's shoulder, and spoke as if I weren't there. "She's in shock, mate. Had a good scare. Got any sugar by chance?" he asked, motioning to Greg's pack.

I wrapped my arms around my wet and bloodstained body, trying to stop shivering.

Greg flung his pack off and dug quickly through it, pulling out a Snickers bar. He unwrapped it and thrust it at me with a worried look on his face. "Here. Eat this, it'll help."

I tried to stammer out a thanks, but my mouth wouldn't form words. It felt heavy and gummy. Why weren't they trying to help Lenny?

"Everyone else gone?" Greg asked Dave as he untied the jacket from his waist and wrapped it around my shoulders.

Dave nodded in the direction of the wooded trail ahead. "Yep, they're all out there."

I shook my head no, but it didn't seem to make any impact in the midst of my full-body quake.

Greg ripped off his shirt. His washboard stomach was taut. He dropped to his knees and dabbed my bloody knees with his shirt. Looking at Dave, he asked, "What happened?"

Dave paused and gave me a long, conspiratorial look. He knew.

I held my breath as he answered, "Meggie here tripped on a snag there." He pointed to the trail behind us.

We both knew there wasn't a snag. Just me and my klutzy feet.

Greg didn't notice as Dave nudged me and continued. "She had me worried for a minute there—thought she was about to slide right off. Huh?"

I nodded at him. The shaking began to subside. Greg doctored my knees with Band-Aids and applied pressure to the gash on my thigh. "You'll be fine, Meg. It's only a surface cut."

I chomped a bite of the candy bar. They were right. The sugar and chocolate surged through my bloodstream. My body let out an involuntary shiver. I wolfed down the rest of the bar. Greg and Dave sat on either side of me. I noticed Dave give

Greg a nod of approval as if they agreed I was no longer in danger of going into full-blown shock.

After polishing off the candy bar, I cleared my throat, inhaled through my nose and tried to refocus on Lenny. "Lenny!" I said, pointing behind me. "Lenny fell."

Greg's face squished in a puzzled expression. "Lenny fell where?"

My energy was definitely returning. Heat rose on my face. "Right here." I motioned to the top of the rock.

Dave looked at me in disbelief. "You fell, Meggie. Lenny's out there with the crew running."

I shook my head, feeling like I'd been caught in a lie. "No, no, Lenny fell. Right after I tripped, I saw him!"

"Are you sure?" Greg asked, removing his hand from the gash on my thigh. "Maybe you got confused when you fell. Saw a bird or something?"

"No! I didn't see a bird. I swear—I saw Lenny." I shook my head, feeling my senses narrowing into focus. I knew what I had seen. "He fell backward off this rock."

Greg shrugged at Dave and pushed himself up. He stretched to see behind and below us. "Nothing there."

Dave returned to standing and peered with Greg. "Nope. I think your eyes were playing tricks on you."

My cheeks blazed with heat. Birds didn't scream or flail backward off the sides of cliffs. "I saw him," I insisted. Despite my cuts, bruises, and blistered ankles, I stretched and stood up. Once upright, I swayed again. Dave and Greg caught me on either side. I brushed them off. "I'm okay."

Swallowing the fear mounting in my stomach, I stood on my toes to get a better view. They were right. There was nothing but water-stained rocks below.

"Come on, Meg, let's get you down and in dry clothes," Greg said, grabbing my arm.

"I'll catch up with the crew," Dave said, starting off in the other direction. "Glad you're okay, Meggie. See you at the other side."

I shuffled my feet over the rocks with Greg leading me by the arm. His touch stirred my stomach into an entirely different kind of nervous flutter.

We'd only taken a step when I spotted a break between the boulders. "Wait!" I shouted. "There!" I pointed to a speck of yellow below.

Greg stopped in midstride. He followed my finger, dropped my other arm, and raced to the rock where I had rested. Carefully, he climbed to the top and surveyed the landscape below.

"Dave!" he hollered. "Get back here!" Then he turned to me. "Meg! Don't move!"

# NINE

Dave bounded under the overhang of rain-drenched moss and leaped up the slippery rock to where Greg peered down. I watched as he leaned over the ledge, looked at Greg and shook his head.

My feet remained firmly rooted to the trail, but they pulled me in Greg and Dave's direction. I was strangely compelled to look.

Greg scampered down the rock and rummaged through his pack. "I might have rope."

Dave turned from his perch and said with a heavy voice, "It's too late. He's a goner."

My knees locked. Lenny was dead. I hadn't imagined any of it. I had, instead, witnessed my first death close-up.

A new wave of tremors washed over my body. Lenny certainly wasn't on my list of people I'd most like to spend time with, but I didn't wish him dead. Gam said death was merely a transition—where our spirits continued on to the next manifestation. To me death seemed brutal and savage. I couldn't see Lenny's body, but visions of his fake tan and slicked hair sprawled on the rocks below flashed through my mind.

Greg dug his phone from a side pocket of his pack and held it in the air, trying to find service. He dialed and positioned the phone in front of him. The speaker reverberated.

An operator's voice came over the line. "911, what's your emergency?"

"This is Greg Dixon. I'm at the summit of Angel's Rest. Someone's fallen. I think he's dead, but we can't reach the body."

The operator walked Greg through protocol and informed him that an emergency crew was on its way.

I heard her say that under no circumstance were any of us to leave until they arrived.

Greg's voice was steady and calm as she asked him a battery of questions about the accident and the victim. "No, no. Definitely not foul play," Greg said into the phone as he paced on the trail.

Dave sat slumped at the base of the rock, watching Greg intently as he spoke with the operator.

Wrapping up the conversation with 911, Greg stuffed his phone into his pocket. "Looks like we're going to be here a while. Better get comfy." He motioned for me to come closer.

My feet didn't budge. I tried to clear my throat, but it was swollen shut. This couldn't be happening. Lenny was dead?

Greg chuckled softly and stepped over to me. He led me, shaking, to the rock. "Give me your pack."

He tugged my pack off. "Sit," he commanded. My knees wobbled as I landed softly on the hard, smooth rock. This felt like déjà vu.

Dave wrapped his burly arm around me in a half hug. "Sorry, Meggie. I know you're shook up. We'll get you down soon." He squeezed my shoulder as he rose. "I better call Krissy. She's probably wondering what happened to us."

He looked around. "I can't believe this. Never had anything like this happen in all my years of producing television."

Running his fingers through his beard, he went quiet for a moment. I wondered if he might cry. Then he seemed to pull himself together. "Must have left my pack up ahead on the trail. I'll be back."

Now I noticed his pack was gone. Why hadn't he been wearing his pack if he was hiking to catch up with the others? I played the scene in my mind. Dave had been standing at the base of the forested trail when I tripped. Did he have his pack on? I scrunched my eyes, trying to visualize what I'd seen. The soggy rain and my intense fear of heights clouded my memory. The only thing I was sure of was that Dave had managed to arrive at my rescue quickly.

But wait, he must have seen Lenny fall. He would have had to run right past Lenny as he was falling. It had all happened so fast. I'd been so focused on the ground and trying not to sail off the edge that I hadn't bothered to look.

Was it possible Dave hadn't seen Lenny? Or was he lying? He could have easily given Lenny a shove and continued on to me. But why? And why had Lenny been standing on top of the boulder? I never caught sight of him before he fell. He must have been on the far side of the rock.

Questions swirled in my head. None of this made any sense.

The rain stopped and sunlight heated the rocks. Steam rose, making the air humid and thick. I had pulled on Greg's sweatshirt when I thought we were descending. It smelled like laundry soap and felt comforting on my body. Now it was slightly damp, having absorbed the moisture from my wet T-shirt like a sponge. I took it off and wrapped it around my knees.

Greg paced. "Can you remember what you saw?"

I blew out a breath of air. "I'm not sure. I tripped and slid over that," I said, pointing at the rock protruding over the ledge. "I was so busy trying to stop I didn't pay attention. All of a sudden, I saw something—what I thought was Lenny—fly past me. The next thing I knew, Dave was helping me up."

Greg squinted toward the forest where Dave searched frantically for his pack. "Hmm."

"What?" I asked, playing with the string on Greg's sweatshirt. "Do you think something's up?"

"I'm not sure—"

"Found it." Dave interrupted him, reappearing with his oversized pack. He flung it in a pile next to mine and Greg's. A walkie-talkie crackled in his hand. He fumbled with the dial and pushed the side button. "Krissy? Krissy, are you there?"

Static sounded from the walkie-talkie. He tried again. No answer. "Maybe I don't have it on the right channel?" He turned the dial again and shouted, "Krissy, come in—"

More static.

"Are you in range?" Greg asked.

"Should be. I talked to her from there." Dave pointed below us to the rock garden where everyone waited for me.

That seemed like days ago. I checked my watch. Only a half hour had passed since I'd met up with everyone.

"Maybe I'll hike up a little and give it another go," Dave said, taking the walkie-talkie with him.

"Come right back, and don't disturb anything," Greg cautioned.

"Yeah, sure, mate," Dave said, giving Greg an odd look.

My feet burned with cold. If we were stuck here until the police arrived, I might as well try to dry my socks. I untied my boots and pulled the laces loose. I pried the first boot off. My sock was soaked light pink. A blister the size of a quarter bulged on my ankle. Two more had burst on the bottom of my heel and were crusted with dried blood. The other foot was equally tortured. Another blister the size of a golf ball had popped on my ankle. Limp skin dangled as it leaked pus and blood.

Greg caught me trying to rip the loose skin free.

"Meg—your feet are wrecked. You didn't try to break those boots in today? Didn't I tell you to check the fit?"

Was it obvious?

"Don't pick at it. You'll make it worse and infect it. Here, let me find you a wrap."

I watched as Greg extracted a first-aid kit and dry socks from his pack. It was like the hiking version of a Mary Poppins backpack. Things kept appearing from its depths.

"Rest your foot here." He directed me to prop my foot on the base of the rock. "This might sting," he said as he squeezed a mini bottle of rubbing alcohol on my open wounds.

I winced in pain and bit my bottom lip to keep from whining. The surge of adrenaline from having him so close helped.

"Next one," Greg demanded as I reluctantly brought the other foot up.

The chilled alcohol stung and sent a tingling pain along my calf. "Let your feet air dry and put these on," Greg said, throwing thick black ankle socks to me.

"Thanks," I managed to squeak.

"How'd your feet get wet?"

"Puddle," I murmured, not trusting myself to talk. Between Lenny's death and trying to keep up with the adventure racers, I was on the brink of a full-fledged panic attack.

He raised his eyebrows but said nothing.

I wondered if Greg suspected my hiking skills weren't exactly what I'd advertised. Thankfully, we wouldn't be able to hash it out because Andrew startled us.

"Hey! What are you two doing here? I thought everyone was long gone." Andrew's cheeks matched his cherry-red sweatshirt, his breathing was labored, and the scent of rancid sweat emanated from his pores. A camera hung around his neck and a video camera sagged on his shoulder.

"Dang, you two don't look so good." Andrew's eyes flashed to my mangled feet and to Greg pacing on a two foot square.

"Where did you come from?" Greg asked.

Andrew pointed behind him with his thumb. "Back there. I shot footage of Alicia and Leaf on the main trail. Pretty good stuff actually. It's kind of a creepy vibe with the rolling clouds. I can't find Lenny, though. Have either of you seen him?"

I couldn't contain my nervous laughter. It was as if a dam of pent-up anxiety broke free inside me. I clamped my hand over my mouth to try and stop myself. It was a bizarre stress response.

"What's with her?"

Greg pulled Andrew close. He said something under his breath I couldn't hear over the sound of my cackle. Andrew's eyes grew wide. He turned to me with a worried expression. Freeing himself from his camera equipment, he struggled up the rock and gasped.

"Oh, crap!"

Greg nodded.

"What happened? Did he slip?"

"We're not sure. Probably. The police are on their way." Greg gave me a hard look—telling me with his eyes to keep quiet.

"Andrew!" Dave scurried over to greet Andrew. He sure had a way of appearing out of nowhere.

"Got Krissy—she's all set. I'll grab the others at Multnomah and be back in an hour. Hey, Andrew, can I chat with you for a minute over this way?" Dave summoned Andrew to the wooded section of the trail.

"What's that all about?" I asked Greg. Did my voice sound shaky or was it just me?

He stopped pacing and sat next to me. "Listen," he said in barely more than a whisper. "Pretend like I'm checking out your feet. Don't look at me."

I resisted a nod and stared studiously at my aching feet,

rocking in place and rubbing my hands along my crossed arms to try to keep it together.

"Something's not right here, Meg. I don't know what it is. Leave it to the police. I don't want you asking questions or talking with anyone other than the police about what you saw. Got it?"

"Sure," I replied, keeping my gaze on my toes. "You think Lenny's death isn't an accident?"

He shushed me as Dave and Andrew made their way toward us. "Maybe," he whispered.

# TEN

It felt like an eternity until the police arrived. I couldn't help checking my blisters every couple of minutes. Greg caught me twice and shook his finger at me. Why hadn't I painted my toes last night? I thought, glancing at my toenails cracked with mint-green polish. Not so appealing.

Dave tried to distract me with tales from his escapades in Australia. "Remember that time, Andrew, when that croc almost chomped off your arm?" He laughed and leaned back on the rock like it was an armchair.

Andrew chuckled and nodded his head.

"Yeah, well, I think you learned your lesson about sticking your arm near a croc-infested creek, right?" He nudged Andrew in the ribs.

Andrew rolled his eyes. "Wait a minute. The only reason my hand was remotely close to the water was because you wanted a tighter shot."

This caught my attention. "Uh, did you film in Australia? I thought the show was *Race the States*?"

"Nah," Dave said. "That was a couple years back. Different project."

"A different project that took six months and never got off the ground," Andrew said with an edge.

Dave ignored Andrew's gripe.

Greg asked, "Did you bring a notebook, Meg?"

"Of course." I nodded in reply, motioning to my backpack.

"Mind if I borrow a couple of pages?"

"Nope—help yourself." I offered him the notebook with quivering hands. This was a time I could really use a zap of Gam's calming energy.

He tore a page from the notebook, grabbed my ultra-fine-point Sharpie, settled on the rock next to me, and wrote furiously.

"What are you doing?" Dave asked, peering over Greg's shoulder.

Greg waved him off. "Nothing. Jotting notes on the climb while they're still fresh in my head."

I suspected this wasn't the truth, but based on Greg's warning, I kept quiet.

The sound of emergency vehicles wailed in a distant echo below us. Hopefully the police would be here quick. It was nearing 3:00. Greg had a welcome party planned at headquarters at 7:00. Surely he'd cancel, though.

Another hour passed before a crew of search and rescue volunteers packed on the summit with us. I counted five, clad in black-and-white checkered flannel shirts. Their heads were helmeted with headlamps secured on top. Their backpacks bulged with glow sticks, survey tape, batteries, compasses, altimeters, maps, rope, and duct tape. Identification badges and orange rescue whistles hung from carabiners attached to their packs. These were the Crag Rats. I'd read about them in my research. In fact, I'd hoped that if I could impress Greg with this first feature, I could pitch doing a story on the Crag Rats.

The Crag Rats defined Oregon search and rescue. The

book I'd read about them touted the fact they were avid lovers of the backcountry, skiing, and mountains. Yep. Confirmed.

They shouted hellos and offered hugs to Greg, who greeted each of them by name and a clap on the back. Greg motioned a boyish-looking member over to attend to my cuts and scrapes, while the rest of the Crag Rats surveyed the scene.

I threw my shoulders back, in response to my rescuer's weathered good looks. He smelled of sunscreen and sweat. He carefully lifted the bandages Greg had applied and said, "Greg did a bang-up job. As always." He took my bruised elbow in his arm and instructed me to bend it left, right, up, and down. "Looks good."

Next, he examined the gash on my right thigh. It must have passed his approval because he pulled a packet of ibuprofen from the side pocket of his pack and told me to swallow two. "It'll help with the swelling."

Dave and Andrew hung back, giving way to the highly organized volunteer group. The team leader barked out orders as the Crag Rats readied themselves for the climb to Lenny's body.

Once anchors had been set, the first responder rappelled down the canyon. He swung his body off the side of the rock face with ease and disappeared over the side of the cliff. His rescue radio crackled confirmation of what I'd expected.

Lenny was dead.

Oh, my God. Lenny was dead. I'd just witnessed someone die right in front of me. I clutched my hand over my mouth and inhaled deeply through my nose, trying to employ every technique Gam had taught me. Nothing seemed to be working to quell my nerves. I couldn't shake the jittery sensation. The team leader radioed to the sheriff at the search base (the trailhead parking lot). "Got a deceased male here. Going to begin the recovery mission. Looks like our best option is to lower him. Call the medical examiner."

With precision, the Crag Rats geared up with ropes and

harnesses. They lowered a litter basket to recover Lenny's body. One by one, they bounded over the side of the cliff.

My young rescuer waved them off and radioed to base camp. He would descend with us. Either he wasn't needed in the recovery effort, or he thought I was in bad shape.

After forcing my injured feet back into my boots, he pulled me to my feet and grabbed my pack. I turned, thinking he was going to help me hoist it onto me. Instead, he wrapped his rescue pack around his chest and threw mine on his back. "I got this. You watch your step."

As we descended, I glanced quickly at the recovery effort below. I could make out the Crag Rats' black-and-white shirts in the mix of bramble and rock. What an impressive crew. These women and men actually volunteered to put themselves in harm's way.

My rescuer stayed right in front of me. Dave and Andrew followed. Greg brought up the rear.

I bombarded my personal Crag Rat with questions all the way down. Who were these mountaineers, how did they train, why did they put themselves in danger? Not only was it potential material to weave into my story, but it was also helping to keep my mind off Lenny.

"We're the first ever mountain rescue team in the United States," he explained. "The group formed in the 1920s and named themselves after the crags in Mount Hood. We have a couple of mantras we follow. The most important is to protect the rescuer first. If it's not safe, we're not going to climb, or we're going to find another route."

"But you raced here, knowing Lenny was already dead." I kept my gaze lasered on my boots, not wanting to repeat another fall.

"Things are never what they seem. We're always going to respond. At heart we're really a bunch of adrenaline junkies. We have to harness danger and use it to our benefit. I can't tell you how many times we've been called out for a heart attack that turns out to really be a bad case of indigestion. You never know what you're going to find."

I wanted to keep him talking because the compelling story of the Crag Rats was distracting me from the terrifyingly gorgeous panoramic view. "Is it hard to race out to a scene like this for nothing?" I asked, limping along carefully.

He shook his head and responded in a solemn voice. "No, that's our other mantra: These things we do that others may live. If there's even a small chance of finding someone alive, it's worth any effort."

The Crag Rats' dedication left me humbled. If they could risk life and limb to rescue (or, in this case, recover) strangers, I could suck up the courage to get myself down without a panic attack.

Dave, Andrew, and Greg lagged behind. I took the opportunity to quiz the rescuer on the cause of Lenny's death.

"You've seen a lot of falls, right? Do you think it was an accident?"

"Hard to say. The medical examiner will have to do an autopsy."

I slid over the loose gravel trail, inched my head near his shoulder and said in a low voice, "Do you think he could have been pushed? I saw it happen. It didn't look right. His body cartwheeled off the boulder."

He shrugged and said, "Maybe. Could have been the way he slipped. Happens more than you'd think."

Going down was worse—much worse. It didn't help that each step sent pain searing up my feet. It was impossible to land without inflaming my blisters. Plus, on the descent we had to hug the right side of the trail, which dropped straight off. Between the agony of my raw ankles and the fear that I'd fall off the cliff, I'd be lucky if I made it back to the parking lot before dark.

Greg caught up to us. I couldn't let him think I was naturally this slow. I lied. "Sorry I'm slow. Kind of tender on my leg."

"Take your time. We're not in a rush." He stood with his hands on his hips. I glanced behind me to see him watching me limp.

Just past the deer trail where I thought I saw someone earlier, Andrew and Dave stopped to remove a GoPro mounted in the trees. Someone had been out there earlier. Maybe it was one of them adjusting a camera.

We continued downward through heavy tree overhangs and winding switchbacks. I lost my footing a couple of times but arrived on the valley floor unscathed. We ducked under caution tape roping off the trailhead, and crossed the street to the parking lot. It was a buzz of activity. A sheriff's car blocked the entrance.

"I'm going to need statements from each of you," a khaki-clad police officer wearing a tan hat said as he approached us. His silver-starred badge flashed on his chest, labeling him as the sheriff. If I'd had to guess, I'd have said he was about Gam's age.

Greg stepped forward and greeted the sheriff, "Hey, Bill, give me a minute, okay?" He pointed his thumb at me and said, "I want to get my staffer here in dry clothes."

Was there anyone he didn't know?

"You got it, Greg. How about I start with you two," the sheriff said, looking at Dave and Andrew.

The sheriff escorted Dave and Andrew to his patrol car while Greg and I made our way over to where his black sports car was parked. He beeped his key chain, and the trunk popped open. He pulled out a yellow climbing fleece, handed it to me, and said, "Head over behind those trees, take off your wet shirt, and put this on."

I limped to a clump of trees and stripped out of my wet shirt. Greg's fleece was warm to the touch. It felt soft on my damp skin and smelled like a new car and pine trees. It hung to my mid-thigh and my hands disappeared in the sleeves. I hugged myself as I limped in the direction of the sheriff.

"Meg! I heard what happened. How are you?" Krissy's voice called out. She rushed from the far side of the parking lot where the van was camped. "They said Lenny's dead? I can't believe it." Krissy tucked an icy-white curl that had escaped from her bun behind her ear.

"It's true," I said, still hugging Greg's sweatshirt around my body. I shuddered, but not from cold, nodding slowly. "Yeah, I saw him fall."

Krissy gasped. She took her petite hands and rubbed my arms as if to help warm me. "I'm sorry. That must have been awful. Come on, I've got tea in the van."

Warm tea sounded wonderful. I let Krissy lead me away from the commotion of the sheriff's interviews. We climbed in. Krissy quickly hit a button that automatically shut the doors.

"Here, this will help," Krissy said, turning the key in the ignition and shooting me a concerned look. Heat blasted from the vents, funneling humid air in my face. I shrugged my hands out of Greg's sweatshirt and held them in front of the vents as if warming them over a campfire. Krissy clicked on my seat warmer. Within seconds, my buns were toasting, too.

"Now you're looking a little better," Krissy said. She reached behind the backseat and grabbed a stainless-steel thermos. Steam erupted from the top as she unscrewed the cap. She poured the boiling water into the lid, which also served as a cup. "Hold this," she said, offering me the cup.

She leaned over my legs to open the glove box. It was crammed with papers, tissue, maps, and gum wrappers. What a mess.

Krissy dug around until she found a tea bag. She shoved all the loose contents in, slammed it shut, and stuck the tea bag in my cup.

Minty herb-infused steam reached my nostrils. The scent reminded me of Gam's kitchen. For the first time in the last four hours, I took a deep cleansing breath in. I took a sip of the burning tea. The hot liquid trickled down my throat and warmed me from the inside.

"I think we can turn this down now," I said, closing the heat vent in front of me. I noticed beads of sweat forming on Krissy's face. Her glasses were fogged up. I couldn't believe she hadn't said anything.

"You sure?" she asked, before turning the van off. "I know if I get cold after a long run I need a while to warm up."

"I didn't know you were a runner." I cradled the tea, finally feeling a touch of calm wash over me.

She screwed the lid tightly on the thermos. "Not anymore. I used to. A little."

I raised my teacup in a half toast. "This is all I need now. Thanks again. I didn't realize how messed up I was."

"I can't blame you. I think I would have gone fetal had I seen someone fall to their death, even if it was Lenny," she said with disdain.

Light rain hit the windshield. I took another sip of tea.

"Do you want to talk about it?" Krissy asked. "Either way's cool. I thought it might be good for you to talk about it while it's fresh."

That reminded me that I needed to talk to the sheriff. Of course that meant leaving the safe haven of the van just as I was finally starting to feel dry.

"I think I better go talk to the sheriff," I said, resting my empty teacup on the dashboard. "Might as well get it over with. Thanks for the tea."

I stretched my back as I stepped out of the car. Every inch of my body ached. All I wanted to do was crawl into bed.

"Where did you sneak off to?" the sheriff demanded as I approached his car.

"I—I—I didn't. I went to change and Krissy offered me tea," I stammered.

"Go easy on her," Greg said, winking at me. "The kid's had the shock of her life today."

Kid? Did he think of me as a kid?

"I'll take it from here," the sheriff said to Greg. He turned to me and tipped his hat. "Sheriff Bill Daniels, miss." A sky-blue patch on his left chest read Hood River County Sheriff with Mount Hood stitched in white and green.

"It's starting to rain. Why don't we have a seat in my car?" Walking around the car, he opened the passenger door and waited for me to sit before he closed it.

"Full name?" he asked as he pushed the driver's seat back and pulled out a small notebook.

"Mary Margaret Reed."

"How do you spell that?"

I spelled my name letter by letter as he scribbled on his notepad. "Reed—hmm. Any relation to Charlie Reed?"

I looked at him with wide eyes. A sudden feeling of heaviness spread down my arms as I took a slight step back. He knew Pops? "Yeah, Charlie's—well, Charlie was my dad."

He tugged a toothpick from a canister resting on the dash. He gnawed it and appraised me.

"A shame we have to meet like this. I knew your dad. He thought the world of you. Talked about you all the time."

He looked like someone Pops would have liked, with his soft eyes, deep wrinkles, and the wooden toothpick clamped between his teeth. His white, scruffy cheeks looked due for a shave.

"How did you know my dad?" I asked. A stabbing pain spread across my abdomen. Just hearing his name made my entire body turn heavy and numb.

A dispatcher came over the radio, barking out code numbers. Sheriff Daniels ignored them, turned down the volume, and said, "Charlie was a good pal. We worked together on that meth story. Until—" He stopped and wrinkled his forehead. "Until, well, he went off the deep end. What a shame. His case file is still sitting on the corner of my desk."

Oh, no, not this. Not Pops's meth madness, as Mom called it. Pops had been a revered journalist throughout the state. He'd worked his way up from covering the street beat to becoming *The O*'s lead investigative reporter. Along the way, he acquired enough awards to fill an entire wall and a handful of enemies—most from the meth story.

Sheriff Daniels distracted me from my thoughts when he put his hand on the small of his back and shifted in his seat. "Sorry, my back's been out for weeks. Can't seem to find a comfortable way to sit."

"You should go see my grandmother—Gam," I said. "She's a Reiki healer. I know that kind of scares people, but it's just moving energy in your body. It could help."

"I may do that. I'll try about anything right now." He cleared his throat, still clenching the toothpick. "Back to business," he said, eyeing me cautiously. "What's your purpose here?"

"I, uh—I'm on assignment for *Northwest Extreme* magazine."

Sheriff Daniels rested his pen on the top of his notebook and appraised me with one eye, "Yep, you look the type." He muttered, "Greg always goes for young reporters. Cheap labor." He picked up his pen. "What did you see up there?"

"I saw Lenny fly off the summit." I paused for a second, watching fat raindrops splatter on the windshield. The sound made me think of Lenny. Although I hadn't heard the impact, he must have landed with a splat. Ugh. I gave an involuntary shudder and said, "I think someone pushed him."

"Chip off your dad's block, huh?" He laughed again but wrote nothing in his notebook.

"Don't you want to take this down?" My voice held an edge. "I heard him scream and then he went sailing past me—but his body cartwheeled. It didn't look like he tripped."

"Had a lot of experience with these kinds of falls, have you?" His eyebrows wrinkled.

"Listen, I'm serious. There's something up with this whole *Race the States* production. Didn't Greg mention anything?"

"Nope. Not a word."

"Well, you should talk to him again. I know he's suspicious, too."

Sheriff Daniels closed his notebook and clicked his pen shut. "I'll do that, Ms. Reed. Don't you worry. Here's what I think. You got spooked up there. Understandable. Happens to the best of us. My advice? Go home. Get some sleep and you'll feel much better by tomorrow."

I glared at him and thrust open the car door. I wasn't imagining things. I might have been young, but I knew what I had seen. I couldn't believe he was completely dismissing me. More like gaslighting.

"I'll follow up if we need anything else for your statement."

I slammed the door shut and stalked over to the van. Greg, Krissy, Dave, and Andrew huddled in conversation.

"How'd it go, Meg?" Greg asked, giving me a questioning look.

"Fine," I said with a half shrug.

"All right, Meggie and Greg, we're heading out to pick up Alicia and Leaf at Multnomah Falls," Dave said. "Meet you for the barbie later?"

Greg assessed the four of us. Krissy's glasses were slightly askew, Andrew's face sweat-stained, and my crunchy hair dried to my head. "Don't you think we should postpone it until tomorrow?"

Dave scoffed. "Nah, Lenny would want us to go on. We can make it a wake. Seven o'clock?"

"I guess," Greg replied, trying to summon a different response from Krissy or Andrew. Neither of them bit. "Okay, if you're sure. I guess I'll see you at seven." Greg ran his fingers through his hair as they all piled into the van.

Krissy maneuvered the van eastward out of the parking lot. I pleaded with Greg, "Why didn't you—" but the sound of a siren cut me off.

The medical examiner arrived. Sheriff Daniels pulled back caution tape to allow the ambulance to enter. There wasn't a body for him to examine. The Crag Rats were still lowering themselves and Lenny's body on the sheer rock face.

"You go home. Take a bath or something. I'll hang out until this is wrapped."

"But why didn't you say anything to the sheriff?"

Greg looked around the parking lot. "Not now. Not here. Go rest. We'll talk later."

Confusion swirled in my head. None of this made sense. Why wouldn't Greg say something to Sheriff Daniels? I could tell from his solid stance I wasn't going to get anywhere by pushing him right now.

I might as well head home. A bath sounded like bliss.

As I tugged my arm out of one of the sleeves of Greg's fleece, his warm, firm hand caught mine. "Keep it."

Before pulling out of the parking lot, I texted Jill. I knew she was in depositions, but I had to tell someone.

> OMG. You're never going to believe what happened. A contestant died. Maybe murdered. I'm freaking out. Call me as soon as you can.

# ELEVEN

Two hours later, my phone alarm blared in my ear. With my eyes shut, I reached my hand out toward Jill's coffee table. Fumbling over a pile of candy wrappers and an empty chip bag (hey, I needed comfort food after today's ordeal), I found my phone and slid the alarm off.

The warmth of my squishy feather-filled down comforter wasn't enough to escape the first image that flashed through my mind—Lenny's body plunging past me. I stretched and pulled my phone close to my face—6:15. The barbecue hosted by *Northwest Extreme* was in forty-five minutes. I'd better get moving.

A text beeped on the screen. Text messages were announced on my phone with the sound of the return key on an old-fashioned typewriter. I should have been born in the 1950s. It suited my style. The high-waisted skirts and clunky typewriters, yep, I was born in the wrong decade. My dream home office, where I'd write my Pulitzer Prize-winning novel, would pay homage to my favorite decade. I kept a secret file folder with clippings of a vintage red Olivetti and of a coral satin flare dress.

One day, when I had my own place, I'd deck my office out with these trinkets of inspiration.

The text was from Jill.

It read:

> Sorry. Been in depos all day. Done by 7:30 or 8:00. Get a beer then? Love you.

Seeing her friendly words brought a smile to my face. But ouch, did moving ever hurt? Angel's Rest killed my quads. I pushed myself off the couch with my arms and hobbled down the hallway to the bathroom.

After a quick shower, I dusted my face with powder, applied lip gloss, blew my hair dry upside down, and tugged on a pair of stretch jeans, a long-sleeved white T-shirt, and my favorite pink puffy vest. My cheeks and lips were chapped and raw with windburn. My eyes felt heavy. I'd have to wear my glasses.

I much preferred my contacts, but when the occasion arose for frames, I was glad I had an assortment to choose from. Without corrective lenses, I couldn't see my hand in front of my face. Fortunately, my prescription hadn't changed since elementary school. I'd amassed an impressive collection of frames over the years. Tonight I opted for a chocolate-brown frame with pink sherbet swirls.

I scribbled a note for Jill, telling her I'd be late but was okay, grabbed my keys, and headed to the office. Greg had invited the *Race the States* contestants and crew, key advertisers, as well as the entire staff, to a welcome barbecue.

It was risky to commit to any sort of outdoor event in April in the Pacific Northwest. Tonight, the weather gods were on Greg's side. Maybe Dave was right—Lenny was sending a message through the weather. The earlier clouds and rain made way for a clear purple evening sky. The sun was low on the horizon and illuminated the Willamette River as I drove to headquarters. Maybe it was the hour-long steamy bath I'd taken prior to crashing on Jill's couch, but the air felt surprisingly warm. I cranked the window and blasted "Mambo Italiano" by Rosemary Clooney.

When I pulled into *Northwest Extreme*'s parking lot, it was jammed with cars. A large white tent stretched across the grassy area in front of the building. Twinkle lights were strung along its edges and portable heaters hummed in each corner. Bistro tables and chairs were clothed in black and six-foot tables lined the edge of the tent.

*Are we really having a party? Lenny just died.* I shuddered. This was wrong.

When Greg took over as editor in chief at the magazine, he moved the operation from a drab downtown office to the converted brick warehouse next to the Willamette River. A walking path from the building's front doors wound for miles along the riverfront, where a jazz quartet played softly on the path. White and pink flowering cherry trees lined the river, littering the sidewalk with pastel petals.

Hickory-scented smoke billowed from four enormous black barbecues at the far side of the tent. Waitstaff in crisp white aprons circulated platters from the barbecues to the tables at the back of the tent. Others circled with trays of appetizers. A line snaked to a fully stocked bar where bartenders were pouring wine and pulling frothy glasses of beer from taps. Dang, Greg knew how to throw a party. I hoped I wasn't underdressed. Scanning the crowd, I waved to a group of my coworkers all dressed casually as well—*whew*.

I hightailed it to the drink line. Armed with a pint, I circulated the tent, in hopes of chatting more with the contestants—I needed more material for my feature and with Lenny's death I needed a new angle. There was no sign of Greg, but Krissy and Alicia were seated at a bistro table near the water. They waved me over. I set my glass on the table and said, "Be right back, I'm going to grab a bite to eat. Either of you want anything?"

"We're good," Krissy said, motioning to the plates in front of them.

My stomach lurched with hunger. I meandered my way through the crowd to the food tables and piled my plate with lemon-grilled chicken, strawberries, grapes, white cheddar cheese cubes, a green salad, a sourdough muffin, and a chocolate cream tart.

"Hungry?" Alicia snarked. Her plate looked like she barely nibbled on anything.

"Yeah," I said, ignoring her judgy tone as I dug into the juicy chicken. "It's been a long day."

I noticed her right arm was covered with scratches. "What happened to your arm?"

She held up her arm. "This? It's nothing. Ran into a sticker bush on the trail."

"It looks like it hurts."

"It's fine," she snapped sharply, putting an end to any further comments.

"We were just talking about what happened up there today," Krissy said, twirling a glass of white wine in her hand. "I still can't believe Lenny, of all people, fell."

"That's called karma," said Alicia, twisting a black cloth napkin in her hand. "Constantly bragging about how skilled and tough he was."

I swallowed a bite of sharp cheese before asking Alicia, "Did you hear anything up there?"

"What do you mean?"

"When Lenny fell. You couldn't have been far ahead, right? Did you hear him scream?" I pulled the stem off the top of a strawberry and popped it my mouth. The cold juice hurt my teeth.

Alicia wrung the napkin with her hands. "No, I didn't hear

a thing. Contrary to what Lenny might have told you, though, I'm actually the fastest. I beat them to Multnomah. Lenny was lagging behind anyway. Called ahead and told us he had to stop for a minute. Maybe he figured we'd wait for him. No way. I kept sprinting."

"That must have been when he fell," Krissy exclaimed. "I bet he stopped to fix a broken lace and slipped." She slugged wine and said, "You were there, Meg. What did you see?"

What did I see? My mind muddled. I tried to replay the events in my head, but everything felt hazy like a bad dream.

"She doesn't want to talk about it, Krissy," Alicia said.

"No, I'm okay. It's just hard to piece it all together." I paused and took a sip of my beer. The smell of hops hit my nose. "I slipped right before I saw him fall. I was distracted, trying to stop myself from sliding over the ledge. I couldn't really see anything."

"What a way to go." Alicia shuddered and threw her napkin over her plate. She pushed herself up from her chair and said, "I'm getting another drink."

Krissy knocked down the rest of her wine and shot up with her glass in hand. "Wait for me. I'll join you."

I felt a hand on my shoulder. "This seat taken?"

I turned to see Greg standing behind me.

"Cute glasses," he said as he set an amber-colored beer on the table and pulled a chair next to me.

Why hadn't I chosen a glass of wine? I was the only person at the table drinking beer.

"You okay?"

"I don't know." I shrugged, answering truthfully. "This whole production feels weird. Why are we still having a party? Doesn't it seem strange that Dave isn't more bothered by Lenny's death?"

Greg rested one hand on his temple. "I'm not sure.

Everyone reacts differently to stress." He coughed as Alicia and Krissy approached the table.

Nodding at Krissy's wineglass, he said, "Perfect Riesling, isn't it? Grapes are grown south of here. The owner's one of our top advertisers."

He stood, nodded to Alicia, squeezed Krissy's shoulder, grabbed his beer, and sauntered away.

"God, I want a boss like that," Krissy said, staring at Greg's backside as he weaved through the room.

From the way Greg squeezed her shoulder, I was pretty sure he returned her feelings. In a strange way it made me feel better. He was my boss, after all. I needed to stop behaving like a lovesick teenager and start acting like the professional journalist he hired.

"What's Dave like as a boss?" I asked.

Krissy slurped more wine. The girl could drink. The room tilted slightly with half of a pint of beer for me.

"Dave's a character. It's the Aussie thing. They play by different rules.

Actually, they don't have any rules." She took another swig of wine. This was good. Maybe if she kept drinking, she'd answer more questions for me.

Alicia stirred a thin black straw in her glass. She appeared bored with our conversation and scanned the room, probably hoping to find another table to join.

"Dave knows the biz," Krissy continued. "You can't take that from him. And he's crafty when it comes to funding. He's found a way to get every single one of his projects off the ground. Trust me; most Hollywood producers can't claim that kind of success. Unless you're a Spielberg or something." She leaned forward and lowered her voice. "The thing is, I'm the one working the deal with the network this time. Not Dave. This is going to launch my career."

Alicia scoffed, mumbling something under her breath.

Krissy ignored her and polished off her wine. "Oregon reminds me of New Zealand. All this greenery and beer."

"I didn't know you were in New Zealand. Were you in Australia, too?" I said, wanting to make a note—everyone in the crew was more connected than I realized. "Is that where you met Dave?"

"No. No, I've never been to either country. Dave talks about New Zealand so much. He hosted another adventure race there years ago. The show garnered a cult following. Oregon is what I imagine New Zealand must be like—forests, beer lovers," Krissy said, holding her empty glass and craning to see how long the line for alcohol was.

Waiters cleared food off the tables and worked the room with champagne and dessert trays. One paused at our table. "Champagne, ladies?"

We nodded as he carefully handed each of us a fluted glass filled with bubbling champagne. I took a sip. The sweet bubbles exploded in my mouth like Pop Rocks.

"That's weird because Andrew told me he and Dave worked on a project that never made it past the cutting room floor," I said. Had Andrew lied?

Krissy snatched a second glass of champagne and downed it. She set the flute on the table and brushed me off. "Oh, don't listen to Andrew. He's always complaining. He and Dave go way back."

The sound of forks on the sides of glasses filled the room as Greg, with a microphone in his hand, addressed the crowd. His tone was somber as he gave a tribute to Lenny. "We lost a great man and adventure racer today." A hush came over the crowd.

Greg talked about Lenny for at least ten minutes. Why wasn't Dave speaking? Shouldn't he be the one to acknowledge Lenny's death?

Greg went on to toast the original ten *Race the States* contestants and thanked everyone for their support in what he said would be "an epic experience. Sure to put the Pacific Northwest on the map as the premiere outdoor adventure spot in the world. Let's do this for Lenny." This was greeted with applause and "For Lenny" from the crowd.

I surveyed the room and spotted Andrew near the jazz band. His hands were flying wildly in the air, obviously arguing with someone. But I couldn't make out who it was. My glasses didn't have the same range as my contacts. I squinted, trying to catch a glimpse.

Alicia swiveled her body and attention to our table. She strummed her nails, caked with dirt, on the tablecloth. "What are you looking at?" she asked in a sullen tone.

"Nothing. I thought I saw a friend of mine."

Alicia snapped her head over her shoulder to the spot I'd been staring at. Andrew's beefy body moved slightly, revealing Leaf, who stalked out of the tent and toward the riverfront with Andrew shaking his index finger after him.

"Old friend, huh?" Alicia asked, shooting me a quizzical look.

I shrugged, stood with my beer in hand, and excused myself from the table. "I need fresh air. Can't waste a spring evening like this. See you two later."

As quickly as I could manage on my gimpy feet, I scooted outside. The sun had sunk in the west. The night air, saturated with barbecue and cherry blossoms, felt refreshingly cool on my face. A slight breeze rustled branches in the trees along the waterfront. I rested my half-full beer on the curb and zipped my vest. Trying to adjust to the darkness, I scanned the grounds for any sign of Leaf. The city lights reflected in the river, but otherwise the path was submerged in darkness.

A tingle of frozen air snuck along my spine as I left the safety and warmth of the tent behind and gimped on the sidewalk to the larger path running parallel to the water. During daylight hours, the path welcomed mothers pushing babies in jogging strollers, die-hard runners, and unhoused people camped out under the oak trees. By night, the path was empty. I looked to my left and right—no sign of Leaf in either direction.

Maybe he'd taken off for his hotel on foot. I decided to give up the hunt but caught movement out of the corner of my eye. Someone was leaning over the edge of the protective wall. The Willamette River ran five feet below.

Typically, the river flowed twenty feet below, but this winter's rain had left the river swollen and flirting with flood stage for the past four months. The river had a history of floods, but for now the retaining wall was holding.

"Hey!" I shouted. "Leaf, is that you?"

The silhouette turned its head, stared in my direction, and bolted into the darkness. This entire event was getting weirder by the minute. A gloomy feeling invaded my body. This was what Gam called a knowing. Like my body knew danger was headed my way.

"Meg, what are you doing out here?" Greg appeared behind me with a flashlight in his hand. The light made tiny yellow spots dance in front of my eyes.

I put my hand in front of my face to block the light. He lowered the flashlight.

"Uh, nothing. I thought I saw Leaf run off. I wanted to ask him something."

"I told you to leave it alone." There was a hardness to his tone that made me flinch.

"I am." I gnawed the inside of my cheek, pointing in that direction. "I just noticed Leaf leave the party and I hadn't had a chance to talk to him since the, you know, fall."

Greg positioned the flashlight to illuminate the path. "Come on, let's get you inside," he said as he chaperoned me to the party. "I'm not kidding around. This could be a dangerous situation."

"But I—I—"

"You said the trail was covered with cameras, right? If Lenny was killed, whoever killed him could have seen you. You've got to play it cool."

I could feel heat rise to my cheeks. Greg really did think of me as a child. "I am playing it cool. I'm telling you, I wanted to talk to Leaf."

"Not according to Alicia. She said you were spying on Andrew and sprinted after Leaf."

We neared the tent. Enough light spilled out from its twinkling lights that Greg clicked off the flashlight.

"Listen, I don't want you involved in this. Why don't you take off? Go home. Rest up. I'll see you at the office tomorrow. Okay?"

"What's that supposed to mean? You don't want me involved in what?" We were interrupted by a rowdy group of climbers all slugging beers.

"Greg! Killer party. Come have a pint."

Greg held a finger. To me, he whispered, "Go home, Meg. Trust me."

# TWELVE

I stormed to my car. Obviously, Greg knew more than he was letting on.

But why wouldn't he tell me? Danger, what danger? He either thought I was a fraud, or worse—he was mixed up in this mess. Sure, I'd made some mistakes but I trusted my journalistic instincts. I was tired of everyone dismissing me. It was time for me to take matters into my own hands and figure out what had really happened to Lenny.

Shutting the car door, I recovered my purse from under the seat. I always left it there, much to Pops's dismay. He was convinced this was the first place thieves looked. But I countered that if they got in, they were going to find it regardless. It's not like I left it on the seat in plain sight.

I pulled out my phone. A missed text from Jill.

Meet us at the bar. Be out late.

Then another:

Matt's coming.

The clock read 9:45. They'd still be there. A beer with Matt sounded heavenly and I needed to fill in my friends on Lenny's murder and Greg's reaction.

My friends equaled Jill, Jill's boyfriend, Will Barrington, and Matt. Matt covered technology for *The O*. We met my junior year (Matt was a year older) when Pops presented as a special guest in our censorship class.

Pops knew all my professors. Matt knew Pops. A fanboy, he brought in a copy of the five-part meth series Pops wrote, "Plague for the Politicians." When Pops spoke to my journalism class, he was still embroiled in the story. Little did he know the fallout the story would bring.

Matt saved a seat for me from that day on with a single stick of silver-wrapped gum. Pops helped Matt land a technology reporting job for *The O* a few months before he was placed on indefinite leave.

Will was a lawyer at the firm where Jill was interning. It was fitting that their names matched. Jill had the annoying habit of morphing into whoever she was dating. I got it. With his Italian heritage and dark-manicured looks, he was easy on the eyes. But I didn't trust him.

Strike one—he carried a black Gucci umbrella. I looked it up; it retailed for nearly five hundred dollars. For a freaking umbrella? No. Strikes two and three—he was an inch shorter than Jill and showered three times a day. Plus, Matt backed me up on this: He didn't trust Will either because Will constantly belittled Apple products and texted on his Android. Absolutely sacrilegious in Matt's book.

We usually met up at least once a week at Deschutes, our favorite brewery. Will tolerated it since they served martinis. I loved it because I could get a pint and a cheese pretzel for happy-hour prices.

I scored a parking space in front of the brewery and spotted them through the bright windows lining the tan-colored brick building. Walking into Deschutes felt cheery even in the dead of winter. Exposed, refurbished wood beams ran the length of the dining room. Archways to the bar featured intricate forest scenes hand-carved with a chainsaw.

I passed through the entryway with windowed garage doors that pulled open in the summertime. The restaurant and bar were humming with diners and from the vibration of industrial fans spinning on the ceiling. Aged wooden kegs and gold-framed beer posters filled the dark maroon walls.

The forty-foot bar, flanked by a Tuscan red tile wood-burning fireplace, was jammed with people. Behind the bar, full-length windows revealed copper brewing tanks. Matt, Jill, and Will were perched on high bar stools around a small mahogany table. A frosted glass chandelier hung overhead.

"Megs!" Matt greeted me with a beer salute and a hearty hug. I tried to ignore the flutter in my chest as I leaned into him, catching a hint of the zippy aroma of his spicy cologne.

Jill swore he'd had a crush on me since the day we met in Journalism 304. I disagreed. It would never work. He had shaggy blond hair, and I had a steadfast rule that two people with the same hair color shouldn't date.

Tonight, Matt's shaggy hair was more unruly than usual, falling in front of his eyes. I tossed it with my hand. "Time for a cut, my friend."

An avid cyclist, Matt pushed his biking saddlebags and helmet to the side and pulled out a stool for me. He grinned and planted himself in the seat next to me. "I know. I know. You sound like my mom. Geez."

Matt wore a shirt reading NO, I WILL NOT FIX YOUR COMPUTER and cargo shorts. Will, who was seated across from him, wore a crisp three-piece suit with a shiny pale blue tie. He sipped a martini and greeted me with a nod. "Hey, Meg."

"Am I ever happy to see you. You're not going to believe my

day." I rubbed my hands together, scanning the table. "But first, I need a beer. Whatchya drinking, Matt?"

"Hop Henge. You want a sip?" Matt held his glass, his fingers smudged with bicycle grease.

"Absolutely." I took a large swig of the honey-colored beer and handed the pint back to Matt. "I think I might need two."

"Spill, Meg. Does this have anything to do with your super-hot boss?" Jill asked.

"I wish. Don't get me started. He's beyond hot, but I'm constantly blabbering and making a fool of myself in front of him. Plus, he's acting really strange."

Matt waved a waitress over. "Hot boss? I thought you were a journalist?"

"Harsh!" I backhanded him on the arm.

Pretending to rub the spot where I hit him, he said, "Lay it on us."

With the promise of a beer on the way, I launched into the details of my day. Had it really only been a few hours ago that I'd witnessed Lenny fall to his death?

Jill was the first to speak after I unloaded on them. She leaned across the table and lowered her voice. "Meg, this is just like a P.D. James novel. If this Lenny guy was really pushed off, that's serious stuff."

Jill was a huge fan of mysteries—especially Brit lit. Her collection of British cozies rivaled her collection of candy.

Will sipped his martini and reached into his suit pocket. He thrust an ivory-embossed business card across the table to me. "One of the partners at my firm specializes in this kind of thing. Call him tomorrow and tell him I referred you."

"I can't afford a lawyer—especially a partner at your firm. Why would I need a lawyer? I'm not a suspect—am I?"

"Doubtful," Will said, repositioning his tie. "Call my friend. He'll walk you through what to disclose. Don't worry. I'll work something out with him."

Jill squeezed his shoulder. I tried not to vomit.

Will didn't even know Jill was an artist. How? How could she be dating someone who she wasn't comfortable sharing every part of herself with?

I blamed her surgeon parents, who were as sterile as the skintight latex gloves they operated in. Sure they sprang for her loft as a graduation present, but not because she wanted it.

Her parents had no idea she was painting. At their urging, Jill studied prelaw and landed an internship at Benson and White, Portland's premier law firm. In secret, she kept her stash of painting supplies hidden in Pops's garage and her inner artist hidden behind her designer suits. He'd been like a second dad to her, encouraging her to pursue her creativity and reminding her that art was supposed to be messy and unstructured. She didn't allow many people into her other world. I was one of the lucky few she did.

"Hold on," Matt chimed in. "I don't think Megs needs to lawyer up. We don't even know if there's been a crime."

"Thanks a lot," I said, kicking Matt under the table. I loved that he always had my back and our playful banter.

"Ouch!" He rubbed his shin. "I'm not saying you're wrong. I think you should slow down and wait to see what the police say."

"You know, I took a criminology seminar last year," Jill said, picking at her salad. "What's the motive here? I mean, Lenny sounds like an ass, but it's a pretty big leap to murder someone because they're a jerk." She paused to dab her field greens with light dressing from a small ramekin. "Do you think he could have been fighting with someone and accidentally got pushed? Go over what you saw one more time."

The waitress delivered a steaming pretzel with a side of warm, spicy beer mustard. Matt set it in front of me. "My treat."

"Thanks," I said, catching his eye briefly as a warmth spread down my neck. I pulled my gaze away, broke off a bite, and dipped it in the sauce. The rich, peppery mustard instantly warmed my mouth.

"Okay." I paused between bites. "Like I said, you know how terrified of heights I am. I didn't know what else to do when I saw Greg coming, and then I tripped. I was so focused on holding my grip that the only thing I saw was Lenny flailing backward over the cliff."

"Did you hear anything?" Matt asked as he whipped out his phone. "I want to take notes while this is fresh in your head."

I shook my head. "No. Not that I remember."

"Think. You had to hear something."

I took a sip of beer to wash down the pretzel and tried to remember every detail of the fall. "Wait, I did hear something. Like a grunt—a deep, throaty grunt."

Matt typed with lightning speed with his thumbs.

Will casually sipped his martini, while Jill leaned across the table, nodding enthusiastically. "This is good. What else can you remember?"

"Yeah," Matt agreed, looking up from his phone. "What about before you slipped? Did you see anything?"

Something nudged at the back of my brain, but I couldn't think of what it was. Had I seen anything? Dave had been standing ahead on the trail; Greg behind me. And Andrew—where had he disappeared to? He vanished for a chunk of time.

Framed TVs above the bar were showing a basketball game. Cameras flashed in the crowd. That was it—the broken camera.

"There was something else," I said. "A broken camera. I saw one of the GoPro cameras that Andrew mounted along the route. It was broken on the path."

Matt typed this new detail into his phone. No wonder he and Pops had gotten along perfectly. They shared a common love of investigating.

Jill clapped. "Matt, be sure to include that one. I've read

enough Miss Marple to know that could be an important clue, even if it doesn't seem like it now."

"Maybe." I nodded in agreement. "But Dave has it."

"Aha!" Matt tapped his fingers on the tabletop and clicked his thumb and index finger into a gun. "The smoking gun. Now we're on to something."

Will scoffed. "You realize you sound like you're acting out a scene from *Scooby-Doo*, right?" He waved the waitress over to pay his bar tab. "Meg, listen. Stop the detective act and call my firm tomorrow. Jill, are you ready? Let's roll."

He grabbed his black trench coat that hung on a hook behind our table and knocked back the remains of his drink. Jill gave me an apologetic look. "See you at home," she said as they hustled out of the bar.

"Don't listen to the suit," Matt said after they were gone. "You're on to something here, Megs. I wish Charlie were here. He'd know what to do. Sorry, I didn't mean to—"

"It's okay." I waved him off quickly, not wanting to allow myself to lean into missing him. "You're right. The cop who took my statement today knew Pops. Said he'd worked with him on the meth story, until he went off the deep end."

"Don't let it get to you. Your dad was one of the smartest people I've ever met."

"That's not what he thought. The second he connected my last name, he looked at me differently."

"You're reading way too much into this."

I shrugged. "Maybe."

The last bite of pretzel sat on the table. I offered it to Matt. When he declined, I popped it in my mouth and washed it down with the flat, warm beer left in the bottom of my glass. "I can't let my mom get wind of this. She'll freak out."

"For sure." Matt nodded in agreement. "Do you want to head out? You look like you could use a good night's sleep." He helped me off my stool and tucked his phone in a pocket of his baggy shorts.

"Thanks," I said, feeling rocky on my feet. "And thanks for the beer. I needed that."

We walked out of the empty bar. Matt waved to the hostess and opened the massive glass door for me.

"I'll email you these notes. Let's hang out tomorrow, okay?"

"Sure. See ya." I hopped into my car and waved to Matt, who stood on the sidewalk waiting for me to leave.

# THIRTEEN

Morning felt like it came early the next day. Jill shook me awake on her way out the door.

"What time is it?" I mumbled without opening my eyes.

Her heels clicked on the floor. Not a good sign. She must have been up and dressed.

"Eight. Sorry. I couldn't wake you—you were out."

I stretched my feet until my toes reached the armrest on the couch. "Yikes. I'm going to be late again." Half opening my crusty eyes, I could make out a blurry outline of Jill rifling through the refrigerator. She wore a tailored cream suit and a matching scarf wrapped loosely around her neck.

Sitting up, I rubbed my eyes and grabbed my glasses off the coffee table. "How is it you look so good this early in the morning?"

Jill laughed. She strolled easily in knee-high, brown leather boots in my direction with a steaming mug of coffee in her hands. "Here"—she offered it to me—"this will help. I made it super strong."

"You're a goddess. What would I do without you?" *Seriously, what would I do without her*, I thought as I scanned the loft, which had been consumed by my mess. I wasn't typically messy, but my stuff didn't fit in the living room. The loft was a spacious one-bedroom with an open-concept kitchen, dining, and living design. It was ideal for a single person. Jill's immaculate entry was cluttered with my rainboots, coats, clothes that needed folding, and stacks of books. I needed my own place.

"As soon as I finish this story, I'm going to look for a new place, I swear."

"Don't sweat it. You've been there for me more times than I can count." Jill rested her hand on my shoulder. "You know I miss him. He was like a father to me, always encouraging me to paint." She paused. "I'm sorry; I know you don't want to go there, but—"

I threw my hand over hers and squeezed it. "He loved you too," I said quietly.

He did. In fact, he was one of the only people, other than me, who encouraged Jill to pursue her art.

She kissed the top of my head and turned to grab her car keys and leather laptop bag. "Listen, I have to bail, but I left lunch for you in the fridge. I don't think you should rush. Drink coffee. Take a long shower. I'm sure Greg will understand if you're a little late this morning."

I wasn't sure if it was the warm coffee bringing me into my body, but I became aware of the fact that every muscle ached. Yesterday's hike and fall had completely caught up with me. I gingerly tried to stretch my arms above my head. Pain shot down my spine. I cringed.

Jill scrutinized me. "See. You're hurt. Do you think you should call in and tell them you're not coming today?"

I slowly reached for the coffee mug. It hurt to move, but the smell of coffee overrode any pain. Taking a sip and savoring Jill's expertly brewed java, I shook my head. "No way. I have to be there. I can't risk this job. Plus, I want to get to the bottom of whatever happened yesterday."

Holding the cup of coffee, I gave her a toast in the air. "Another couple cups of this, and I'll be good to go. I promise."

She looped her laptop bag around her arm and gave me a skeptical look on her way out the door. "You be careful, Meg."

I followed Jill's advice and nursed two cups of coffee before hobbling my way into the shower. The warm water rejuvenated my angry skin. A thick scab had formed over the gash on my leg and my entire body was freckled with an assortment of purple bruises.

Fortunately, I didn't have much on the agenda, other than meetings. I should be able to plop myself in the conference room or at my desk for the bulk of the day and write. Of course, with Lenny's death I had no idea whether the *Race the States* schedule would be altered for the week.

I didn't feel like eating breakfast, so I stuck a granola bar in my purse and grabbed the lunch Jill packed. *I'm so lucky to have Jill*, I thought, peering into the brown lunch sack—there was a soda, a hard-boiled egg, whole-wheat crackers, a banana, orange slices, and a dark chocolate.

Limping my way down the concrete stairs to my car took twice as long as normal. I should note here I didn't do elevators. Ever. I refused to ride in those death traps.

Maybe I should have reconsidered. Each step I took made me want to toss those damn boots in the dumpster. I clung to the handrail and hopped step by step until I made it to my car.

The radio announced there had been an accident with one of the contestants in town for *Race the States*. They didn't release Lenny's name or give any more details. This would be big news for the local media. As the main sponsor for the event, *Northwest Extreme* was likely to be swarming with press, all reporting "live" from the scene.

The quest for the first and best live shot had transformed journalists into ambulance chasers who spent their days crouched in front of police scanners. If I had to live on ramen noodles for the next ten years, I refused to take that route. A Pulitzer would rest on my desk someday, and I'd never get there covering house fires or teenage drag-racing.

As I pulled into the parking lot, four satellite vans blockaded one end.

Yep. The media were on the story.

No sign of last night's event remained. The tent and twinkle lights had all been packed away. Instead, reporters jockeyed for position in front of the steel doors. Great. How to get past them without showing any sign of physical weakness?

*Suck it up, Meg,* I told myself as I grabbed my lunch and shut the car door.

I used a trick Gam taught me years ago—I took a deep cleansing breath in, imagined firm roots originating from my core and continuing deep into the ground, squared my shoulders, and walked forward with purpose. "Fake it 'til you make it." I could hear her voice in my ear.

Carefully treading with painfully perfect posture, I squeezed through globs of reporters sporting their individual station jackets and too much makeup.

"Hey there!" a young brunette reporter bellowed as I pushed my way past. "Do you work here? Can you comment on yesterday's tragic accident?"

I shook my head and tried not to make eye contact. Within seconds, I was surrounded by a mob of microphones and shouting reporters.

"No comment," I muttered as I approached the front doors. They seemed so close, yet not close enough for my short arms to reach, especially as I was willing my core to stay stable. The heavy steel doors burst open, and a lanky hand pulled me inside.

"You didn't answer any questions, did you?" Greg asked as he slammed the doors shut behind him. I could hear pleas for a comment or exclusive interviews echo outside.

"No way," I said, releasing my stomach muscles and heaving air out of my lungs. "I was trying to get away from them and hoping they wouldn't notice I'm hurt."

Greg's eyes softened. He rested a hand on my shoulder. "I'm sorry. Not surprised you're hurting this morning. The day after is always worse. You don't need to be here today. Take the day off. Type your notes from home. I can sneak you out the back if you want."

"No. Not at all. I'm cool. I didn't want to give the vultures out there anything to jump on." I sucked my belly in again. "Plus, I need to work on the feature. I've got tons of notes and photos from yesterday to go through."

"If you're sure?" Greg scowled.

I nodded. "For sure. See, I brought a lunch." I held the brown bag. Why did he make me feel like I was back in school whenever I spoke?

Greg glanced at his watch. "You've got time to get your notes done. We're planning to gather in the conference room for a working lunch and to figure out where"—he paused—"we go from here."

He peered in the direction of the open workspace in the center of the building and checked behind him. "Like I said last night, Meg, stay out of whatever's going on with this Lenny situation. I want your notes and a rough draft of your intro on my desk by the end of the day. Got it?"

Resigned, I gave him a half nod and hobbled off to my desk.

Before I could do anything, I had to sort through the stack of paperwork on my desk. I'd spent a chunk of time prior to yesterday's hike researching each contestant. The resulting notes were scattered all over my desk. This called for organization in the form of color-coded file folders. I would never have admitted it to her, but I was pretty sure I developed my organizational skills from my mom.

One of the many things I appreciated about working at

*Northwest Extreme* was the office supply room. It was packed with file folders and standard office supplies. I knew it didn't sound glamorous, but a well-stocked supply room was nothing to scoff at. Writing for the student newspaper in college meant we had to bring in our own staplers and pencils. Those added up surprisingly fast.

I passed by the conference room on my way to pick up file folders and noticed Andrew scrutinizing a camera. A pile of GoPros was scattered on the table. I poked my head through the glass doors.

"Hey, Andrew! What are you doing here this early?"

He startled and quickly flipped off the camera. His eyes looked bloodshot, and his disheveled sandy hair stuck up in all directions. The room smelled of bacon. Two crumpled fast-food wrappers lay in the middle of the table.

Andrew saw my eyes linger on the discarded wrappers. "Breakfast of champions, eh? Don't tell Dave I was eating this crap, okay? He hates it." Grabbing the wrappers, he formed them into a tight ball, swiveled around in his chair, and swished them into the garbage can in the far corner of the room.

"Nice shot." I grinned. "Don't worry, your secret's safe with me." I snuck a peek behind me to be sure Greg wasn't near. He wasn't. Good. This was my chance to see if I could learn more about Andrew.

I entered the room and slumped into the empty chair next to Andrew. I wanted to know what he'd been intently watching. Maybe if I commiserated with him, he'd be more willing to open up.

"I order mochas with extra whipped cream all the time," I confessed.

Throwing his head back, Andrew laughed. He rubbed his round gut and appraised me. "Yeah, but you're not working on a beer belly like me."

"You're in Portland; it's basically a requirement that you drink a beer," I assured him.

Andrew stood and stretched. He lumbered to the windows and peered out. "It is a beautiful city you have here."

I couldn't disagree. Light clouds dusted the powder-blue sky. Pink buds burst from the tips of cherry tree branches, and the normally reclusive Northwest sun danced reflectively on the river.

"Don't get used to this. The rain will be back any minute." It took every ounce of self-control not to reach over and switch his camera on. Andrew was clearly absorbed in thought as he gazed out the windows.

"You never answered my question. What are you doing here this morning? I thought we were all getting together for a debrief at lunch?" My eyes focused on the cameras.

Andrew froze. Turning to face me, he said, "Uh. I don't know if I'm supposed to tell anyone."

"Tell me what?"

"I guess it doesn't matter. Krissy's going to flip out anyway, so I suppose everyone will know."

"Know what?"

"Dave told me I have to review all the B-roll I shot yesterday. I guess the sheriff wants to take a look at the film I shot. It's a beast of a project to go through all this."

He laughed nervously and turned back to the pile of cameras.

I reached for a camera and examined it. "How long will it take?"

"Forever." Andrew shuffled from the window and slumped in his chair."

"Why's Krissy going to flip?"

"Who knows how long this will set back production? The sheriff could hold on to these for weeks. Kind of hard to shoot a

TV show without them. Don't think it's in the budget to buy replacements."

He clicked a camera into his viewing screen and hit play. "She freaks out about schedules and stuff. I guess she thinks the race is going to hit it big. I keep telling her to relax, you know?"

"Yeah, well, that could be a big delay. I don't envy her. Or you, for that matter. I'll let you get back to work. In fact, I need to do the same. I've got a ton of notes to type from yesterday that are due, like, now." I pushed on my palms to help my stiff body remove itself from the chair.

"Catch you later." I waved as I backed out the door.

Andrew's eyes followed me. Had Dave really tasked him with reviewing the B-roll, or was he up to something else? Those cameras could reveal what happened to Lenny.

And because I was such a klutz, they could show me looking like I had considered faking a fall before I actually fell. Great. Just great.

# FOURTEEN

Hopefully Greg wouldn't get his hands on the footage. I headed for the supply room. It was time to focus on my assignment, anyway. File folders. That's what I needed. And to impress Greg with my stellar writing skills.

The office was a flurry of noise and activity. Ad sales reps negotiated rate cards over the phone, a product demo had torn a couple of writers from their desks to catch a glimpse of the latest in sub-zero sleeping bags, and the rest of the *Northwest Extreme* writing team was on deadline—headphones on, fingers flying across keyboards. The magazine boasted the largest circulation of any adventure publication.

I shoved piles of notes to the corner of my desk. My stomach growled.

Right, I skipped breakfast. Pulling the granola bar and my headphones out of my purse, I crunched the zesty "health" bar and plugged into Ella fitzgerald's "A fine Romance." I tapped my feet to the beat. I had to concentrate on not singing the lyrics aloud. This seemed to annoy my coworkers.

Now for my notes. Where to start?

Lenny. Who knew? Maybe Greg would want me to pull together an obituary of sorts. I labeled the file with a black Sharpie pen and wrote LENNY RAY on the tab. Digging through my stack of notes, I found a bio of Lenny that Krissy had provided.

Here's what I had on Lenny:

Lenny Ray, originally from New Jersey. A self-described jock and adrenaline junkie. Age twenty-seven. Claims to be a professional bodybuilder. His *Race the States* bio included a lengthy list of awards from various bodybuilding and wrestling competitions around the United States.

Again I wondered how a bodybuilder ended up in an adventure race. And how did Lenny make enough to take three months off to compete? Was Dave paying the contestants? Everything I'd read in prepping to cover the events asserted the contestants weren't being paid. I was sure winning a nationally aired television race could lend itself to endorsement money. And of course there was the million-dollar prize to claim at the end of the race, but the winner took it all. How could Lenny (or Alicia and Leaf) afford to not work for three months? Could Alicia or Leaf have killed Lenny in order to narrow their odds of winning the prize money?

I clicked open a browser window and typed Lenny's name into a Google search. Immediately, a photo of an overly tanned and greased Lenny appeared. The caption below the photo read, LEN THE CON, AKA SWEET NOSTRILS, WINS AGAIN. I printed the article and hustled over to the copy machine to pick it up before anyone else had a chance to read it.

The piece ran in the *New Jersey Herald* six months ago. It was a fluff story about local boy Lenny's rise from regional competitions to placing second in the International fitness and Bodybuilding Federation Mr. Europe Grand Prix and a win at the New York Pro. Again, it didn't make sense this beefcake would have any interest in an adventure race. No wonder he'd been huffing up the trail. Bodybuilders and pro wrestlers aren't exactly known for their superior cardio abilities.

I skimmed the rest of the article. My eyes homed in on the final paragraph hinting the Ray family might have mob ties. Their Italian diner had been the site of two shootings and a hotbed for mob activity. I highlighted the last paragraph, circled Lenny's mob name in red pen, and made a note on the side to contact the reporter who'd written the story. I shoved the article and all the notes I'd collected on Lenny into the folder and stacked it on the corner of my desk.

Next up, Alicia Abbott.

Alicia Abbott, originally from Atlanta, Georgia. Her bio didn't list an age, but I suspected she was in her early thirties. She spent her high school and collegiate years skiing competitively. As a professional skier she bounced around the globe, with stints in Canada and Switzerland working as a ski instructor, and three years training for the Olympic ski team—she didn't make the cut. Next week she planned to travel to Utah to resume her training.

The glossy photo attached to her *Race the States* bio reminded me of a CIA agent. Alicia's long torso and shorter legs exuded strength. In the photo, her hair—the color of black leather—was pulled into a long ponytail, her arms swinging stiffly at her sides and her eyes hiding behind pilot sunglasses. I sensed she held an innate ability to shape-shift.

Could Alicia have had something to do with Lenny's demise? How had she gotten the scratches on her arm? What motive could she possibly have, other than the fact that Lenny was a jackass? That didn't seem like motive for murder. Maybe a cold shoulder, but pushing someone off a cliff? No way.

I couldn't find much more on Alicia, other than a few articles about her skiing accolades. For the sake of thorough research, I went ahead and printed them out too. Adding those to my notes and Alicia's bio, I rested her neatly packaged file folder on top of Lenny's.

Next, Leaf Green.

Leaf's straggly hair and aging, doped-up eyes greeted me from the clutter pile I was slowly making my way through. Now here was a contestant whose involvement with *Race the States* intrigued me for entirely different reasons. At age thirty-seven, Leaf was the only contestant from Oregon and he certainly fit the part of organic hippie. What I didn't understand was how he had the drive to sign up to race around the country. Every movement Leaf made appeared to be in slow motion. Obviously, he possessed an enviable talent to scamper up trees and scale cliffs, but I didn't see him as a fierce competitor.

His *Race the States* bio touted he'd launched one of the first lines of hemp clothing in Oregon. His clothing line had been picked up by a major retailer and was due to roll out nationally in August. What the bio didn't list was his infamous regional fame.

During the spotted owl debate ten years ago, Leaf and a group of his friends staged an elaborate sit-in in an area slated for clear-cutting. He spent four weeks living in a makeshift tree house in an attempt to stop the deforestation. After a lengthy battle in court, he also spent a chunk of time in prison for his stunt. What was Leaf doing on a show like *Race the States*? And why did he insist that the show was an eco-challenge? Nothing in the race material I read mentioned anything about being green.

I read on to discover that Leaf had been suspected of a number of eco-terrorism acts around the state but never officially charged. I scoured the internet for more history behind his antics. A grainy mug shot of Leaf from last year popped onto my screen. It gave me the shivers. His face looked rough and not just from the lack of a shave. It didn't take long to print out a stack of news stories on Leaf and add them to my file on him. No time to read them now. I'd save that for later.

From there, I was left with bios and headshots of the seven other contestants who'd previously been eliminated from the race. I decided for the time being to file them together and leave it at that. A sense of accomplishment washed over me as I looked at my organized file folders. I should probably tackle my notes from yesterday next, but instead, I pulled out three new folders and labeled them: DAVE SHEPARD, ANDREW BLACK, and KRISSY MILES.

I wanted to gather everything I knew while it was fresh in my head. I didn't know yet how any of it might fit into my story, but if Greg asked, I'd tell him I thought we might end up doing a sidebar about the making of *Race the States*. That would warrant compiling background information on the production crew. And speaking of Greg, what was his involvement with *Race the States*? I wondered how I could find out how much money Greg had invested in the race as a sponsor.

What did I know about this motley crew? I searched through my files until I found the original packet Greg had given me. There wasn't much on any of them. I'd have to look online.

I started with Dave.

Dave Shepard, sixty-something, from Sydney, Australia. *Race the States* was his baby and a project he'd been working to get it off the ground for five years. Krissy mentioned Dave had produced a similar show in New Zealand. Indeed, the internet was awash with info on Dave's original series: *Eco Race*.

*Eco Race* ran for eight years in Australia and New Zealand. If the message boards were any indication, it was well received. I found several fan sites begging for its return. Plus, it won a Logie (the Australian version of an Emmy).

So, Dave had produced a green show. Had he convinced Leaf that *Race the States* would be an eco-race, too?

As I worked my way through the maze of connected articles online, I discovered a photo of Dave and Andrew in the Outback. I wondered if this was the site of Andrew's near miss with the croc. I also learned that Dave had been a professional climber before venturing into reality television. The last thing I found was an interview with Dave about *Race the States* in which he said he was most nervous about recreating the show in America due to our stringent liability laws. New Zealand and Australia are much looser with personal safety issues, so he surmised that would be his biggest hurdle here in the U.S.

Interesting tidbit. I printed it out and stuck it in with my other notes on Dave.

The clock on my laptop read 10:45 A.M. I needed to wrap up these files quickly and move on to my notes. I linked my hands together and stretched them over the top of my head. Ouch. I'd forgotten how stiff I was.

Andrew Black—the camera operator from Canada. What did I know about Andrew? He and Dave had worked together on previous shows. This appeared to be a point of contention for Andrew when it came to taping schedules and his personal safety. What was his relationship with Dave really like? It was hard to determine from the outside whether they were close friends capable of easy banter or whether Andrew was really frustrated with Dave.

Other than the fact that he was in his thirties and originally from Canada, I knew little about Andrew.

An internet search didn't yield much more information other than a list of programs he'd been the videographer for.

What I did know was Andrew and Lenny had tangled right before Lenny's fall, and Andrew's whereabouts were unknown. Had Andrew been on the deer trail?

I quickly scribbled on a piece of paper and moved on to the last crew member, Krissy Miles.

Krissy served as the executive assistant on the shoot. I didn't really know what the role entailed. I spent fifteen minutes searching online. From what I could find, executive assistants ran the gamut from sitting at a front desk in a big studio to coordinating the entire shoot. I put Krissy in the latter category. Otherwise, she'd told me she was from L.A. and had been working in Hollywood for six years. I couldn't find much else on her. Warner Brothers listed her as an assistant on a couple of projects. Printing those out, I placed them in Krissy's file and stacked all the files neatly on the corner of my desk.

Whew, that was complete. I made a mental note to see what more I could find out about the production crew. Next, I began uploading the photos I took of the climb. As the photos uploaded, I typed my trail notes. My fingers flew over the keyboard. Though I was a long way away from the real guts of a story, the process of pulling details together sparked my energy. I finished compiling all my notes two minutes before noon. Without editing, I clicked save and shut off my monitor. Time for lunch.

I grabbed the lunch Jill packed me from the fridge and hurried into the conference room. Midday light streamed in from the long windows, casting little shimmers on the glass tabletop.

"Hey, lassie, how are you this morning?" Dave greeted me with his usual jovial tone and a beaming smile. His outback hat was still absent from his head. No one else in the room shared his chipper demeanor. I couldn't blame them.

Andrew didn't bother to glance from his slumped position in the same chair he'd been in earlier. Alicia Abbott picked at a salad. Leaf Green's lunch looked as unappetizing as possible. He dumped whey protein into thick green sludge in a cup and chugged it. It smelled like rotten grass and yeast. I shuddered and chose a chair on the opposite end of the table—far away from his health drink.

Greg and Krissy hadn't arrived yet. Was she trying to get him alone?

I opened my lunch sack and cracked the hard-boiled egg Jill had tucked in for me. I noticed a drop of blood on the pristine white egg. Where did that come from? I rested the egg on a paper napkin and assessed my hands. The skin underneath my right thumbnail was chapped and bleeding. Add it to the list. I sucked the blood off my thumb and bit into the egg. It tasted like iron. Grabbing an orange slice with my left hand, I was careful not to let the juice touch the cut on my thumb. The flavor of the tangy, sweet orange took away the bitterness of iron. It didn't take away the palpable tension in the room.

What was up with this group? Awkward silences made me skittish. I became uncomfortably aware I was tapping my foot under the table. So much so, the floor beneath me shook.

"Where are Greg and Krissy?" I asked to break the silence.

Alicia shrugged. Andrew cast a hard look in my direction. Leaf ignored me. Had I done something to piss them all off? Or was the reality of Lenny's death sinking in? Finally, Dave said, "Should be along here anytime."

I crunched on a cracker. It sounded like I was chomping on nails. The door pushed open and Krissy clicked in on three-inch heels. Greg followed right behind. She giggled flirtatiously and thanked him for being such a gentleman (to open the door for her). Gag.

"Sorry I'm late," Greg announced, seating himself at the head of the table. He easily conveyed authority simply with his posture. Alicia sat upright. Leaf put down his slimy drink. Andrew mustered enough energy to remain only half-hunched, letting out a little grunt as a greeting.

Greg didn't seem to notice the effect his unassuming power had over this crowd. "Krissy and I have been on the phone with our vendors and partners to figure out the best plan for moving forward with this project given yesterday's"—he paused—"events."

Taking a sip of water from the glass in front of him, he continued. "At this point it's up to the sheriff when and how we move ahead."

I caught Dave looking desperately at Krissy before he interrupted. "Now listen, mate. As we discussed last night, we have to keep filming. We have to keep a good face in public. It's like what they say in Hollywood, 'The show must go on.'"

Krissy cracked open a can of iced tea. "Maybe they said that twenty years ago, Dave."

Greg held up his palm. "Let's all take it easy. I'm not suggesting we cancel the race, but Krissy's made it clear several events are going to have to be reworked. Plus, until we get the go-ahead from the sheriff's office, none of us are doing anything."

"These laws. How do we get around this? I can't have the racers waiting around for your sheriff to make a move." He gestured around the table. "I've got a lot of money riding on this."

"I don't see we have much choice." Greg pursed his lips. "The good news is Krissy's been able to move most of our scheduled events back a day or two. This might impact the kind of press coverage we can generate, but frankly, I'm not worried about it. With Lenny's accident on the front page of every media outlet in town, I don't think we're going to have a problem getting people out."

Dave tried to keep his tone light. "Is your sheriff going to cover all my costs of extra hotels and food?"

"I wouldn't get your hopes up. I think what we need to do now is refocus." Greg gave Dave an exasperated look and turned his attention to the far end of the table. "Krissy, can you hand out the new schedules?"

Why was Greg so involved in rescheduling the race events? Shouldn't Dave be working with Krissy?

Krissy opened her black leather laptop bag and pulled out a bundle of packets, which were passed around the table.

After everyone had a packet in their hands, Greg said, "I think you'll see in reviewing these, Krissy has done a fabulous job of restructuring the race finale. At this point we're slotted to continue with the next event on Sunday, but that's subject to change based on what we hear from the sheriff."

There were murmurs as we leafed through the packets.

"We're supposed to hang around for the next three days?" Alicia asked. "What kind of race is this going to be with two of us anyway?"

Greg shifted in his chair. "Afraid so. I've been in contact with our vendor partners to see if any of them are willing to host you. I'm pretty sure we can get you a tour of the Nike campus and potentially get you out on the river one afternoon. I'm waiting to hear. I'll let you know once I do," Greg said. "As far as finishing the race goes, that's up to Dave."

"Dave," Alicia demanded, "what do you say? How far is this delay going to push the finale? I'm due to start training in Utah next week. I can't miss the first week."

"No worries. We're not canceling. I'll have a little chat with that bugger of a sheriff and see if we can't get this thing moving."

Krissy raised her index finger. "Uh, that's not going to work, Dave. Regardless of whether or not the sheriff gives us the green light to continue shooting, this new schedule isn't flexible. I've been up since the crack of dawn rearranging. Do you realize the level of work that goes into coordinating an event like this? For God's sake, we're shutting down part of a highway and closing portions of two state parks."

"That's all right—I know you can work your magic again if you need to, Krissy."

Krissy slammed her packet on the table in front of her and stood in a huff. "No! No, I can't, Dave. And I'm not going to! I'm tired of being the only person on this team who cares about this production. We need to send the network our rough cut in three weeks. The schedule is complete. No changes." She threw her laptop bag over her shoulder and stormed out the door.

"Don't give her a thought," Dave said with a half laugh. "She's worked herself into a tizzy. She'll come round." He left his copy of the schedule sitting on the table, pushed his chair back, and said to Leaf, "Got a minute to take a little walk on the river, mate?"

Leaf looked behind him at the sun-filled sky, then skeptically at Dave. "I guess."

Greg held a finger in the air. "Before everyone leaves, I'd like you each to schedule a chunk of time with Meg. As you know, she's the lead on this feature, and since we have downtime I'm sure Meg would appreciate any background information she can garner on each of you."

With a mouthful of chocolate, I couldn't say anything to Greg, but I gave him a curious look. He winked.

Wasn't that exactly what he told me not to do? I thought I was supposed to stay away from the contestants, not cozy up to them. As soon as this meeting was done, I hoped to have a one-on-one with Greg and figure out what in the world he was thinking.

"I'm getting in a run," Alicia declared, leaving the conference room and her uneaten salad on the table.

Andrew didn't move. He mumbled under his breath to Greg. I picked up Dave's schedule, tossed my lunch and the remains of Alicia's in the trash, and chased Greg to his office.

"Got a minute, Greg?"

"Sure. Shut the door behind you."

I followed him in and closed the door. "I don't get it. I

thought you wanted me to stay away. Now you're telling them to come spend time with me?"

Greg peered over my head to the common workspace. He leaned over his desk and spoke in barely a whisper. "I heard from the sheriff, Meg. He thinks it's a simple accident. Doesn't sound like they're going to investigate much more, but I also heard a rumor this morning that might make them reconsider. I need you to do more research into *Race the States*. Get as much info as you can."

A combination of fear and excitement built in my stomach. "Okay, I can do that."

"Wait before you go diving in. Be strategic. I read through your portfolio before I hired you. And I know you learned from one of the best. You can dig, but don't do it publicly. Got it?"

"Sure, of course." I nodded solemnly, but internally I was beyond confused. It felt like whiplash to have him telling me to leave the case alone one minute and giving me the green light to pursue it the next.

"No, I don't think you do. I'm serious, Meg—not a word about this to anyone. When you're talking to that group, it's only under the premise of your story. Understood?"

"Yep." I resisted the urge to salute.

His phone buzzed on his desk. I watched him pick it up and look at the number. "Hold on a second. I need to take this."

I pretended to be very interested in the posters on his office wall. Greg pushed to his feet and walked over to the far side of his office.

"What do you need?" he asked the caller. "How much?" His voice jumped. "No way. Listen, I can't talk now. I'll call you later."

He strode over to me with a wide smile. "Sorry about that, Meg. Time to get back to work. I need your rough draft as soon as possible. We're tight on this one."

I nodded and gave him a thumbs-up. "You got it."

"One more thing before you go. Anything you find—anything—you tell me first."

"It's a deal." I tried to calm the eager energy pulsing through my body. This could be the story of a lifetime.

"Hey, Meg?"

"Yeah?" I turned around.

"You have chocolate on your chin."

*Oh, my God. I'm an idiot.*

# FIFTEEN

I knew immediately upon returning to my desk that something was wrong. My neatly stacked files were strewn across my desk. My red pen was lying on the floor. My monitor was glowing. I'd turned it off—hadn't I?

I scrutinized the files on my desk. Nothing noticeable was missing.

Next, I pulled up the notes I'd typed from yesterday's hike. The entire file was missing. Had I forgotten to click Save?

I checked my deleted items. It wasn't there. Maybe I'd saved it in the wrong folder. I did an auto-search for "Race the States." The search window text read, 0 RESULTS FOR RACE THE STATES.

Was I seriously sleep-deprived? Had I experienced a time slip and landed in an alternate universe?

Had someone gone through my stuff? Why would they delete my notes?

I scanned the office. Most people were out at lunch; only a handful of my coworkers sat hunched over their desks. No one looked when I stood and surveyed the space. There wasn't any sign of someone trying to sneak out of the office. Maybe I was being paranoid? Someone could have accidentally knocked the file folders off my desk on their way to lunch—I guessed. But if someone had gone through my computer—that was creepy.

That's when I noticed a bunch of the photos I had uploaded were gone, too.

I spent the next hour retyping my notes, and this time, not only did I click Save, but I also emailed a copy to my personal account and to Matt. There wasn't compelling information or evidence in my notes—at least none that I could think of. There was a play-by-play of the hike, lots of extraneous details about the landscape, and the brief interviews I conducted with the contestants near the summit—all stuff I'd use to craft my rough draft for Greg.

Was I overlooking a major detail in the notes? I didn't think so. What about the photos? I scanned through the originals on my phone. Nothing jumped out. It was just a bunch of shots of the trail and everyone posing at the summit.

I glanced at my watch—the time read 2:25. The rest of my afternoon was cleared thanks to the change in schedule. I wanted to get a walk in and go see Gam.

This time I wasn't taking any chances. I resaved the document, logged off, and shut my laptop down. I bundled my file folders together with a large rubber band and shoved them in my tan-flowered laptop bag. There was no way I was leaving them here. Giving a wave to my coworkers, I headed for the front door.

Freedom washed over me as I pushed the heavy doors open and stepped out into the muggy spring air. The drive north to Gam's condo didn't take long. She lived in a two-story riverfront condo on the Washington banks of the Columbia River. Her eclectic new-age bookshop was right around the corner, connected by a three-mile walking path along the river.

Whenever I visited Gam, I always got a walk in. I kept a gym bag in my car with my tennis shoes and headphones. Usually, I parked in the far lot near the start of the waterfront trail. From there, it was two and a half miles to Gam's condo and another half mile to the shops and restaurants.

Today, I considered driving all the way to Gam's. My body was sore and my blisters were raw. But the glorious April sun beckoned me. What the hell, I'd take it slow. Gam would say my body would rebound faster with a hit of natural vitamin D.

I grabbed my gym bag from the trunk and carefully applied extra moleskin to my blisters and laced my tennis shoes. Thanks to Pops, my car was equipped with a first-aid kit, jumper cables, and a spare tire, as well as an emergency blanket and bottled water. As he always said, "You never know when you might hit trouble. Better safe than sorry."

I felt sorry for my feet. They sparked with pain as I tugged my laces tight. Good thing I hadn't told Gam I was coming. This might take a while. Still, the sun on my neck felt like magic and a walk would help clear my head. I plugged my headphones into my ears and started on my way.

The multipurpose path was a popular spot on sunny days. It paralleled the Columbia River. Sailboats packed the waterway between banks, and planes eased and tilted their way in for landings. The sound of rumbling trains and departing jetliners was oddly relaxing.

On a busy afternoon like this one, with bikers, runners, and elderly couples out for a stroll, it was a place I could completely check out.

Monuments retelling the tales of the tribes who used to live along the river were strategically placed with stunning views of the mighty passageway to allow travelers to pause and consider history.

I usually ignored these. Having grown up in the region, the

stories of early adventures are part of my makeup. But today, I opted to take a short rest and read one of the markers. It pointed out the fishing talents of the Indigenous Americans who lived on "the river of trade." A far cry from today's motorized boats that sped over waves and strong currents in search of salmon.

*Onward*, I urged my body. What would Gam have to say about Lenny? She was intuitive and could read me by simply closing her eyes. She'd be able to tell me what I should do.

I turned with the path as it curved its way closer to the water. Here, cottage-style condos rose on my left. The condos were painted slate with bright white shingles and trim. They seemed like they should be in New England, not the Pacific Northwest. Gam's was the last one on the far end.

Most of the decks held outdoor furniture, barbecues, windsocks, colorful plastic Adirondack chairs, and potted palms. Gam's deck housed an assortment of hanging chimes, gongs, sundials, a statue of the Buddha, and hand-thrown ceramic pots with healing plants. You couldn't miss it.

The muted whitewashed decks of her fellow condo owners blended with the background. Gam's deck was a kaleidoscope of color. I loved it. Her neighbors hated it.

She was constantly attending condo association meetings in defense of her deck. When she first purchased the condo after my grandfather died ten years ago, she tried to paint it purple and teal (her two favorite colors). She lost that battle but carved her color mark on her deck. Passersby often stopped to admire her unique spin on outdoor living.

A twelve-foot statue of Sacagawea carved out of stone loomed behind Gam's condo. Sacagawea's hands were enclosed as her gaze rested on the mighty river. Gam chose her corner location not only due to its proximity to the beach, but also because she said she slept easy at night knowing Sacagawea's ancient spirit was watching over the land.

A heron flew overhead, its wingspan stretched longer than a

small car, casting a shadow on the sidewalk. It landed on the peak of Gam's condo. Of course.

I knew Gam would still be at her shop, so I didn't bother to stop at her condo and continued on. Two restaurants with beachfront property were buzzing with happy-hour crowds. As I passed by, the smell of the grill and beer hops made my stomach growl. Maybe Gam would want to join me for a burger once she closed the shop.

Gam's store, the Light and Love Bookstore, was tucked between a coffeehouse and a gelato shop. The door jingled as I entered. I breathed in the scent of herbal tea and noticed the lights were turned low, which was a sign that Gam must be doing a session in the back room. New age music chanted on the overhead speakers.

"Margaret, is that you?" Gam's voice called from the back room.

"Sure is. How did you know?" I chuckled.

"Finishing with a session. Be with you in a few. Keep an eye out. I think someone's coming in to buy a new animal card deck by the register."

I poured myself a cup of green tea. Gam had tea on all day. Customers were welcome to help themselves to a cup while they perused the shop. She kept a kettle and a collection of her own pottery on an antique desk near the front door.

The Light and Love Bookstore was the only new-age shop in town. Gam had developed a loyal client base over the past ten years. She offered specialty classes on theta healing, meditation, Reiki, finding your spirit guide, and more, as well as hosting private individual sessions. She didn't like to be called a psychic, preferring the term "healer."

"Psychic" meant directing someone's future, the opposite of her approach.

She said, "The future is mutable, Margaret. We're always at choice. Which holds great promise and hope for change."

Her shop was as eclectic as her condo. She sold gems, crystals, drums, essential oils, teas, and a vast collection of new-age books and card decks. I made my way behind the counter with my tea. Gam kept new shipments and special orders for customers by the cash register. An animal deck with a photo of a lion sat next to an unopened delivery box.

A woman breezed in.

"Can I help you with anything?" I asked.

She shook her head. "This is my first time in. I think I'll look around."

"Feel free. Help yourself to tea." I motioned to the tea set by the door.

I busied myself opening Gam's latest delivery—Celtic jewelry. The woman declined my offer of tea and spent the next ten minutes browsing through the card decks on a spinning rack. She looked disappointed as she turned to leave.

"You're sure there's nothing I can help you with?" I called.

"Well," she said, coming close to the counter with a sheepish look on her face. "I've actually been trying to find these animal cards. I saw them online, but they've been sold out forever."

I laughed. The woman looked surprised and slightly offended.

"No, sorry," I said as I held up the animal deck. "You wouldn't be looking for this by chance?"

"Yes! That's it."

"Great. Sounds like it was meant to be." I handed her the deck and rang up the sale.

"I can't believe it. I should have come here earlier. I tend to do more of my shopping online, but this is cheaper. I'll be back," she said with a happy wave as she trotted out the door.

Gam might not have liked the term "psychic," but she had an uncanny knack for predicting the future, even when it came to what new customers might want to buy.

The door to the back room swung open. I could hear Gam instructing her client to drink plenty of water and take it easy for the evening. They emerged from the back room and made their way to the counter.

My jaw dropped as I saw who Gam was escorting. "Sheriff Daniels. What are you doing here?"

# SIXTEEN

Sheriff Daniels twisted his body from side to side. "Your grandmother worked on my back. Feels mighty spry. Thanks for the tip."

"You bet," I said, tucking a sales receipt into the cash register. "I didn't think you'd really come."

"Glad I did." He picked up a drum and ran his roughened hand over the smooth leather. "Glad you're here, too. Got a minute?"

Gam caught my eye as she bustled behind the counter. "You two chat. I'll finish up here."

I traded places with Gam. Sheriff Daniels returned the drum to the rack. Reaching into the breast pocket of his uniform, he removed a spiral notebook.

"I've been reviewing your statement," he said. "Remind me again, what exactly did you see at the top of the cliff?"

"Um"—my voice sounded unsteady—"not a lot really. I slipped. I didn't see much. The only thing I remember is Lenny's body." I couldn't finish. A wave of dizziness came over me. It felt as though the room was tilting on a wild sea.

I held the counter to steady myself.

"I know this isn't easy," he said, intentionally looking away. "Take your time."

My nostrils flared as I inhaled a deep breath.

Gam held her index finger and thumb together in the air. It was a sign to center myself. She'd taught me the simple centering technique of firmly pressing my index finger and thumb together when I felt nervous.

I jammed my fingers and thumbs together. "I remember Lenny's body sailing over the ledge."

"Mm-hmm, and was he facing forward or backward?"

I closed my eyes. It wasn't an image I wanted to conjure up. Until this moment in time, I hadn't realized how deeply I'd been avoiding replaying Lenny's death in my head. How was he facing?

I didn't have to think long. I knew he was facing me. "Backward," I said with confidence.

"Okay," Sheriff Daniels responded casually while making a note. The way Lenny fell had to be significant.

People didn't tend to fall backward over cliffs. Another shiver ran down my spine.

"You good?" asked Sheriff Daniels, looking up from his notebook.

"Uh-huh, I'm fine."

"Can you think of anything, anything else you may have heard or seen? If something seems insignificant to you, it might be important."

"Well..." I hesitated.

"Yes?"

"On my way up, probably about a mile before the summit, I could have sworn I saw someone on a deer trail."

A look of excitement washed over Sheriff Daniels's face. "Man or woman?"

I shook my head. "Honestly, I'm not sure. Whoever—or

whatever—I saw ran by too quickly to make out any details. Sorry."

"No need to apologize. Anything else?"

"To tell you the truth, this whole production seems strange to me. I think there's more to the story than meets the eye."

Raising one bushy eyebrow, Sheriff Daniels gave a half laugh. "Like your father, aren't you?"

I crossed my arms and frowned, not a response Mom would have approved of.

His voice dropped. "I meant that as a compliment. I thought a lot of your father. Please continue."

"Well, first, there's Andrew, the camera guy. He and Lenny got in a pretty wicked fight right before Lenny took off for the summit."

"A physical fight?"

"No." I shook my head. "Andrew threatened Lenny—told him if he didn't quit with the attitude he was going to make him pay.'"

"Go on."

"Then he showed up out of nowhere on the summit right after Lenny fell."

Sheriff Daniels put his pen down and pulled a silver canister from his pocket. He popped a wooden toothpick between his teeth.

He offered one to Gam. She declined.

"Please continue," he said as he returned the canister to his pocket.

"Well, then there's Alicia. She has scratches all over her arm. She told me she got them from a sticker bush, but she's pretty cut up. I don't know how she could have done that on the main trail."

"Okay."

I wiggled my fingers. The centering exercise worked. I felt much calmer as I unburdened myself to Sheriff Daniels. I also knew more than I realized. "Earlier, I was doing some background work on the piece I'm writing, and I learned that Leaf has a criminal record. And Dave is strangely focused on filming. The whole thing seems off."

Gam was reviewing an inventory sheet, but I knew she was listening intently.

"Oh, and speaking of Dave. I remember seeing him pick up a broken camera on the summit right after Lenny fell."

Sheriff Daniels continued to write in his notebook.

"There's one more thing. I think someone went through my files. They were thrown all over my desk."

Sheriff Daniels stopped writing and pulled the gnawed toothpick from his teeth. "You sure?"

Gam looked up from the inventory list as I said, "Yeah, I'm sure. I had them all stacked neatly. I went to a meeting and when I came back they were all messed up."

Sheriff Daniels stuck the toothpick back in his mouth. "Hmm. What was in the files?"

"I don't know. A bunch of background info on the contestants and show."

"Anything missing?"

"I'm not sure. I'd just started to compile everything. But I know someone went through my machine. They deleted the photos I took yesterday and all my notes from the climb."

"Mm-hmm." He wrote something in his notebook. "I'll be sure to take a look."

He tipped his hat to Gam and said, "See you tomorrow."

To me he said, "I'll be in to interview everyone again tomorrow." He handed me a business card. "Here's my number. Anything comes up, you call me. In the meantime, be on alert. I'm treating this as a homicide."

# SEVENTEEN

After walking Sheriff Daniels to the door, Gam rushed over to me and squeezed me in a huge hug.

At seventy-one, Gam bustled with more energy than most people half her age. You'd never have pegged her as a new-ager. No robes or flowing skirts. Mom inherited her love of fashion and shopping from Gam.

I inherited my lack of height from her. She stood eye-to-eye with me, dyed her hair obsidian, wouldn't leave the house without eyeliner, and tanned on her deck for fifteen minutes a day when the sun was out to maintain her olive complexion.

She pulled away from the hug and looked at me with skeptical eyes. "Shall we put the Closed sign on the door and cozy up for a little chat?"

Feeling like I might cry, I looked at my feet and nodded.

Her black pantsuit with purple and silver sequins sparkled as she turned the sign on the door.

"New outfit?"

"Don't you love it? I spotted it weeks ago but the price was way out of my budget. I asked the Universe to lower the price, and guess what? I went back yesterday, and it was marked as half off. Yahoo!" She pulled a crystal gemstone from her bra. "This little helper did it. Give me two minutes." She bustled to the kitchen and returned with a fresh pot of tea and a Tupperware container full of homemade cinnamon cookies.

"Here"—she thrust a cookie at me—"have a cookie. It'll help. Why don't you fill me in?"

I munched on the spicy sweet cookie and downloaded the last two days while Gam sat intently listening.

When I was done, she closed her eyes, took a deep breath, and said, "first, let's give you a zap, shall we?" She put one hand on my knee and the other on her heart. "Be right back."

In Gam-speak that meant she was leaving her physical body to go "up" into the spiritual world. From my vantage point, I saw her close her eyes, tilt her head, and sway slightly. A surge of warmth radiated from her hand and buzzed down my leg. After five minutes she took another cleansing breath, sat straight, opened her eyes, and brushed her hands together. "Did you feel that?"

"It feels like my entire leg is being heated."

"Yahoo!" Gam clapped her hands together. "That means it worked. Hopefully, your blisters and leg will feel better. I'll give you another zap before you go." She paused while she poured herself a cup of tea. Taking a sip, she sighed and said, "Now, Margaret, about this Lenny situation. I don't like it."

"Did you see something, Gam? Do you know who killed Lenny?"

"Slow down. You know it doesn't work like that." She ran her thumb over the crystal hanging from her neck. "First of all, my worry for you in this has nothing to do with what I may or may not be picking up on from the Universe. It's simple. You're a twenty-three-year-old young woman who's starting out in her first job. I don't think it's wise to align yourself to such negative energy."

"So you do see something?" I leaned closer to her on my chair.

She gave a half laugh and took another long, slow sip of her tea. "What I'm picking up on is your energy, my dear," she said as she got to her feet and hurried to the back room. "Wait a minute. I have something for you."

She saw something. She didn't want to tell me. I knew better than to press her.

She came back and held out an opaque pale blue stone about the size of a small apple but oval in shape. "This is blue calcite. It's a powerful cleanser. You can sleep with it under your pillow or keep it next to your bed at night."

I took the stone from her. It was heavy and cool in my hand. "Thanks."

"Let's pull a card for you and see what animals are showing up." She took a golden embossed card deck and cut it in half. "Choose one."

I tugged a card from the fanned deck.

"The cougar!" Gam clapped her hands together. "That's a power animal."

"What does it mean?"

"The cougar shows up to remind you of boundaries—to think before you act and stay on track. I'd say that's a pretty clear message, don't you?"

She thrust the card into my hand. "Keep this."

Putting her hand on top of mine she said gently, "I love and adore you, Margaret. I know you'll listen to your heart and your spirit guides. If you stay open, the Universe will lead you to what you need to know."

"Of course, Gam. Thanks for listening. I'm sure I'm blowing it all out of proportion, anyway."

Gam pursed her lips and looked as if she were going to say something more, but stopped herself. She squeezed my hand

and said, "Good on ya! Now, how about a burger before you head home? They've been calling me all afternoon."

Later that evening, after a burger with Gam, I read through the contestant files at Jill's place.

"I don't get it," I said to Jill as she sat next to me on the couch, touching up her clear polish manicure. The smell gave me a slight headache. "Why would anyone want to go through these bio sketches I did on the contestants? There's nothing here you couldn't find from doing a pretty basic online search."

Jill held her hands out to examine her work. She twisted the cap carefully on the polish and blew on her nails. "But that's it—you did the searching. Maybe whoever went through your stuff was counting on the fact that no one would dig any deeper than the show."

I dropped the files on my lap. "You could be on to something. Yeah, what did I find that Krissy hadn't already compiled for their *Race the States* bios?"

"Maybe you should cross-reference them?"

"Great idea. Do you want to help?"

"And have a chance to play Miss Marple—uh, yeah, of course I want to help. Hey, what about the photos? Those could be even more important. What did you shoot out there?"

"Um, I took a bunch of pictures."

My phone buzzed on the coffee table. Mom's picture flashed on the screen with each ring. A familiar swirl erupted in my stomach. I could only imagine what she wanted to lecture me about now. "Guess I better answer, huh?"

Jill scrunched her face and handed me the phone.

"Mary Margaret Reed!" Mom's voice was laced with frustration on the other end of the phone. "I've been at the club and heard *Northwest Extreme* is involved with that hiker's death. Do you know anything about this?"

If there was one thing my mom hated more than anything else, it was being scooped. She prided herself on being up to date on the latest gossip. This was of particular use for her at the club, as she liked to call it.

The club actually had a name—Downtown Athletic Club. While there were many athletic facilities in the area, the Downtown Athletic Club was the premier social club. From hosting business luncheons to bar mitzvahs, seeing the club's logo on an invitation bought you immediate cred. Memberships were exclusive, expensive, and by referral only. When she left Pops, she wormed her way in. She launched a successful real estate agency right before the housing market tanked. I was pretty convinced she traded commission payments for club membership.

The worst part of the club was that Jill's boyfriend, Will Barrington, and his family were longtime members. Somehow, Mom managed to work this well-known fact into any conversation we had, reminding me that finding someone successful like Will was the right move for my future. Shudder—never. I'd rather be broke and couch-surfing forever.

"Nice to talk to you too, Mom," I snarled. Ever since Pops's death, Jill had been urging me to go to counseling. She seemed to think I had unresolved "issues." She was right. We did have issues. The problem was I had no interest in resolving them.

"Don't you talk to me in that tone, Mary Margaret."

"It's not a tone. What do you want?"

"I want to know what in the world is going on at this so-called magazine."

I banged my phone on the couch before responding. "It's not a so-called magazine. It's a legitimate, internationally recognized publication."

"Darling." Her voice sounded syrupy and fake. "I'm not knocking your little job. I just wish you would take your career more seriously, and give up this little magazine for a real job.

There's no career path in writing for you, especially if these if the news reports are true. I'm worried about you."

Oh, my God, I was going to kill her. If there were a way to commit murder by phone, I'd be all in. She was a genius at twisting compliments into passive-aggressive put-downs.

"Thanks for your concern, but there's really nothing to worry about. One of the contestants in an adventure race fell on a hike."

"It is true?" She sounded almost delighted. "The women at the club aren't going to believe it. What else do you know? Who was it? Were you there? Did you see it happen?"

"Enough. I can't tell you any more. The police are still investigating."

"Oh! There's an investigation? This is juicy. Wait till the ladies hear about this at brunch. When can you tell me more?"

Great—just what I needed. My gossip-hungry mom stalking me for details she could share with her ladies who lunch.

"Seriously. You're ridiculous. I need to go."

"Wait! Before you hang up, let's put a date on the books for lunch. You can't stay mad at me forever."

Yes, I could.

When Pops became obsessed with the meth story, his reporting prompted national television coverage and several documentaries. Portland was painted as a hub for an insidious drug infestation sweeping across the country like a swarm of locusts. Every reporter at *The O* covered the story. *The O*'s investigation translated into three hundred stories dedicated to the subject. Congress passed tough anti-meth legislation and a media storm brewed.

Pops dug deeper into international drug trading, backing off meth. Things imploded when major news outlets like the *New York Times* claimed *The O* used false statistics in order to inflate the story.

At the center of the controversy, Pops convinced his editor

the real story was how high-ranking government officials were involved in funneling drugs through the Northwest. *The O* refused to run the piece. Pops was put on a temporary leave of absence. He shuttered himself in the farmhouse with stacks of discarded papers littered on every inch of free floor space. Mom walked out.

"Margaret, are you there?" Her voice came over the phone.

"Yeah."

"I wanted to tell you I found the most amazing rhinestone brooch for you. I've been looking for it everywhere. Your father and I bought it at that antique shop we used to take you to in Newport. It'll go beautifully with your pea coat. I can swing it by this week."

"I'm busy."

She sighed. "Okay, take care, sweetheart, and call me when you can."

Flinging my phone at the pillows on the couch, I spiked my hair with my fingers and let out an audible groan.

"That bad?" Jill asked, carefully placing my phone back on the glass coffee table and giving me a soft smile. "You know, she really does mean well. Don't let her get to you."

I shot her an incredulous look, "And how do you suggest I go about doing that?"

Jill jumped to her feet. "I know!"

Her ivory silk pajamas swirled around as she skated on thin moleskin slippers over the hardwood floors to the kitchen, where she rifled through the cupboards. I watched her remove boxes of organic cereal, couscous, brown rice, and steel-cut oats from the shelves. The girl lived on a diet of health food and sugar. It was an odd mix, but somehow it worked for her.

She stood on her tiptoes and stretched her lanky arm to the back of the shelf.

"Aha! Got 'em!" she shouted and stuffed the boxes of health food back into the pantry. Sliding to the couch, she dropped bags of candy on my lap—dark chocolates, marshmallows in the shape of yellow chicks and pink bunnies, and sour jellybeans.

Shrugging off my look of surprise, she said, "What? It's my secret Easter stash." Unwrapping the pale blue foil, she popped one into her mouth and handed another to me. "The cure for your mother is always sugar. Eat this and forget about her."

The rich, creamy chocolate melted in my mouth. Jill was right. There was nothing I could do about my mom other than ignore her. Entering into any debate with my mom never ended well, at least for me.

"Come on," Jill said, stuffing a sugar-coated marshmallow in her mouth. "Let's go through your notes and see if we can figure out why anyone would have been interested in them. We need to think like a Masterpiece Mystery detective. What would Miss Marple do?"

"No idea. What?"

"Hang out in the village—listen, follow the clues. We can do this, Meg."

After an hour of combing through my files and consuming enough sugar to put us both in diabetic comas, we weren't any closer to finding anything new.

"I'm beat. I think I'll call it a night," I said, closing the files and stacking them on the coffee table.

"Get some rest," Jill said, patting my knee. "Do you mind if I take these to bed with me? I want to have one more quick look."

"Knock yourself out." I handed her the files. "It's doubtful you'll find anything. I've looked through these a hundred times."

Jill finished off a handful of jellybeans and said, "Let's go back to the photos. There must be a photo of something someone didn't want you to see. Do you remember what you took photos of?"

"Everything, the trail, the contestants. I already looked

through them. There's nothing there." I scrolled through my phone to prove my point. "Wait—what about the deer trail? I took a picture there. Maybe someone saw the flash?"

"That's it!" She stopped with the files in her hand. "Meg, you realize what this means. The killer knows you saw them."

# EIGHTEEN

I awoke the next morning to the smell of coffee and an empty loft. Jill had left a pink sticky note on the top of my files next to the coffeepot. It read:

*Call Matt ASAP. I sent him these last night. Coffee's on. See you tonight. Smooches.*

Pouring myself a cup of Jill's rich brew, I grabbed cream from the refrigerator and sank onto the couch.

Jill had highlighted the page numbers on the bottom of my notes. In the margin, she'd written:

*Look what I found. Three pages missing!!!*

She was right. Three pages of Alicia's file were missing.

I had carefully numbered each page I'd printed out from my Internet search. It was something Mom used to do when I was little. She'd help Pops with his research, organizing his files with different colored pens and writing numbers on the bottom right corner of every page.

Pages 24-27 were missing from Alicia's file.

Alicia must have been the one who went through my files. But why? The only thing I'd found on her were old skiing articles. Could Alicia have killed Lenny? Her arms were all scratched. Maybe she'd cut them pushing Lenny off the cliff. But she was long gone by the time I reached the summit.

Between sips of coffee, I sent a text to Matt.

He responded right away.

Meet at Marchelle's in 45?

I slammed down the rest of my coffee and raced to the shower. Marchelle's was a coffee and hemp shop Matt and Pops loved to inhabit. It was located in a converted barn, outside of town, close to my childhood home. The shop was a hub for conspiracy theorists and pot enthusiasts.

Yesterday's sun had been replaced by a solid wall of iron-gray clouds stretching from the skyline to the ground. I could tell rain was on the horizon, from the way the wind freed blossoms from the trees, whipping them like confetti dancing in the air. The sky turned darker and darker as if I were driving into the night.

When I arrived, Matt waved from an overstuffed, shabby green chair in the corner of Marchelle's. He sat next to a wooden stove churning out heat and smoke. His slate-gray helmet with neon-yellow caution signs rested at his feet. Matt and his bike were rarely less than a few feet apart from each other. He rose to greet me.

"I got you the usual," he said, giving me a hug and handing me a chipped ceramic mug. "Coffee straight, black, right?"

He smelled like mint gum and earthy aftershave. His arms were firm and reassuring around me. I stayed in them a moment too long. Realizing this, I quickly shrugged him off and sank into the chair next to him. "Black coffee?" I scowled.

He punched me playfully in the arm. "I'm kidding. It's a mocha with extra whip."

"Thanks." I grinned. "You're the best."

"You hungry?"

"Kind of." I paused. Had I eaten? No, I guessed I hadn't. "Yeah, I could eat."

"I was thinking quiche, if that's okay with you? Marchelle has a sundried tomato and goat cheese special today."

"I'm in." I nodded. Honestly, anything sounded fine.

"Okay, be right back. Don't move." Matt moved toward the rustic counter to place our order.

Was Jill right? Did he really have a crush on me? We'd been friends for so long it was impossible to imagine Matt (or any other male for that matter) lusting after me. I wasn't that kind of girl. I was the best friend. Jill was the leading lady.

Matt returned with a plastic giraffe. He placed it on the scratched circular table between us to mark our order and scooted his chair close. "Jill filled me in on the latest."

I looked around the room to see if anyone was paying attention to our conversation. The space was cluttered with tattered books, hemp clothing for sale, candles, and fliers taped to the walls, promoting upcoming wellness seminars, hemp cloth-making classes, a meditation workshop, and political house parties.

Pops used to love this spot. I could almost picture him standing at the counter, ordering a chai latte with a pencil in his ear and a newspaper tucked under his arm. An ache, worse than being stabbed repeatedly by a jagged knife, cut through my stomach.

As a kid, Mom took me to *The O* once a week to meet Pops for lunch. We'd grab ham and cheese sandwiches from Marchelle's and eat them at his desk. I remember puffing up with pride when his editor stopped to shake my hand and say,

"Your dad is my best writer. Follow his lead and we'll have you on the team one day too."

I attributed my burning desire for truth-seeking to Pops. When he was on a story, we didn't see much of him. It made Mom furious, but she was focused on social climbing and his work helped launch her into new circles. Gam said it was love at first sight with them. Maybe it was. I didn't remember it that way. I remembered them like static between radio stations—always searching for the right call letters but mainly stuck on the annoying buzz.

*Keep it together, Meg.* I looked away from the ad and returned my attention to Matt.

"I don't know what to think," I said to Matt, suddenly paranoid people were paying attention to our conversation. Another glance around the room confirmed they weren't. "I keep going back and forth. My boss is acting weird. Gam warned me not to get involved yesterday. I swear someone went through my files. Jill thinks the killer saw me. But at the same time, I feel like I'm being ridiculous."

Scooting his chair a couple of inches away from the smoldering fire, Matt wiped smoke out of his eyes and coughed. He put a hand on my knee and looked me intently in the eyes. "Something's up here, Megs. I know it. You need to stop blowing it off and start watching your back."

Instinctively, I turned to look over my shoulder. We both laughed.

A woman with long braids and a floor-length flowered skirt delivered two steaming slices of quiche to our table. She stuffed the giraffe in her apron pocket and gave a little bow as she backed away.

"You didn't need to get two," I said to Matt, cutting off a bite of the dense quiche and blowing on it. "I would have split one with you."

Matt blew on his quiche, too. "That wouldn't be any fun. Plus, you look like you could use protein this morning."

Yes, I could. The savory quiche melted in my mouth. The sweet tang of the sundried tomatoes blended with the creamy goat cheese. I let out a little groan and dug into another bite. Content to eat our breakfast in silence, Matt kicked back in his chair with his quiche resting on his lap. I devoured mine in about five bites and proceeded to wipe the cheesy residue on my plate with the crust.

I dusted crumbs off my hands and sat back in my chair. "Okay, what did you discover?"

Holding a finger as he chewed his last bite of crust, Matt put his empty plate on the table and reached into his laptop bag. The bag was made of an industrial waterproof nylon in sap green. It had tiny green alien men along its black straps and packs of gum bulging out of the side pockets. He pulled out his iPad and clicked it on. He slid his finger over the slick screen until he landed on a folder. Tapping it once, a spreadsheet appeared on the tablet. "Look at this," he said, expanding the spreadsheet with two fingers. "When Jill emailed me last night, I went ahead and did more research on *The O*'s internal servers into *Race the States*. Both the cast and crew." He thrust the tablet into my hands.

"Take a look at these numbers, Megs. *Race the States* is bleeding out cash. There's no network funding. Dave's fronting the money from his own production company. But his company's in trouble. I found this scanning through files they submitted publicly to find venture capital last month. No one bit. *Race the States* is totally broke."

I scanned through the profit and loss sheet. Numbers in the thousands and hundreds of thousands flashed on the screen. Since numbers weren't my thing, it was hard to decipher. But the glaring red negative number on the bottom of the spreadsheet did not require a math mind to interpret it. *Race the States* was in deep financial trouble to the tune of over two million dollars of debt.

I stared, barely breathing, with my mouth gaping open, at the screen. This was huge news. Did Greg know? Did Krissy or Andrew know? Obviously, Dave knew. He'd been hiding the fact that the company was going bust, but from who and why?

Could this have anything to do with Lenny's death? Now I was more confused than ever.

"What do you think this means?" I asked, handing Matt his device.

He carefully placed it inside his messenger bag, grabbing a stick of gum while hunched over. "Want a piece?"

"Not unless you think I need one? Is that a subtle message I have quiche breath?" I made a funny face.

Matt tore off the gum wrapper and scoffed. "Not at all." He took a quick glance around the room again. I could smell the refreshing scent of mint on his breath. "Your friend Dave at *Race the States* is in it up to his ears. Honestly, I don't know what it means. I'm going to keep looking. But I do know he's not giving you or anyone else the whole story."

"Do you think this could have any connection to Lenny's murder?"

"It might. And until we know more, you need to be careful."

I gave Matt a skeptical look. "Now you're sounding like my boss."

"The boss you have a crush on?"

"Stop it." Was it just wishful thinking or did he sound a touch jealous?

"I'm serious, Megs. We're talking about a ton of money at stake here. People do irrational things when it comes to money, and I don't want you in the middle of it. Remember that story I wrote last fall about the CEO of that biotech startup who was murdered for the technology?"

"Yeah."

"That's what I'm saying—*Race the States* probably stands to pull in millions of ad dollars if one of the major networks picks it up. Plus, like Jill said, if you got a photo of the killer on the trail, they could come after you next."

I swirled the chocolate sludge on the bottom of the ceramic mug. Was I actually on the trail of something more than just my story?

"Yeah, and about your boss, how much is *Northwest Extreme* paying for sponsorship?"

"I don't know. I can't seem to get a handle on how involved Greg is with the show. I mean, I know he has exclusive sponsorship, but does that mean he put up the million dollars for the prize money, or is that coming from Dave?"

"I don't know. See if you can find out. That could be important."

Our waitress stopped at our table to clear the empty plates and ceramic coffee mugs. I put my face in my hands and rubbed my temples.

"There's one funny thing I found," Matt said after the waitress was out of earshot. "Lenny gave himself the name Sweet Nostrils from an online mobster name generator site."

"What?"

"Yeah. I did you. Do you want to know what your mobster name would be?"

"Uh. Yeah, obviously." I grinned. "Lay it on me."

"Wait for it." He held up a finger, giving me an impish smile. "Dead Eye Maggie."

"Oh, my God. That's awesome. Can you call me that from now on?"

"Absolutely."

"What about you?"

He cocked his head to the side and slanted his eyes. "East-Side MP."

After cracking ourselves up, Matt continued. "Here's what I

want you to do—lay low, but see what else you can find out about the contestants. I'm going to head into the office and see what I can pull up on Dave through *The O*'s archives and our journalist's toolbox." He chomped his gum and bounced his left knee as he spoke. "You see what you can learn about *Northwest Extreme* and I'll text you as soon as I know more. Deal?"

I bit my bottom lip, a habit Mom hated. "You really think I could be in danger?"

Getting to his feet, Matt pulled me up with ease. "Yes, I do. And I think you should be careful, Megs."

He walked out the door. I stood by the woodstove, inhaling the scent of old wood. Three people had warned me to stay out of this mess. first Greg, Gam, then Sheriff Daniels, and now Matt. Could they all be wrong? Probably not. Something was definitely amuck at *Race the States*. I was determined to figure out what it was.

None of them had witnessed a man falling to his death.

Plus, I had to do it for Pops. I hated the way that Sheriff Daniels said Pops "went off the deep end" and looked at me with pity. Maybe if I could solve what happened to Lenny, it would help restore Pops's name. I was in the best position to learn more.

Gam always claimed my intuition ran deep. I had an uncanny knack for nailing people on the spot. I'd watch my back, but no way was I going to lay low.

# NINETEEN

After an uneventful afternoon at the office, Greg called an emergency team meeting in the staff room. I'd been caught up in working on my draft, which was now overdue, and didn't notice the time. My phone buzzed on my desk, sounding an alarm. I was ten minutes late. Shoot. I slammed my laptop shut and raced to the conference room.

Everyone was in deep conversation as I pushed the heavy doors open. Sheriff Daniels stood at the head of the table. He glanced at the clock and then to me, before pointing at an empty chair next to Krissy. I slunk in and hunched my shoulders as I sat.

Sheriff Daniels cleared his throat. "As I was saying, we cannot rule out foul play at this point in time."

Dave let out an audible groan. No one else made a sound. Krissy tapped her fingers on her knees under the table. Andrew's gaze was fixated out the window. He didn't seem to register that anyone else was in the room.

Alicia threw her head on the table and sobbed under her breath to no one, "I'm never getting out of here, am I?"

I noticed Andrew started to say something to her, but stopped himself.

Greg's eyes were focused on the paperwork in front of him. I tried to catch his glance, but he didn't look up.

Leaf, on the other hand, held his piercing brown eyes on mine as if challenging me. I looked away briefly and glanced in his direction again. He was still staring hard at me. I gave him a puzzled look. He shook his head and glared. What was his problem? He'd been avoiding me since I tried to chase him down after the party.

Sheriff Daniels continued. "At this point, we're treating this as a homicide investigation. After we're done here, I'm going to need fingerprints and to take each of your statements individually." He motioned to the table where a fingerprinting kit sat ominously.

Andrew scoffed. Krissy examined her nails.

"I appreciate your cooperation," Sheriff Daniels said. "And as a reminder, no one is to leave the state until we get more information from the coroner's office and can make a determination in the case."

Rain pounded outside the windows, which were sweating from the heat of our combined bodies behind closed doors. Muggy air and tension hung in the room.

"One more thing," Sheriff Daniels said, pushing up the brim of his hat. "We've copied all the footage you shot. My deputy has your cameras to return, so you can keep filming."

He glanced at the torrential rain outside. "Guess the good news is that means you'll be able to get out in our lovely Northwest weather."

"What about the news folks?" Dave asked. "You're not planning to let them loose on this, mate, are you?"

"Good question." Sheriff Daniels nodded to Dave and addressed the rest of us. "No, we're not informing the media of anything, but as I'm sure you're all aware, there's heavy interest in this story right now. I recommend if asked, you simply respond by saying 'No comment' and leave it at that."

Dave clapped his hands together. "That's right. Listen to this here sheriff. We need to keep this under wraps. Can you imagine the ratings?" He elbowed Andrew, sitting next to him, still staring out the rain-splattered window. "We can tease it up for weeks."

Alicia pounded her fist on the table. "Look, I didn't like Lenny any more than the rest of you, but come on, Dave, have a little heart. The man was murdered and you're talking about ratings."

"It's not—"

Cutting him off in midsentence Alicia glared at him as she said, "I want off this ridiculous show. I'm done."

She stood and huffed toward the door. Sheriff Daniels raised his right index finger. "I'm sorry, miss, but you can't leave until I tell you otherwise."

"This is absurd."

Sheriff Daniels tipped his hat in Greg's direction, ambled over and put his hand on Alicia's shoulder. "Come with me. I'll take your statement first."

Alicia brushed his arm off her shoulder and stomped out of the room. "Fine."

"I'm going to need the rest of you to stay put. I'll try to make this as quick as possible."

He strolled out of the room. We all sat dumbfounded. finally, Greg disturbed the awkward energy. "You heard what Daniels said. I'm jumping on a call. You're all welcome to hang out here or at one of the hoteling stations until he's ready for you." He looked at his watch. "I'll stay until he's finished with his questioning to lock up."

Gathering his papers, he stood and turned to me. "Meg, I think there's a box of nutrition bars in the staff room. Can you grab them and bring them in here in case anyone's hungry? And don't forget I need your rough draft."

Glad for any excuse to be out of the stifling room, I jumped to my feet. I could feel Andrew's and Leaf's eyes burning into me as I went to snag the Powerbars. Out of the corner of my eye, I noticed Leaf lean over to whisper to Andrew, who responded with a rough shake of his head and a finger to his lips. What was going on with those two?

The staff room was a total mess, as usual. *Northwest Extreme* received daily shipments of sample products from vendors vying for free press. Due to slumping ad sales, Greg had laid off the admin whose job it had been (among other things) to go through product samples and deliver them to the appropriate team member. This left the staff room in a constant state of disarray.

Shipping boxes were piled next to the refrigerator, which was plastered with fliers for upcoming runs and bike tours. The circular white-topped lunch table and two of the matching chairs were also stacked with products like breathable ankle socks and neoprene water bottles. A state-of-the-art reclining bike no one wanted to claim rested in front of the soda machine. Products arrived at such a breakneck pace, often they were left untouched for weeks.

I searched through the cluttered counter with trail-sized energy gel packs in new flavors—blue raspberry and cherry cola. Gross. I shuddered, pushing the box aside. Next I found lemon gum samples enhanced with caffeine and other "naturally occurring" energy boosters. The only place I wanted caffeine was in my coffee, not in my chewing gum. Underneath a box labeled New Goo, I found the nutrition bars. Was "new goo" something one consumed or used to repair shoes? I didn't want to find out.

As I grabbed a handful of bars, I noticed a cracked GoPro

camera buried at the bottom of the box. What was it doing here? It looked like the broken camera Dave had tucked in his pocket. How did it end up in the staff room?

I tucked the bars and camera under my arm and headed to the conference room.

"Here you go." I tossed the bars on the middle of the table. "I recommend the blueberry crunch. It's pretty tasty," I said, trying to keep my tone light.

"Thanks, Meggie." Dave reached his tanned arm for a peanut cluster bar.

"Hey, did you lose a camera? I found this in the staff room." I held up the camera.

Dave bit into an energy bar. "Nope, don't think so. Andrew?"

Andrew didn't even look at the camera when he said, "That's not one of ours."

"Are you sure?" I asked. "It looks like it's been used."

Andrew tugged at his headphones, but didn't make eye contact with me. "I'm sure. I had to count all our cameras to give to the sheriff. None were missing."

Dave coughed. "Think I'll step out for a little freshy for a minute."

Andrew laughed stiffly and said something so low none of us could hear. Dave eyed him with a look of warning on his way out the door.

One of them was lying.

My watch read 5:15. Doing quick math in my head, I calculated there were seven of us to interview. Looked like I'd be here a while, which was fine because I had work to do on my draft. Giving the story some space had brought some new ideas to the surface. I tucked the broken camera into the pocket of my dress and returned to my desk.

The common area was deserted. Most of the writing staff

set their own hours—often covering events in the evening or on weekends. Aside from the small ad sales department, who worked traditional hours, everyone else popped in and out unless we were close to deadline. The week before an issue dropped, the office was a buzz of activity—clicking keyboards and a constantly full coffeepot. Since we didn't have any admin staff, most of us used our personal phones for research and interviews. Greg covered our monthly cell bills. It was easier for him to reach us on assignment. At our last staff meeting, he'd told us he was officially cutting out our landlines. No one used them anyway.

I was surprised when I returned to my desk to see the red light on my phone lit up. Apparently Greg hadn't discontinued the service.

Picking up the black phone, I punched in my voicemail code and waited. A gruff voice jolted me upright in my chair. "Listen, you bitch. Stay out of this, or you'll be sorry."

I looked around the room and shivered. The voice was indistinguishable. Someone clearly had tried to disguise their voice. It sounded like a man but I couldn't be sure. Clicking Play again, I listened intently. The background sound crackled and the repeated words made me shudder.

What should I do? Sheriff Daniels was interviewing Alicia in the accounting office. Greg would probably take me off the story if I told him. I couldn't let that happen. With another glance around the room, I pressed the Save button and put the phone down.

I shoved the camera in the back of my top drawer. Why would Andrew deny it was one of their cameras without even looking at it? I'd have to tell Sheriff Daniels about it.

Could I really be in danger? Or was someone trying to scare me off?

Obviously, someone thought I knew more than I did.

What about the fact that *Race the States* was in the red? I was on to something. I only wished I knew what, and what I should do.

Could it be Alicia? I needed to ask her about my files. Maybe she was done with Sheriff Daniels and I could catch her before she left.

I skirted around Greg's office to see if Alicia was still in the accounting office. She wasn't. Neither was Sheriff Daniels.

Where did everyone go? Goosebumps formed on my arms as I scanned the empty hallway and returned to my desk.

Just as I pulled out my chair, I felt a tap on my shoulder and jumped.

"Sorry, Ms. Reed," Sheriff Daniels said. "Didn't mean to scare you."

"That's okay. I'm on edge. I just got a nasty voicemail telling me to back off."

Sheriff Daniels pulled a chair on wheels from my coworker's desk next to me. He held an arm to stop me. "Wait a minute. Someone threatened you?"

"Uh-huh."

"Did you save it?"

"Yeah. Do you want to hear it?"

"Of course. I need to hear it." He rolled his eyes and gestured toward the phone.

I picked up the phone and punched my voicemail code. Pushing the speaker button, I set the headset on the base and turned to watch his reaction. An automated female voice-recording came through the speakers. "You have no new messages."

What? Frantically, I punched buttons. It must be in the saved messages. "Hold on a sec," I said, feeling my cheeks flame as Sheriff Daniels looked at me with concern. "It must be in my saved messages."

He nodded.

The woman's voice sounded again. "You have no saved messages."

"I don't know what's going on," I shouted, looking wildly around the empty office. "Someone must have erased it. I just left my desk for five seconds."

Sheriff Daniels put a firm hand on my shoulder. "Do you remember what they said?"

I couldn't believe this was happening.

"Not word for word, but basically knock it off or I'd be sorry."

He looked from me to the phone. "I'll take a look around. Run prints on your phone. Have you talked to anyone since our conversation yesterday?"

"No. Not really. I did learn that Dave's in financial trouble, but I didn't tell him that."

"Good. Don't." With a quick glance over his shoulder, he continued. "I don't know what you've discovered that has someone spooked, but I don't want you talking to anyone about Lenny from here on."

I gulped and nodded. "There's something else." I pulled the broken camera from the back of my drawer. "I found this in the staff room. It looks just like the one I saw on the summit. Andrew and Dave both claim it's not theirs."

He examined the cracked, plastic GoPro. "I'll see if my tech team can scrub it."

Sheriff Daniels stood. He started to pat my shoulder and stopped himself with his hand midway in the air. "You're free to go. Stop by the kitchen and have your prints taken before you leave. My assistant should have it set up. Ms. Reed, please stay out of this."

I slunk into my chair and rested my head in between my hands. What the hell was going on? Pulling the receiver off the base, I punched in my voicemail code again, hoping the message might magically reappear. When the automated voice repeated, "You have no new messages," I slammed down the phone and pushed to my feet.

Someone wanted to scare me. It was working. But as to listening to Sheriff Daniels's request—no way.

# TWENTY

Fingerprinting didn't take long. I exited the building with black residue on my fingertips and a seething stomach. Was someone trying to scare me, or just make me look like an idiot?

Before I headed home, I needed air and space to think. I maneuvered my car out of the parking lot and in the opposite direction from the Pearl. Despite the misty rain, I rolled my window down and blasted Sinatra.

I drove aimlessly for about fifteen minutes. After my arm lost feeling from the frigid, wet rain, I finally succumbed and rolled the window up. With no particular destination in mind, I soared along the highway, mesmerized by the rhythmic motion of the wiper blades and Sinatra's crooning lyrics. Commuter traffic had already returned home. I imagined cozy families enjoying soup and crusty bread as I breezed by hillside homes lit from the inside on the gloomy evening.

Before long I was en route to the Gorge, following the Columbia River. Birds scattered above my windshield as jets rumbled to land at the Portland airport. A tree-covered island divided the river as I sped past big-box stores and outlet malls.

A paper mill puffed out pristine white clouds of waste into the air.

I felt myself being drawn to the old historic highway as highway signs directed me to the route. *Why not?* I thought, as I turned onto the scenic road. At 7:00, I had at least a half hour of daylight left. Plus, I figured I could return via the freeway, which would shave off fifteen or twenty minutes.

Every five minutes, a car would pass by me in the opposite direction—toward town, but otherwise, the highway was void of traffic. The wind picked up as I continued east. fir trees bowed as I passed. I switched the wiper blades to high and hunched forward over the steering wheel to see through the foggy windowpane. Maybe this wasn't such a good idea.

Ignoring the nagging voice urging me to turn around, I zoomed around slick corners. Wind forced the car over the centerline. A horn blared. I clutched the steering wheel and directed the car on the right side of the road. My rear defrost had been on the fritz for a while. Thick steam enveloped the back. There wasn't much hope of it clearing, unless I rolled all the windows down.

Suddenly, headlights appeared through the foggy window, headlights that looked like they were about to touch my bumper. Crap, there was no space to pull over. The margin between my car and the moss-covered guardrail was less than a foot. I eased my foot off the gas, slowing in hopes the car would pass.

It didn't.

My heart rate quickened around "s" curves. The car behind me kept on my bumper. I couldn't make out the driver through my foggy window. The intense beam from the headlights filled my entire backseat. I hit a straight stretch of road and rolled my window down again. Pellets of arctic water ricocheted off my skin. I clutched the steering wheel with my right hand and stuck my left hand out the window. I frantically waved with my left hand to motion the car ahead of me.

The car didn't budge. It made a revving sound with its engine and lurched close to my bumper. I dug into the wheel, bracing myself for impact.

A new switchback of curves lay ahead. I decided to step on the gas. Maybe if I sped up, the car would back off. Rain from the open driver's side window pelted my head. Water dripped down my cheek. I didn't dare remove a hand from the wheel to wipe it away. Sailing around a curve at 60 mph (twice the posted limit), I was sure I would lose control.

Yellow caution signs warned of falling rocks.

Somehow, I managed to stay on the road. The car tailing me remained less than a foot from my bumper.

As soon as we escaped the curves, I motioned for it to pass, again.

This time when I stuck my arm out the window, it flashed its lights to high beams and laid on the horn. I jumped forward, my seat belt cinching around my neck. The sound of the horn echoed through the empty forest, bouncing off the windy trees. My hands shook.

I didn't know what to do. The first trail entrance was probably at least another five miles ahead. I could pull into a parking lot when I got closer, but until then, I was stuck. There wasn't a sign of another car as far as I could see.

At that moment, the car behind me revved its engine again and surged toward me. I slammed on the brakes and fishtailed over into the left lane.

The car flew forward in the right lane, its horn blaring as it passed me. I tried to catch a glimpse of the driver or the car, but it was too dark to see anything. Another horn blared. This one sounded different. I returned my gaze to the road in front of me in time to see a car headed straight for me in the left lane. I swerved to the right lane and skidded to a stop.

*Whew, that was close.*

Each muscle in my body twitched in shock. I was okay.

The car had slammed to a stop literally inches from the guardrail. Another second and I would have smashed right into it. Was that what the car tailing me was hoping for?

I needed to move. The sun had completely sunk in the sky and the remaining dusky light barely made it through the thick trees. If a car came up behind me, they'd never see me in time to stop.

Before I continued on, I needed to check my tires. The force with which I'd pressed on the brake pedal left my right calf muscle tight. I could smell burning rubber and hoped my tires weren't destroyed. Exhaling deeply, I carefully exited, checking behind me to be sure no one was coming. The wind blew strands of hair in my eyes.

First I checked the front of the car. Smoke or steam, I couldn't be sure which, given the smell from the tires, billowed from the sides of the hood. My headlights lit up the moss-covered guardrail, revealing deep cracks and chunks of missing cement. I wondered if the barrier would have held on impact. My left eye twitched.

Damn, I wished I knew something about cars. I quickly checked the driver's side. I couldn't fit between the car and wall, so I crouched near the front tire. It looked okay—I guessed. Hopefully, they would hold long enough to get me home.

Light from the opposite direction reflected on the windshield. A car slowed on the left side of the road directly across from me.

I stood. Spots danced across my vision. I could feel my entire body sway.

I grabbed the hood of the car to steady myself.

"Hey! You okay?" the driver on the other side of the road called.

"Yeah, I'm fine. I was run off the road. Trying to make sure my car's okay before I continue on."

"Run off the road?"

I nodded. "You didn't happen to see a speeding car go by, did you?"

"Sure did," the driver yelled across the highway. He looked to be in his seventies and wore a cowboy hat on his head. "Stupid kids. They flew past me."

He was probably right. It wasn't someone out to get me. More likely a group of teenagers out for an evening joyride and messing around.

"Did you see what the car looked like?" I asked.

The driver leaned out the window. "It was pretty hard to tell since they were flying by, but it looked like a van to me."

A van, like the *Race the States* van? "Was it white by chance?"

"Yep. Sure was."

My heart skipped a beat. I stood in the rain dumbfounded. Someone from the crew must have been following me. Had they meant to scare me? Or was something more sinister at play? Had someone actually tried to harm me?

If so, who? Who had access to the van? I'd seen both Krissy and Dave drive it, but did anyone else have a set of keys? Could Alicia have followed me out here?

"You better get moving. Not a safe space to be stopped." The driver motioned to me.

"Thanks." I waved as I made my way to the driver's side. "I appreciate you stopping."

He tipped his hat and drove off.

With a quick look behind me, I made sure the road was clear before opening the driver's side door and jumping in. I turned the engine and steered the car to the center of the lane. My hands felt clammy on the wheel. I exhaled to try to get my heart rate to return to normal.

Kids. It had to be kids. Right? But if it really had been teens out for a joyride, you'd think they'd have blown past me. Why would they tail me for miles and try to run me off the road? That didn't sound like teenagers messing around.

A mile ahead, I spotted the turnout to the parking lot for the always-popular Multnomah Falls. I could hear the roar of the falls before I could see it. Although it was late in the evening midweek, the parking lot was still three-quarters full. Tourists with cameras and backpacks trekked from the parking lot under the highway to the falls.

I steered the car into an empty space with a view of the Multnomah Falls Lodge across the street. Pops had loved the lodge. He used to take me out this way for Sunday drives and hot cocoa.

One of the first filler pieces I'd written for *Northwest Extreme* was about the lodge. It was constructed in the 1920s with Cascadian stones and Oregon timber. Its long slanted roof, cobblestones, and peekaboo windows reminded me of a German village. The day lodge consisted of a gift shop and coffee shop. For visitors who were more inclined to fine dining, the restaurant served world-class meals in the fireside room with heart-stirring views of the falls. In the summer months, a patio opened with the powerfully peaceful sounds of the falls for the backdrop to dinner.

Multnomah Falls attracted over two million visitors from around the globe each year, easily making it Oregon's premier tourist attraction. The vast majority of visitors never made it to the top, since the falls actually consisted of two steps. Most visitors made the short paved climb to the Benson Bridge, which rested above the base of the falls. It was not my favorite spot. The rustic moss-covered bridge was built of cement with slats for viewing the 64-foot drop beneath your feet. It did offer spine-tingling views of the first step that plummeted 542 feet above, but it was not for the faint of heart.

One summer, when I was about ten or twelve, Pops and I hiked to the Benson Bridge. He held my hand the entire way—urging me on despite my fear. I remember his salt-and-pepper beard, the tilt of his wire-frame glasses, and how he smelled like citronella.

Throngs of tourists in raincoats pushed past us. When we finally made it to the foot of the Benson Bridge, he leaned over and said, "Maggie, you've made it this far. Won't you feel proud of yourself for standing above the mighty falls? I'll hold your hand the whole way."

He was commendably patient with me (and everyone else he encountered). "Take your time, sweet one."

I remembered the feel of the spray from the icy water. Gam had told me the legend of the falls. Indigenous Americans believed it was created for a princess who desired a private space to bathe. I imagined princesses adorned with jewelry, diving from the bridge into the pool of glacial runoff at the base. Flying freely through the narrow carved-out cliffs, they waved to the birds floating in the sky and the trees jutting from the basalt rock. Landing without a splash headfirst in the pristine water, they swam to the bottom of the deep pool to touch the slippery rock base. Returning for air, they glided in the sun for hours.

If the princesses in my vision could dive into the plunging falls, I could walk across a bridge. finding my determination, I thrust my hand in Pops's and crept onto the bridge. His hand was rough and his fingers stained with newsprint. He didn't let go despite my nails digging into his skin.

It took us twenty minutes to walk the span of the bridge. Pops held true to his promise, coaxing and encouraging me the entire way. Once I was safely on solid ground, he treated me to a chocolate-swirled ice cream cone at the base of the falls to celebrate my mighty accomplishment.

Shaking myself to the present, I realized I'd completely forgotten about that trip until this moment. I turned off the engine and pried my hands from the steering wheel.

I needed to get out of the car. Maybe a coffee or soda from the gift shop would settle my rattled nerves.

I pulled my raincoat over my head and clicked the locks shut. Scurrying on a pedestrian bridge leading to the lodge, I passed by tourists with drenched hair returning from the jaunts to see the falls. Small hungry children whined and pleaded with their parents for candy bars and rainbow-colored lollipops. A group of tourists with name badges posed for a group photo. I couldn't believe this many people were out past dusk on a random April evening. My eye continued to twitch. I rubbed my index finger on the thin skin near my temple but couldn't get it to stop.

The gift shop was equally packed. I ignored the collection of postcards, thimbles, and Oregon black raspberry jam at the front of the store. A woman's voice came over the speakers, announcing the shop would be closing in five minutes. Customers should please bring their purchases to the counter. This excited the foreign crowd as a line quickly queued.

I pushed my way to a wall of snacks and refrigerated drinks. I'd skipped dinner. It was 8:00. Grabbing a bag of chips, a soda, and tropical candies, I turned to take my place in line when someone bumped into me.

"Ooh, sorry," I started to say when I locked eyes with Andrew.

His black raincoat dripped water onto the floor around him. He looked winded as if he'd been running. His cheeks flushed red and small beads of perspiration formed on his forehead.

"What are you doing here?" I demanded, my mouth hanging open. He wiped sweat from his head.

I took a step back.

He stared at me for a second before glancing around the store. "Scouting locations for Krissy."

Fear rose in my throat, tightening my vocal cords. I swallowed hard, trying to loosen them. What were the odds Andrew would be at Multnomah Falls at the same time as me? He must have tailed me. Was he trying to send me a message?

"You look kind of shaken up. Is something wrong?" Andrew's words sounded innocent and thoughtful, but the snarl on his lips made me quiver.

I bit my lip. "No," I lied. "Grabbing snacks for my drive home." I held the bag of chips. "How'd you get out here anyway? Weren't you supposed to give your statement? And wait, you don't have a car." My eye twitched rapidly.

He laughed. "I got a ride. Cool place. Are you sure you're okay? You seem kind of weird. Is something wrong with your eye?"

"I'm fine. Really hungry." I tore into the chips.

"Looks like you've got the junk food bug too." Andrew held up a handful of candy bars, chips, and nuts.

Where was his camera gear? I'd never seen him without his earpiece and camera.

"Are you planning to film here at the falls?"

"Nope. Krissy sent me to prep the trail for the next shoot. She told me to scout this area on the way back. You know her, always focused on the best shot. She must tell me ten times a day, 'On this production, we err on the side of coverage first.'" He said this in a high-pitched tone, mimicking her voice. It unnerved me.

"It's not even her production. Dave's my boss, but don't tell her that."

"Well, I better get moving," I said, backing away, with a mouthful of chips.

"You do that. Be careful out there. Roads are slick." He

lumbered his way to the front doors and cocked his head over his shoulder as he pushed them open.

I drew a breath. Did he mean that as a warning?

Andrew had most definitely followed me here and run me off the road.

Now I needed to figure out why.

# TWENTY-ONE

The next morning, I awoke with a start, sure I was late for work again.

Remembering it was Saturday, I let out a long breath.

Still, I had more work to do on my feature. I needed this story to be perfect—to wow Greg with my writing abilities. The best way to do that was to return to the scene of the crime.

I sent Matt a text.

Time for a quick hike this morning?

Matt's phone, like his bike, never ventured more than an inch or two away from his body. He must have been asleep or in the shower since he didn't respond within seconds of receiving my text.

While I waited for Matt's response, I padded into the kitchen and filled Jill's ebony teakettle with water. French press sounded like the morning revival I was in need of. Water fumed on the stove as I ground nutty chocolate-scented whole beans. Jill's kitchen could have belonged to a five-star chef. It was outfitted with top-of-the-line appliances and gadgets, like the fancy grinder I held in my hand. With the exception of the grinder (Jill was as addicted to coffee as I was), the professional kitchen tools were completely wasted on Jill. Her meals consisted of salads and gobs of candy. Most of her culinary accessories sat unused in drawers lined with French parchment paper.

The kettle screeched on the stove, causing me to jump and spill freshly ground coffee on the pristine counter. Last night's run-in with Andrew had me shaken. I wished Jill were home. She was spending the weekend at Will's beach house. Her note promised she'd check in later.

I punched in Sheriff Daniels's number. I had to tell him that Andrew was stalking me. His phone went straight to voicemail, so I left him a message explaining my encounter with Andrew at Multnomah Falls.

Scooping the spilled coffee into the stainless-steel composting bin, I shook the rest into the base of the French press. As I carefully poured scalding water over the aromatic grounds, my phone dinged.

I secured the lid of the French press and slowly pushed the grounds to the bottom. This process struck me as magical. I was literally turning ordinary water into thick coffee with my hands. I sucked in the aroma through my nose and resisted the urge to pour myself a cup immediately. It needed to linger, but it smelled like heaven.

Allowing the flavors of the grounds to mesh with the steaming water, I hurried over to my phone.

Matt's message read:

YOU want to HIKE?!

I shot back:

No. I need to go back to Angel's Rest. You game?

Sure. An hour?

Perfect. Meet here?

Nope. On my bike. Gotta change. My place. 10:15?

Done. See you soon.

I looked at my watch. It wasn't quite 9:00. Plenty of time to enjoy my coffee and shower.

A little over an hour later, I pulled into Matt's driveway. He lived in a row of townhouses on the east side of the river where rent's half the cost of the Pearl. The area was cute, with bungalows, tree-lined streets, and train stops every few blocks. Matt typically biked over the Hawthorne Bridge to *The O*'s headquarters downtown. Or on a rainy day, he could hop on MAX and take the train across.

I tugged on my boots. This was the first time since our disastrous hike I'd attempted to put them back on. Three layers of Band-Aids and moleskin should do the trick.

Matt stuck his head out the balcony doors from the top floor, "Hey, one sec. I'll be right down. You want me to drive?"

"Sure."

I locked my car and grabbed my day pack from the trunk. The early-morning sun had baked yesterday's rain off the pavement. Sunglasses were a necessity. Hard to believe after last night's deluge. I dug through my bag for a pair of brown-rimmed shades and pushed them over my nose. Maybe I could hide my fear behind them. The thought of climbing Angel's

Rest again made me short of breath, but I had to impress Greg with sensory details of the trail and rugged landscapes and I also wanted to see if I'd missed something on the trail. And the fact that I was willingly climbing the peak again must mean I'd gained a small notch of confidence in my outdoor skills, right?

Matt bounced down the stairs in his standard attire—shorts and a Geeks Rule T-shirt. "Changing" must have meant swapping his Converse for the hiking boots laced on his feet. "Nice outfit, Megs. You look like an official adventurer."

I gave him a pose, twirling in a circle in my expensed hiking gear and boots.

"I can't believe you're willing to go for a hike." He walked around the side of his red truck and unlocked the passenger side door. "Hop on in," he said as he held the door open for me.

In the sunlight, his blond hair was streaked with white. I realized it was much, much lighter than mine. Perfectly acceptable for dating. We were off by at least three shades.

"I know. I'll fill you in on the drive. It's kind of a long story."

"Got it." He secured my door and disappeared behind the truck.

It took longer than it should have for him to get in. I unbuckled my seat belt and turned to look out the window. He was kneeling in front of my car, examining the headlights.

"What are you doing back there?" I called from the window.

"Your bumper is kind of crooked, and your front tires look really worn down." Matt stood and came around to the driver's side. The truck leaned to the left as he squeezed in. "You need a tune-up."

I laughed.

Matt looked at me in surprise. "Look, I'm only trying to keep you safe."

"Sorry," I said, reaching over and patting his knee. "It's not that." I sighed. "It's a long story. You want to head out to the Gorge and I'll fill you in?"

Matt maneuvered the truck in the direction of Angel's Rest. I filled him in on the events of last night.

When I finished, he shifted around a corner and gave me a wary look. "Megs, this is getting serious. But why go back? I don't get it."

"I need a few more details for my story and I want to see if there's anything on the trail. It's not raining. Maybe we can make our way to the deer trail? Maybe I can figure out what the missing photo is. Andrew had to have left a clue somewhere. I'm convinced that he did it."

We caught air. The truck hit a small bump in the twisted road. Old-growth tree roots snarled to the surface of the cracked pavement. I held on to the side handle above my window, narrowly avoiding hitting my head on the top canopy.

"Sorry about that," Matt said, shifting once again, slowing. "You're playing with fire here. I think it's time to call the sheriff."

"I did. I left him a message this morning. You don't understand." I hated the pleading tone in my voice. "I have to find real evidence. I know it's Andrew. I need to prove it."

"Don't freak out when I say this, okay?"

"I won't. What?"

"I'm serious. You have a tendency to... well... flip out on me."

The truck lurched. A small deer sprinted across the highway and disappeared into the trees on the other side of the road. Matt's quick reflexes spared both us and the deer. According to Gam, seeing a deer in the wild was a sacred blessing. I'd take any sign I could get.

"Good save." I exhaled and hit the dashboard.

"That was a close one." Matt clutched the steering wheel, his eyes focused on the road ahead.

"I promise, I'm not going to freak out. Tell me what you're thinking."

"Okay, here's the deal." Matt didn't glance in my direction. His gaze stayed firmly glued to the highway. "Maybe you should listen to your boss and leave it alone. This is getting too dangerous.

"But," I interrupted, "I thought you said we should work on this together."

"I know, I know. Calm down. See, you're doing it." Matt laughed and beamed at me before returning his focus to the road. "I'm not saying you can't look into the contestants. I mean, you have to for your feature, but you can't just go around accusing someone of murder."

He steered past a group of hikers parking on the side of the road.

"Here's the thing, Megs. I have a feeling you're wrapped up in this because of your dad. It's like you have to prove something. I'm worried about you."

Rather than inflaming me, his input made sense. He was right. I did have something to prove, for Pops, for myself. I stared out the window, allowing his words to sink in.

I'd never forget where I was when I received the call about the accident.

I'd been packing my college apartment. For months, Jill and I had plotted our post-graduation plans. We were heading south for a month. Her internship wasn't due to start until early August, and I had no job prospects at the time. I'd scrimped and saved enough cash from my collegiate newspaper job to afford gas and food for the road trip. Plus, thanks to those glossy graduation announcements Mom forced me to send out, checks from relatives and family friends poured into my mailbox for weeks before graduation. As much as I wanted to join my friends at weeknight bar raids, I opted to tuck it all away for our post-grad blowout.

Our plan was to pack everything. I'd drop off my stuff and store it in the farmhouse until we returned. Jill had already secured her Pearl apartment. She'd leave her stuff there, and we'd hit the road.

Thirty Days South, we named our trip. Starting from Portland, we'd drive south, wherever the road led us. We'd eventually land in Mexico, but whether the route took us through California or Texas, we'd let our instincts decide. We had to do something radical before we dove into the working world.

Then the call came.

I was sitting on my bedroom floor between half-filled cardboard boxes. finals were complete. The window was open, letting in the June sun, the scent of blooming strawberries in our window boxes, and the sound of college kids initiating summer vacation. I'd dumped the contents of my dresser drawers in front of me and was trying to decide which ratty collegiate T-shirts to keep and which to deliver to the Goodwill on our way out of town.

My phone beeped—Mom. Ugh. She probably wanted to lecture me for the hundredth time on how much better use of my summertime I could make job hunting versus embarking on a childish trip.

"Maggie." Her voice was shaky. She never called me Maggie. Pops called me Maggie. Something was wrong.

"What's going on?" I clutched a tie-dyed T-shirt in my hand. It could probably go.

"Are you sitting down?"

I looked around the cluttered space. "Yeah... why?"

"It's your father. There's been an accident."

I dropped the T-shirt and punched the speaker button on my phone. "What kind of an accident?"

"He was on his bike. Riding to town. Someone hit him."

Pops was regimented when it came to safety. He had more lights on his bike than a small plane. He always wore a helmet.

A mild calm came over my body. He'd probably broken his arm or something.

Pops rode his bicycle all around town. He owned a beat-up rust-red pickup truck, but he preferred his bike. The bike was like his second child. He spent hours in the barn tuning it. I wasn't sure how professional cyclists would categorize the bike —a hybrid? Pops found it at one of the swap meets he frequented. It was a classic road bike he outfitted with dirt-track tires. When I'd stop by for Sunday dinners, I'd usually find him in the barn, covered in grease. He liked to tinker. He said it cleared his mind, made room for the words to come out.

Dead air came through the phone. The sound of my classmates laughing on the common lawns outside felt sinister.

"What is it? Did he break something?"

More silence. I grabbed the shirt again and balled it in my hands. "What's wrong?" It felt like my throat was closing in. "Mom?"

"He's dead, Maggie. He's dead."

Not possible. It couldn't be true. Not Pops. He was safe. He was always safe on the road.

"Maggie? Did you hear me?"

My hands felt funny. I'd wrapped the T-shirt tightly around them, cutting off all circulation. They were turning purple in color and losing feeling. I didn't care. "It can't be true."

"I'm so sorry."

The next weeks were a blur. I wasn't sure who packed the rest of my stuff. Probably Jill or Matt. I moved in a daze through the funeral. We canceled our road trip. I moved in with Jill, unable to face seeing the farmhouse without Pops or his bicycle in it.

Instead of spending the summer on the road, I curled in a ball on Jill's couch. I didn't shower for days. I ignored the sound of children playing in the fountains below and the long evenings of sunlight. I refused to speak to Mom. She called daily. I hit Ignore.

Jill begged me to come to barbecues, a weekend at the coast, or for coffee outside on the deck. Gam urged me to join her for walks along the river, healing workshops, or for a slice of her homemade cherry pie. I refused. Pops was gone. My world had tilted on its axis and I didn't care if it spun itself into oblivion.

No tears would come. I tried pinching myself. I tried force —an attempt at guttural sobs like dry heaves. None would flow.

After weeks of cocooning myself in Pops's blue-striped pajamas without consideration of a shower, Jill dragged me into the tub. She'd drawn a warm bath infused with jasmine oil, lit candles, and opened the bathroom windows to allow the evening breeze to enter. My sleep (the little I'd been conscious of) had been tangled with nightmares and strange dreams. I must have dozed off in the bath, lulled into a moment of peace from the water cleansing my sweat-stained skin. It might have been a dream. It could have been a vision. But with my head resting on the cotton pillow Jill secured to the edge of the claw-foot tub, I allowed my eyes to close. My entire body froze as if I'd been paralyzed. For a second I panicked. I tried to wiggle my toes. Nothing. I tried to move my head from side to side. Nothing. Pops's deep, kind voice resonated in my ears. I relaxed into paralysis, afraid any slight movement might make his voice disappear.

"Maggie." Pops's voice brushed over my forehead as if his soft words were stroking it.

*Please don't let this moment vanish.* My mouth didn't betray me. I spoke the words in my head. *Pops, I'm here.*

"Sweet, sweet Maggie."

Water spilled from my eyes, cascading down my motionless cheeks where it collided with the lukewarm bathwater.

"Maggie, I'm here."

I wanted to shout, *Pops, I'm here too!* Words wouldn't form on my lips.

Instead, salty tears flooded them.

"It's time to carry on, sweet one. It's time to carry on."

Feeling surged through my body, burning the tender cells on my skin. From here grief erupted in violent sobs. Jill raced into the bathroom. She stopped midstride when she saw me sobbing, dropped to her knees on the tile floor next to me, and stroked my damp hair.

"It's okay, Meg. This is good," she said over the sound of my wails.

After that night, I spent a chunk of the next week sobbing, attempting to purge grief from my body. It didn't exactly work. Grief stuck with me like a loyal dog, but I learned to walk with it. I learned how to cry in the car and avoid cheesy commercials, especially those with dads hoisting their daughters on their shoulders or anything by Hallmark. Slowly, I accepted Jill's and Gam's offers of getting out of the apartment.

I channeled my building rage at Mom. Pops's death was her fault. If she hadn't left him, maybe he wouldn't have ridden his bicycle to town. Maybe they'd have met us in Mexico for a week to celebrate my graduation. Instead, my entry into adulthood had come full force. I was a college graduate without a home, a job, or a parent.

Matt cleared his throat expectantly. "You still with me, Megs?"

"Sorry." I whisked tears from under my eyelids and flipped my attention in his direction. "You're right about Pops. You're right about it all. I'll be more careful, I promise."

"Whew." Matt let out a long sigh. "I thought you might bite my head off."

"Am I that bad?" I winced.

"Not at all. Well, maybe sometimes when you get an idea

stuck in your head. It's one of the great things about you, actually. You're tenacious. You go after things. But on the flip side, you can have a tendency to have narrow vision sometimes."

I blushed at his one-sided compliment. Gam always claimed each of us had a yin and yang in terms of our strengths and weaknesses. That they happened to be the polar opposite of each other, and our ultimate goal in this life was finding the perfect balance between them.

Hundred-foot evergreen trees stood like soldiers guarding the base of the forest. This was the place Andrew tried to run me off the road. In contrast to their ominous waves in the wind last night, they appeared regal and sturdy in the pollen-filled sunlight.

"Your job is to keep me honest. Deal?" I socked him in the arm.

He faked pain and grinned. "You got it."

When we reached the parking lot at the base of Angel's Rest, a vision of my beat-up body wrapped in Greg's sweatshirt raced through my head. Had it really only been three days ago I'd been interrogated at this spot? Time was flying at lightning pace. It felt like that was weeks ago.

All the caution tape had been removed from the base of the trail marker. No one would have any idea a crime had occurred here. A stranger venturing up the path wouldn't have to fight the memory of seeing a man's body sailing to his crushing death. *Good God, Meg, what are you thinking?*

Maybe this hadn't been the best idea. Not only did the thought of the trail's rocky ledges and switchbacks send a wave of nausea up my esophagus, but I hadn't expected to have a surge of memories push to the forefront of my mind.

I hesitated at the trailhead, casting a wistful look at Matt's truck. I wished there were more cars in the parking lot. Where was everyone? It was Saturday, after all. Hopefully the trailhead would fill up soon. Sure, it was daylight and I had Matt with me, but if Andrew really saw me as a threat, what would stop him from coming after us today?

I froze. “Forget it, Matt. This was a stupid idea. I don’t know what I was thinking. I can’t go back up there.”

Matt grabbed my hand and led me slowly upward. “Come on, Megs. We’ll do this together.”

# TWENTY-TWO

It was amazing how different the trail appeared. Maybe Matt's presence and firm grip helped to subdue my fears. Or it could have been the sunlight and sound of spring finches flitting between the trees.

As we ascended, Matt pointed out a gigantic osprey nest and eagles soaring overhead. We stood to watch them float with ease through the cloudless sky. Matt prided himself on his outdoor background. His obsession with nature was in stark contrast to the geek-inspired lifestyle he led. Although I knew this about him, it always surprised me when his ranger roots came seeping to the surface.

He should have been the one working at *Northwest Extreme*—a point verified by the contents of his day pack. An oddly perfect assortment of gadgets. Maybe I should talk to Greg about having him write a nature geek column?

He tracked our pace, distance, ascent, and calories burned on an app. A set of high-range binoculars was secured in a side pocket of his pack.

"Try these suckers out. I got them a month ago and have

been dying for a chance to use them." He handed me the tiny binoculars.

Adjusting the lenses, I tilted them to the sky. Trees and greenery flashed in front of my eyes, making my head spin. I spotted the eagles above and gasped. I could make out the details of each individual feather as they soared thirty feet above us.

Matt grinned. "Cool, yeah?"

I weighed them in my hands. "Yeah, and light."

"Technology, my friend. Technology."

"Listen, I'll admit these are pretty sweet, but when are you ever going to need them in the real world?"

"Today!" Matt beamed and tucked them carefully into the side pocket of his pack.

I huffed as Matt effortlessly sailed over small logs and loose rocks along the trail. He kept glancing back to make sure I was still following him.

"I'm good." I waved him on with my hand, pausing to catch my breath. "Keep going."

"You want to jump out in front?" Matt asked. He stopped and waited for me.

"No, no, keep going. You're making me move. If I lead, I'll be too slow."

Matt shook his head. "You're half my size—literally. Your legs barely come to my knee."

"I swear, I'm fine. I want to keep going."

"Well, at least drink this. Your face is bright red." Matt offered a fresh Gatorade bottle.

The flavor of salty lemon-lime gave my energy a burst. I didn't remember feeling this scorched or sweaty when I was here with the *Race the States* crew. Of course it had been rainy and windy that day.

Plus, I had trudged along at my own pace. Keeping up with

Matt was a challenge, but I didn't want to let him see how much I was struggling.

After another fifteen minutes of switching back and forth on the dirt trail, we came to the first rocky clearing. This, aside from the summit, was my least favorite part of the hike. Today sunlight blazed on the rock-covered exposed cliff. The heat generating from the black rocks was probably enough to fry an egg.

I made the mistake of looking down. My heart hammered in my chest.

*Please don't let me hyperventilate.*

"Follow my lead," Matt called. "And stay close to the right, okay?"

I nodded. No one, with the exception of Jill and Matt, knew about my deep-seated fear of heights. He tried to play it off like this was a dangerous section of trail, when without me he'd fly over the narrow gravel path on his mountain bike.

I drew in my breath as I cautiously moved onto the loose gravel path. Little rocks kicked under my feet and scattered over the side of the cliff. The sound of them bouncing down the cliff like Planko blocks encouraged me to hurry. This stretch of path ran for about one hundred yards. But it felt like a mile to safety on the other side.

"Are you sure this is a good idea, Megs?" Matt asked. He stood with one foot propped on a rock. "You look pretty shaky. I think it's too soon to be here after what—happened..." He trailed off.

"I'm sure. I've got this. If I don't face my fears, I'm going to end up sitting on Jill's couch eating candy for the next month."

Matt looked unsure. The sound of a dog barking echoed above. I jumped and let out a little scream.

"This is a bad idea. You're jumpy. I think we should turn around. Seriously, Megs, you're going to get hurt. Not because of any danger on the trail, but because of your own stubbornness."

"Please, Matt. Please. I've got to do this. I have to take another look. I'm sorry I'm jumpy. I promise I'll be more careful."

Matt patted the rock he'd been resting his leg on. "Come sit down for a sec at least?"

Happy for the reprieve, I flung my pack on the ground. It went tumbling toward the edge since it wasn't weighted down with all the extra gear I'd brought along on the first hike. I'd learned my lesson. Keep it light.

The sight of my pack resting precariously on the side of the cliff made my mind flash to Lenny. How was I ever going to get that image out of my head?

"Are you sure you're okay?" Matt said, offering me half of a granola bar. I declined.

"You look like you're off in space somewhere." He bent on his knees so his eyes were level with mine. Holding my gaze, he squeezed my hand and said, "What's going on with you today? Is it your dad? Are you thinking about Charlie again?"

I squeezed his hand for a brief moment and dropped his grasp. "I miss him. It's hard, and with Sheriff Daniels—it's all coming to the surface again. I feel like I owe it to Pops to figure out what happened to Lenny. Maybe it'll clear up some of the mess." I looked away. "Plus, if I don't, that image of Lenny flying off the summit is going to become permanently implanted in my brain. I didn't like the guy, but I almost feel responsible for him. Does that make sense? Plus you know what it's like to be on a story. I feel like I can solve this. I have all the pieces—I just have to fit them together."

Not meeting my eyes, Matt shook his head and said, "Yeah, I get it."

"Gam talks about the connectedness of the Universe all the time. I think because I'm the last person who saw Lenny alive, maybe we're connected in a strange way. I have to figure out who killed him because if I don't, I'm not going to be able to let it go. I can't explain it, but I need to solve his murder."

Pulling me to my feet, Matt brushed dirt off my pack and helped me secure it over my shoulders. "Suck it up, little one. We'll get to the bottom of this."

We continued at a noticeably slower pace. Matt kindly made no mention of this fact.

The hard-packed trail wouldn't reveal any footprints of those who trod before us. After last night's rain, the dirt was solid under the overhang of high trees. The sun's warmth had baked the trail in an hour.

No other hikers passed by as we ascended. After another ten minutes, we came to the spot where I'd seen someone on the deer trail.

"Here, Matt," I shouted, pointing to the small offshoot of a trail leading deep into the woods. "This is the deer trail. This is where I saw someone and took the photo."

"Hmm." Matt dropped his pack. "It's pretty dense. I don't think a photo would show anyone back there."

"Yeah, and it happened so fast. I caught a flash of red but couldn't even make out if it was a man or a woman. Do you think we should go back there and look around?"

Matt unfastened the side pocket of his backpack and grabbed his binoculars. He squatted to see through the trees and blackberry vines.

"Looks okay to me," he said, tucking his binoculars away. "We probably won't want to stray too far from where we can see the main trail. It looks like this is a pretty established path, but don't go off of it—got it? These woods are littered with poison oak. That's the last thing you need right now."

"Got it. Stay on the trail; keep sight of the main path. I can do this."

We had to crouch in order to avoid hitting our heads on the trees and vines twisting along the deer trail.

The trail was nothing more than a six-inch-wide path worn by herds of deer and other wild game using this route between the upper falls of Multnomah and their burrows deeper in the woods. It was evident humans typically didn't traverse this way.

Matt held long tree branches and prickly vines as we weaved our way deeper beneath the trees. Sunlight disappeared and I lost sight of the main trail.

I had an eerie feeling we were being watched. Stopping at the sound of a squawking bird overhead, I turned slowly in a circle, checking to see if anyone was hiding in the thick brush.

A tree snapped and the bushes to my left quaked. "Did you hear that?" I whispered.

He held a finger to his lips to silence me and pushed me to my knees with his other hand. Carefully he drew his binoculars out and scanned the area where the bushes had been disturbed. I could feel my heart pounding in my throat. The woods were eerily silent. Too silent.

After surveying the area all around us, Matt returned his binoculars to his pack and helped me to my feet.

"Probably a spooked animal. I don't see anything out there."

Unconsciously, I put my hand on my neck to feel whether my pulse rate had slowed. It hadn't. My veins bulged to the beat of my racing blood.

"Do you think we should turn back? I can't see the trail anymore."

"It's up to you. As long as we stay on this, we're fine to follow it a little farther."

I glanced behind me and agreed. "Okay, how about five more minutes, and if we don't find anything, we turn around?"

"Works for me." Matt plunged ahead through the dense foliage, seemingly unfazed.

With every snap of a twig or chirp of a bird, my stomach

dropped. What if Andrew had followed us again? I couldn't shake the feeling something or someone was stalking us—conveniently buried in the cover of the forest canopy.

About the time I was ready to call it quits and work our way to daylight and the security of a well-traveled trail, Matt stopped in midstride. "Hey, what's that?" He pointed to a low-lying tree branch about a yard off the trail. A tan object dangled from it. Was it a bandana or a ripped shirt?

We made our way closer, and as my eyes focused on the object dangling from the tree, I let out an audible gasp.

"Oh, my God, Matt, that's Dave's hat!"

"Are you sure?"

I plucked the hat from the tree. It was weathered—clearly it had been out here for days. Dirt and leaves were caked to it. It felt damp to the touch, but the mesh material it was made of was waterproof. I brushed off the debris.

There was no mistaking it was Dave's hat. That could only mean one thing; Dave had been out on this trail. But why?

# TWENTY-THREE

"How do you know this is Dave's?" Matt asked, taking the hat from my hands and examining it carefully. "This could belong to anyone."

"It's Dave's," I assured him. "He wore it everywhere—at the restaurant that first night I met him. Most people don't wear hats inside Shared Table. Plus, he mentioned he lost it the other day. I haven't seen him wearing it since..." My brain replayed the meet and greet and our last meetings at the office. "I haven't seen him wear it since Lenny died!"

Matt turned the floppy hat inside out and read the label. "I think you're right. Look at this."

It read, MADE IN BYRON BAY, AUSTRALIA.

"Told you." I punched him in the arm.

"What are you, five?" Matt bantered with a grin.

"Better question: What do you think we should do with it?"

"Well, we've already touched it, so I guess we take it with us and you call Sheriff Daniels and tell him as soon as we get back."

"I know, real evidence," I said, grabbing the hat. "I don't get it, though. Dave's been vocal about losing his hat. If he thought it incriminated him in any way, why would he go around announcing he'd lost it?"

I crushed the hat in my hands. Upon releasing it, it popped back into its original form. The tag claimed it was a bestseller in Australia, made of durable waterproof canvas with a coiled spring wire fitted inside the brim. I wrapped the dusty cotton chin cord around my finger and thought.

Matt peeled back vines and craned his neck. "Yeah, and what's a hat doing on an offshoot trail at least a half mile below the site of the murder?"

"Well, we know Dave's in financial trouble. What if he came out here to meet Lenny? Maybe I saw him. He and Lenny got in an argument and the hat came off in the fight?"

Matt looked skeptical. "Why would he come all the way out here to meet Lenny?"

"Let's say Lenny found out Dave was broke. Maybe he threatened to go public?"

"You could have something there," Matt said, rubbing his chin. "Lenny discovers Dave's in too deep. Dave follows him out here and threatens him. But that still leaves the issue of Lenny getting pushed off the summit. We're nowhere near there," Matt said, motioning in the direction of the main trail.

"Yeah, and I saw Dave. I don't think he could have pushed Lenny. He was right there when I fell. I looked away for a split second."

Matt tilted his head to one side and paused. "Well—I suppose it's plausible he could have given Lenny a quick shove when your attention was focused on the fall. It wouldn't take long."

A thought spiraled through my head. "Do you think this trail connects with the main one? Could Dave have raced here to beat Lenny to the summit?"

My words were coming out rapidly. I heard myself smashing them together. "What if... what if Dave planned the whole thing? Think about it. He freaked out he didn't have the cash to finish the show and scrambled to find new venture capital. He'd invested his entire life into *Race the States*. Would that warrant murder? If he believed Lenny was going to tell everyone his secret?"

"I don't know." Matt shrugged. "Sadly, people have probably killed for less."

We both stood there, pondering our next move. I had no idea how long we'd walked along the deer trail. My body was spent. I was covered in sweat, and my cheeks were burning. I wanted to turn back, but I also was desperate to see whether the trail looped upward and connected to the main trail.

"What about this trail?" I asked, pointing to the twisting tracks leading deeper into the middle of the woods. "Do you think there's a way it connects higher up?"

"It could." Matt turned in the direction of the main path. "There are tons of trails like this used by animals. I think we should head back now."

It took us fifteen minutes to return to the main trail. I was sure an experienced hiker could have done it in five. Not me. The dark sense of foreboding eased in my body as sunlight began to pour in through the trees. I could hear other hikers not far above us, laughing.

What did I know? Andrew had followed me and tried to run me off the road last night. Was it a warning or was he trying to kill me? Dave had been hiding on the deer trail the day Lenny had been murdered. I had one solid piece of evidence: a hat. As much as I'd rather hoof it to the parking lot, I had to reach the summit.

"You have time to continue on to the top?" I asked Matt once we made it back to the main trail.

Matt checked his watch. "Sure. We're not far off, are we?"

To tell the truth, that day was such a blur I couldn't remember if we were five minutes or five hours from the summit. I looked and noticed the tree line was thinning ahead. We must be close. Around the next bend, the rocky field leading to the summit exposed itself. I swallowed hard. This was the worst part of the climb by far.

"Ah! We're close." Matt's voice was laced with enthusiasm.

I didn't respond. The voice in my head quaked—*Turn around.*

The jagged granite and basalt formations looked completely different drenched in midmorning sunlight and free from the drama of *Race the States* contestants. I clawed my way over the rocks, digging my nails in wherever possible. A dark layer of dirt spread underneath my fingernails. The weight of my pack was light, but the weight of the week's events bore down on me. I had to make it to the summit. Maybe I should fling my pack over. Gam would call that an energy cleanse.

Matt reached the narrow ledge of the summit first. He waved casually and watched as I inched along the face of the rock.

"You want a hand?"

"No, I'm good."

He turned his body to the east. "Dang! It's been a long time since I've seen a day this clear. You've got to come check out this view. It's spectacular."

"No chance," I muttered under my breath. My legs shook. I tried to overextend my knees in an attempt to control the involuntary shaking. I'd made it to the exact spot where I'd fallen.

Noticing my quivering wooden legs, Matt gave me a look of concern and hopped to where I stood. He wrapped his arm through mine. "This is the spot, I take it?"

I couldn't form words with my mouth. "Mm-hmm."

"Should we turn around?" Matt tried to keep the worry from his voice, but squeezed tighter on my arm.

"No, I've got this." I leaned forward a couple of inches to see over the rock blocking my view.

The cliff dropped off. Looking straight out from this vantage point gave me the false perspective that I could swan dive straight into the Columbia River 1,500 feet below. I shuddered. In actuality, the massive boulders where Lenny fell scattered about fifty to a hundred feet below. Would there be any sign of his death, or had the Crag Rats and this week's rain washed away all evidence of his demise?

"Can you see anything down there?" I asked Matt.

"No." Grabbing his binoculars, he said, "Wait here. I'm going to climb to the top of that rock to get a better view." He pointed to a ten-foot boulder.

Waves of nausea and déjà vu swam through my body. I'd come this far and it didn't seem to matter. No sense of closure overcame me. If anything, I felt worse.

"Can't see anything from up here," Matt called as he scrambled down the boulder. "There's a smaller rock here where someone could have hidden."

Plopping next to me, he rubbed my back. "If you're up for it, there's one more thing I think we should do. But only if you're up for it."

"Sure, I'm up for anything," I lied.

Matt laughed and threw his hands in the air. "Seriously, Megs! Do you think I'm an idiot? I know you're not okay, but I do want you to see something. Also, you're adorable when you try to lie." He chuckled, stuck his tongue out, and crossed his eyes.

He thought I was adorable? My cheeks flamed again, but this time from the heat of energy pulling me toward him. His goofy expression made me break into an uncontrollable bout of giggles. I knew it was a stress response, but I couldn't stop laughing. My sides ached. My cheeks hurt. I hadn't felt this good in the last three days.

"That's more like it." Matt rose to his feet, grabbed both of our packs and flung one on each shoulder. "But that's not what I want you to see. I'll take these the rest of the way. Come with me."

I sprang to my feet, energized by the release of laughter. As soon as my eyes were parallel with the horizon, my entire body swayed. I'd momentarily forgotten I was 1,500 feet above the river far below.

"Steady there." Matt grabbed my arm and held me upright.

"Must have stood too fast." I tried to cover. "Air's lighter here at the summit, right?"

Matt wrinkled his nose. "No, we're not high, and we're not even at the summit."

"What?"

"That's what I want to show you. Come on."

I followed Matt across the narrow ledge and into the wooded dirt trail upward for a quarter of a mile. This was the path that Alicia and Leaf had taken to Multnomah Falls.

The route was much less traveled, with gnarly vines and thick ferns covering it. We came to a junction where the main trail veered left. Matt led us on a smaller trail. "This is Foxglove Hill."

"Where are we going?"

"Hang on, it's not far."

We continued a small trail that wasn't much wider than the deer trail we'd been on earlier. We hiked over fallen logs blocking the path, which was overgrown with moss-covered tree branches. I wondered how Alicia and Leaf had managed this stretch sprinting, or if they'd stayed on the main path.

We appeared to be winding our way deeper into the forest. A boggy stretch of wild salmonberry bushes overtook the path. We trampled over them. Leaf would be pissed.

Coming to another junction, Matt pointed to a wooden sign reading DEVIL'S REST.

After a quick, steep climb, we were completely boxed in by creepy spider trees with moss-covered trunks.

"This is Devil's Rest?" I asked.

"Nope. Trust me. We're close."

"I thought Angel's and Devil's Rest were the same trail."

"Nope." Matt turned around to make sure I was close enough to hear him. "As you can tell, this is a much quieter trail. Amazing views. You can see all the Washington mountains from the top."

A small Forest Service sign marked the west end of Devil's Rest trail. We followed the trail down a steep bank to the east and to a spur trail. Where in the world was Matt taking me? And did he know how to get back?

Coming to a stop by a small clearing, Matt said, "This is it."

He dropped our packs on the trail and bent over. Huge evergreen trees colliding with low-lying ferns blocked the view of the river, but a section of them seemed to be hollowed out.

He pulled me with him into what reminded me of a rabbit hole.

The clearing revealed a stunning view of the river, Mount St. Helens, Mount Adams, Mount Rainier in the distance, and a glimpse of the rocky summit we'd been sitting on twenty minutes ago.

"Check out these views." Matt motioned his hand outward, then pointed to the heavily wooded forest. "Devil's Rest is another half mile or so straight up."

He explained that day hikers opted to trek to the rocky formation known as Angel's Rest. But Devil's Rest was the summit of record. The trail connected with Latourell, Multnomah, and Horsetail Falls, then looped around to Angel's Rest and continued to the parking lot at the trailhead.

This made for the perfect hiding spot.

From here the killer had the vantage point of seeing Lenny reach Angel's Rest. It would have been a sprint to push him over the ledge, but possible.

Definitely possible if the other contestants had already

continued to Multnomah Falls. Unless you were specifically heading for this little lookout point, it would be easy to miss, especially at the rate they must have been running.

Could Dave or Andrew have hidden here? Lying in wait for the ideal opportunity to send Lenny sailing to his death? What about Alicia? Was this how her arms got scratched? Or Leaf? He was from Oregon. He probably knew about Devil's Rest.

Devil's Rest. The name sent a shiver up my spine. I didn't believe in the Devil. Nor did Gam, but the irony of its sinister name wasn't lost on me.

# TWENTY-FOUR

After an hour and a half of lagging my way to the parking lot with Matt, we made the return drive to Portland in near silence. Deep in thought, I barely noticed as we flew past the spot where Andrew ran me off the road last night. Finding Dave's hat and discovering the secret summit at Devil's Rest had to fit together somehow.

Before I knew it, the familiar sight of Portland's cityscape and bridges came into view. I looked in surprise as Matt steered the car into his complex. "We're here already?"

He gave me a knowing look. "You've been lost in thought. What are you plotting?"

"Nothing."

Raising an eyebrow, he said, "Yeah, right." He pulled the keys out of the ignition. "Don't go chasing after Dave. You're taking that hat to the sheriff, right?"

Flashing both my thumbs, I said, "Right. You got it. Thanks for tagging along. See you later." I scooted off with Dave's hat hidden in my backpack before Matt could say anything else.

I'd formulated a plan. I needed to run to the office and pick up a copy of the schedule to find out what the contestants were doing this afternoon. I also wanted to get Greg a new draft by the end of the day. I had some new ideas for my story. Once I took another pass at my feature, I could hunt Dave down and confront him about the hat.

The short drive to *Northwest Extreme* went by without notice. I slid into an open space in the empty lot without memory of how I'd arrived. Gam called this a state of waking meditation. I called it dangerous.

As I stepped out of the car, I heard screeching.

The white rental van came tearing into the parking lot. It took a corner too hard and tilted onto two wheels. I braced myself for impact, shutting my eyes. Nothing happened.

I peeked through my right eye, leaning on the hood of my car. The van bounced on all four wheels and skidded to a stop an inch in front of me.

Tire tracks traced its route from the street, and the smell of burning rubber hung in the air.

*What the hell?*

A pristine white circle glared in the middle of the dirty van. The *Race the States* logo was missing.

Krissy jumped out of the driver's seat and raced over to me.

She clenched her fingernails between her teeth and dug her thumbnails into her chin. "I'm sorry! Are you okay?"

"I'm awake," I said, ruffling my hair with my fingertips. "I was jonesing for an afternoon coffee, but I don't think I need one now. What happened?"

"Whew," Krissy said, removing her fingers from her mouth and wringing them together. "I didn't think I was going to be able to stop in time."

"Me neither."

"I don't know what happened. All of a sudden, the gas pedal stuck. I couldn't get the brake to push. finally, I grabbed the emergency brake."

Loose hairs spilled from her normally coifed ponytail. Her

striped pale-blue and lemon-yellow broadcloth shirt had come untucked. Her glasses were askew.

"That was close." My body hummed with pent-up adrenaline. She could have seriously injured me—or worse. I let out a little shudder. Was that her plan?

"I know. I'm so sorry." She brushed imaginary dust from her shirt.

"What are you doing here on a Saturday anyway?" I didn't trust her flustered act for a minute.

"I'm going over details for the finale with Greg."

"Have you been driving the van the entire time?" I couldn't hide the doubt creeping into my tone, but she had nearly run me over.

"Pretty much," she said, re-positioning her glasses on the bridge of her nose.

"Are you sure no else has had access to the van?"

She looked at me quizzically. "Why?"

"Maybe someone tampered with it?"

"Why would they do that?"

"Well, you know with what happened to Lenny. There's a killer walking around. What if the killer left evidence in the van or something? You're sure no one else has driven the van?"

Krissy tucked her subtly hemmed cotton shirt into her skirt and pleated it in front with her hands. Straightening her skirt had the same effect on her body. She stood with her shoulders erect. "Well, I did loan the keys to Dave last night. He said he wanted to run a few errands."

"What about Andrew?"

"No, Andrew hasn't driven it."

"You're sure?"

"What's the deal? Do you know something I don't? The van's registered under my name. That means I'm responsible for it. I'm not about to let everyone run around town with it."

"No." I quickly changed the direction of the conversation.

"I think I'm freaked out, you know? This whole situation with Lenny has me rattled."

Krissy's lips pursed. She reached out and put a hand on my arm. Through clenched teeth, she said, "Don't you give Lenny a thought. He wouldn't have given you one."

"Probably not." I shrugged.

"That man cared about one person and one alone—himself. Plus, he was a buffoon—I doubt anyone tried to kill him. He probably fell backward trying to pose with flexed biceps. Are you heading in?"

I followed Krissy into the office. She was right. Lenny had acted like a self-consumed ass in the brief interactions I'd had with him.

"Ah, I see Greg beat me here." She turned and made a beeline for Greg's office. "Take it easy."

I left Krissy cooing over Greg and headed straight for my desk. The message light on my phone wasn't lit, but I picked up the handset and listened anyway. No new messages. At least that was a minor celebration. Hopefully, whoever had left the warning and chased me had decided I didn't know enough to be worth the energy.

I sat down to collect my thoughts and think about layering in a new imagery for my story. I wanted readers to feel like they were on the trail with me. I added scenery details and fleshed out Angel's Rest. When I was done, my mind drifted back to Lenny's murder.

I missed Pops. He'd know what to do. I tried to keep the memory of that fateful day in the deep recesses of my brain. Gam called it denial. I called it self-preservation. I could hear her voice in my head, urging me to mine my memory—to allow the pain and tears to push to the surface. I did that once. I couldn't do it again. Not yet. It was much easier to live in denial, telling myself Pops was on an extended vacation. He'd be home soon.

Forget what Matt said. I had to confront Dave. If I could corner him and catch him off guard, I'd be able to tell if he was lying. This time, I wasn't taking any chances. I picked up the phone and called Sheriff Daniels.

"Daniels here."

"Sorry to bug you again, Sheriff, but I have an important piece of evidence for you. My friend and I just happened to hike Angel's Rest this morning and I found Dave's hat on a deer trail. I'm not sure what I should do with it."

Sheriff Daniels cleared his throat. "Ms. Reed, what part of 'Stay out of my investigation' did you not understand? You and your friend 'just happened' to hike my crime scene?"

"Well, it wasn't closed off."

"Young lady, you know very well that's not what I mean."

Maybe calling Sheriff Daniels wasn't the best idea.

"Now, Ms. Reed, I want you to bring that hat down to the station and stop meddling with my investigation. Is that clear?"

"Yeah," I mumbled.

Sheriff Daniels's voice became softer. "The last thing I need is another body on my hands. I've got my deputy questioning Andrew as we speak about what he was doing at the falls last night. I need you to leave this case to me and my team."

"I understand."

After hanging up with Sheriff Daniels, I found the updated schedule and scanned it to see what, if anything, was on the docket for the evening. Nothing for Dave on the schedule. Or for me, for that matter.

Grabbing Dave's hat and leaving my desk untouched, I headed for Greg's office. I could see through the glass that Krissy had unbuttoned the top two buttons of her shirt and hiked her skirt well above the knee.

Greg positioned his chair from behind his desk right next to Krissy. They laughed like old chums as I poked my head in through the glass doors.

"Sorry to interrupt." I glanced behind me. "Do either of you happen to know where Dave might be?"

"Didn't know you were here." Greg waved hello over his shoulder. "Last I heard, he was off to climb. Not sure where. You know, Krissy?"

Krissy's tone was cool as she snapped her head around. She'd removed her glasses. Her steel-blue eyes looked fresh and twice their size without her glasses. "He went to an indoor climbing gym, downtown somewhere." She turned to Greg. "I needed him out of my hair, if you know what I mean. I can't get anything done with him underfoot." She smiled coyly and laughed. "Bosses. What are you going to do?"

Her laugh—almost a cackle—reminded me of Mom's.

Greg winked and pointed at me. "That's what this one says about me.

Right, Meg?"

"No, no, never," I stammered.

Krissy narrowed her eyes as if to say, *Leave us alone.* I offered my thanks and made a quick exit. I could have sworn Krissy made a reference to me being childish as I backed out the door.

"Meg," Greg called.

Oh, God, what did I have on my face now? "Yeah?" I winced.

"I need your next draft. As in—today!"

"I know. I'm totally on it. I've already made a bunch of changes and should have something for you to look at soon."

I knew I could bang out the rest of the draft quickly, but despite what I'd already written, I was stuck on the right angle to take—lean hard into Lenny's death or gloss over it and focus on the race? A bit of both?

Pops said his best writing happened when he wasn't writing. So what better distraction than working on a murder case to help inspire my writing? I'd go find Dave and confront him about *Race the States* and his hat. Sheriff Daniels knew everything, so there was little risk of Dave lashing out at me.

Tracking Dave shouldn't be too difficult. There were only a handful of climbing gyms in the area and only two downtown. I pulled up both downtown locations in my phone and opted to start with The Wall. It was a ten-minute drive from headquarters. Plenty of time to take a quick spin through the gym and finish my rough draft.

The Wall reeked of chalk and old sweat. A scrawny high-school kid manning the reception desk eyed me when I walked in. "You here for the newbie class?"

"I'm looking for an Australian guy. His name is Dave. He's about six feet, graying hair, beard. Talks in a deep Aussie accent. Have you seen him?"

"Nope." The kid pointed to the clock on the wall. It was made from carabiners and climbing rope. "The newbie class started fifteen minutes ago. They're the only ones in the gym."

"Thanks anyway." I turned to leave.

"You should come and check out the newbie climb. It's a killer."

I offered him an appreciative nod, knowing there was no way I'd climb for entertainment.

The other downtown location was called The Ledge. It had opened six months ago. *Northwest Extreme* covered the grand opening. One of the laminated magazine covers in Greg's office was a spread of the bash.

The Ledge smelled new. There was a faint scent of coconut in the air coming from the tanning salon next door. Neon-green signs plastered the walls with information on classes and gym member records.

A forty-something hard-bodied woman in tight black spandex and yellow climbing shoes greeted me at the front desk.

"I'm looking for an Australian guy," I repeated.

"Oh, sure. You mean Dave?" she asked.

She knew him by name? "Yeah, is he here?"

"Yep, right there in fact." She pointed her finger to an exposed climbing wall.

I craned my neck to see to the top where Dave was perched.

"You want to climb? We have a discounted rate going. After five it's the regular rate."

"I'll wait for him, thanks."

"No problem. You can have a seat over there." She nodded to a couple of egg-shaped chairs in the lobby.

"One question," I asked hesitantly. "Do you know Dave?"

"Nah, not really. He's been here a bunch the last week. Competitive, that one. Tries to break his time, using new holds." She chewed on a pencil and leafed through a scheduling book on the desk. That gave me an idea.

"Has he been here every day this week?"

"Uh, I'm not sure. Maybe."

"Do you know if he was here last night by chance?"

She took the pencil out of her mouth and looked quizzically at me. "Why do you want to know?"

I'd come on too strong. My mind raced for an excuse. "I'm trying to plan a surprise party for him." I surprised myself with this easy lie. "I can't seem to figure out his schedule. I was wondering if he's here around this time? That might be a good way to get him to the party." I grinned with what I hoped was an innocent smile.

Nodding, she flipped through the scheduling book. "Looks like he was here from six until about eight last night."

"Great. Thanks so much," I said as I moved to have a seat in the cushion-filled egg chair.

Dave couldn't have been the one in the van last night if he was here.

Unless he left early?

I slunk in the chair to watch Dave swing expertly down the wall. From this vantage point he looked like he could be in his early thirties. His well-defined calf muscles pushed off the wall as he sat in the harness and glided to the ground.

Catching sight of me, he waved as he unhooked his gear. What was I going to say? I should have thought this out more.

I took a quick breath in as he ambled over to me. He stopped to flirt with the receptionist.

"Hey, hey, Meggie. What are you doing here? Do you want to scramble up the wall? I'll get you hooked up." He stood with one foot propped at a 90-degree angle on the chair next to me. I shifted a little, feeling trapped by the weight of his body towering over me.

"I'm not here to climb, Dave. We need to talk."

There. I'd said it.

He laughed heartily and slapped his knee. "You're a quick one, aren't you?" Pulling the egg chair with his foot, he sat and leaned forward on both elbows, invading my personal space.

I tried to scoot my chair. It wouldn't budge, banging against the wall.

"What do you want to know, Meggie? I'm all yours."

I hunched my shoulders and placed my hands on my stomach, what Gam called my power zone. "I know your secret, Dave."

This sent Dave into a fit of chuckles. I gave him my firmest look. He recovered and mimicked my serious face. "You've got spunk. Has anyone told you what a cutie you are?"

I paused and raised my eyebrows at him. Then I threw my arms around my chest, waiting for him to respond.

"Ah, don't want play, do you? All right. Tell me, what secret is it that you think you know?"

"You're broke," I blurted out, folding my arms and watching him carefully.

Dave's eyes surveyed the room. The receptionist was staring at us, leaning over the desk, trying to eavesdrop. When she met Dave's eyes, she busied herself with the log book.

"Now what would make a nice little girl like you say a nasty thing like that?" Dave's voice was even, but I noticed his right eye twitched as he stroked his silver beard.

"I'm not being nasty. It's my job as a reporter to learn everything I can for my story, and I happened to learn *Race the States* is out of cash. Why is it that no one else seems to know this?"

He lowered his voice and leaned closer to me. "Listen here, and listen good. You don't know what you're playing with here."

I could tell from the measured cadence of his Aussie speech he was working hard to maintain his composure. I'd rattled him. Time to push a bit more.

"From what I heard, it's more than rounding up funding. I heard you're personally in way over your head. Is that what Lenny discovered? Is that why you pushed him over the ledge?"

"You think I killed Lenny?" Dave laughed. "That's a good one."

His laughter irritated me. He wasn't taking this seriously. "Do you have another explanation?"

"Meggie, I don't need one."

I held my position firmly—arms crossed, eyes piercing, pretending I wasn't shuddering internally.

Dave moved even closer to me. I could smell dried sweat on his skin and a hint of tobacco on his breath. "You want a story?"

"Of course." I nodded.

"I'm the last person on the planet who would want to kill Lenny. He and I were talking about partnering up. He planned to fund the whole project."

My jaw dropped. I couldn't fake my shock. Dave and Lenny partners? Questions swarmed in my head. Like, how did Lenny have that kind of cash?

"That's right," Dave continued, looking smug that he'd stunned me with his revelation. "I never would have hurt Lenny. He was my way out of this one. Not sure what I'm going to do now. I've been on the hunt to find somebody else with a chunk of cash. Lenny and I had big plans for future shows all over the globe. Bummer, he's gone. A real bummer."

"Does anyone else know Lenny was going to fund the show?"

"Nah. I like to keep my cards close to the chest if you know what I mean."

"You're sure? No one else on the crew? What about Andrew? I thought you two were good friends. You didn't mention anything to him?"

"Not a word, Meggie. Not a word. I'm telling you, this is showbiz. Happens every time. Money always comes through. No sense in worrying the crew."

Whether Dave liked it or not, someone knew and used that information to kill. But why?

Lenny funding the show would have benefited all the contestants. His backing would have guaranteed the show aired. Unless someone didn't want the show to air? That was a direction I never considered. Who might that be? Leaf had made his irritation with the lack of environmental awareness on the show clear. Alicia had threatened to quit.

"We got us a deal, right? Not a word about money to anyone?" His words weren't in his usual relaxed tone.

"Yeah, I promise. I won't say a thing to the crew." What I didn't say out loud was that I couldn't say the same about Sheriff Daniels.

"I'm going to scale that wall over there again and see if I can't scrounge up another sponsor while I'm at it." Dave stood.

"You're hoping the gym will fund the show?"

"You never know." Dave sneered. "Money comes from all kind of places. Not a word." He pressed a finger to his lips, his eyes growing cold.

"Wait," I called.

He turned to face me.

"I found your hat."

"What?" He froze for a moment. "Where did you find it? I've been looking all over for it."

"I found it out at Angel's Rest. On a deer trail. Now it's with the sheriff."

"Huh?" Dave looked confused.

"It was way out in the woods. Probably at least a quarter mile off the main trail. I found it hanging in a tree."

"How did it get out there?"

"I was going to ask you the same thing. What were you doing out on the deer trail?"

"Nothing. I wasn't on any deer trail. Must have blown off of me."

*Right*, I thought to myself. *It slipped off your head and blew a half mile away into dense tree cover. Highly unlikely.*

"I thought I saw someone on that trail the day Lenny died."

"Wasn't me. Wasn't me." He bent in a slight bow and looked at me with hard eyes before racing off toward the climbing wall.

I returned to *Northwest Extreme* to finish my draft for Greg, but I couldn't let go of my conversation with Dave as my fingers flew over the keyboard. I used it as fuel as my story took shape. I wasn't sure if he was telling the entire truth about funding *Race the States*, but I suspected that he'd been on trail. The question was, had he accidentally lost the hat, or had someone planted it there?

# TWENTY-FIVE

The next morning, I startled awake to the sound of my phone ringing at 6:00 A.M. Gam's face flashed on the screen. *Sunday, Gam.* Why couldn't I sleep in, on the one day it was OK to do so? I slid my finger over the phone and answered with a croaky voice.

"I'm so glad I caught you."

Caught me? Without her early wake-up call, I would have slept another two hours.

Gam thrived on little rest. She claimed it was genetic, but obviously I didn't inherit the no-sleep gene. Most mornings she arose at 4:00 A.M. and spent an hour meditating before walking three or four miles on her treadmill. Normal people would shuffle half-awake to hit start on their coffeepots by the time Gam had meditated, exercised, and cooked a full breakfast.

"I know you're not going to like this," she went on, not bothering to ask if I was awake. "You need to go to your father's house. Your mother is prepping the farmhouse for an estate sale. She asked me to call you, which I think was quite thoughtful of her. It's time, honey."

My jaw clamped. Tightness spread from my cheeks through

my temples. "No way, Gam. I haven't been back since—since, you know."

"Honey, I know. But it's time. I think this is the Universe's way of forcing you to face this."

"I can't, Gam. I'm not ready." The tightness in my head spread like a cobweb through my brain. It left me feeling tingly and lightheaded.

"I understand, but it's time. Your mother can't leave it sitting empty. This needs to happen. Would you like me to come with you?" Gam's voice held its usual calm forcefulness. Although she stood not much taller than five feet, her power towered over her. Strangers on the street adjusted their bodies unconsciously to her presence, giving her a wide circumference, moving to the edge of sidewalks as she passed.

A couple hundred years ago, she would have been labeled a witch, probably burned at the stake if she'd lived in the Northeast. Her present-day healing energy naturally drew people to her, but only on her terms. One look at her serene, commanding face told you she'd pack a mighty punch if you crossed the line.

When I was seven, Gam took me to a spiritual retreat. Pops pushed for me to go. Mom refused. She didn't approve of Gam's career choice either. I could see it in the way she snuck to a different line at the checkout in the grocery store. She'd try to shush Gam under her breath when Gam offered to put her hands on a stranger's back.

"Would you like me to give you a little shot of Reiki?" Gam would ask, rubbing her hands together and rocking slightly.

Mom covered her eyes with her hand and hissed, "No, they don't want you to touch them."

Gam would close her eyes as a warm smile tugged at the edge of her cheeks and she'd rest her hands on the stranger's back. I couldn't tell if she had transported to a higher plane when she tapped into the energy of the great spirits she talked of. Or if she enjoyed pissing Mom off. Probably a bit of both.

Pops and Gam teamed up on Mom. I remembered many fights when I was a young child. Mom was infuriated that Pops sided with Gam. Pops was incredulous that she didn't appreciate Gam's divinely guided talents. How were they ever a couple?

One night, Mom flew around the living room flinging Pops's newspapers in the air, threatening to throw them in the fireplace. "You're as out of touch with reality as my mother!" she shouted, ripping one in half. "I can't stand it anymore."

Sitting with his long legs stretched out on the couch, Pops chuckled as he pulled a well-worn pencil from behind his ear and said, "There's nothing out of touch about your mother. In fact, she's one of the most grounded people I know."

Thinking on that now, I wondered if he meant that as a dig at Mom. His words launched a new tirade. "Do you know what she did today when she picked our daughter up at school? Do you?"

I ducked behind the doorway so they wouldn't know I was listening. "No, dear." Pops shook his head and tapped the pencil on his salt-and-pepper beard. "What did she do?"

Mom slammed a stack of newspapers on the top of the fireplace mantel. "She got out of the car and hugged the oak tree in the front of the building. Hugged. A. Tree."

"Mm-hmm, and?"

"She hugged a tree. She started talking to it—the tree. Telling it what a wonderful spirit it was and how glad she was to be able to spend this time together. Poor Mary Margaret. What will her friends or teachers think? Her grandmother is hugging the trees. Fortunately, I hurried her into the car before Mary Margaret came outside. I don't think she noticed. Hugging trees. Good Lord, hugging trees."

"You know, at the end of the day, I think there are much worse things you could spin yourself up on, rather than worry about your mother hugging a tree." Pops crossed his legs and returned the pencil to behind his ear.

This infuriated Mom more. She grabbed the stack of newspapers from the mantel, flung them in the air and stormed out the front door. I poked my head around the corner. Newspapers floated to the floor like individual magic carpets. I imagined myself riding them.

"You can come in, Maggie," Pops called.

I stopped to pick up a paper that landed in front of my feet. "Leave it," he said, and patted the couch. "Come here, little one."

The newspaper left black ink stains on my fingers. I crawled onto Pops's lap. He stroked my head and said quietly, "You know your mom loves Gam, don't you?"

I hung my head.

Pops took his warm, callused hands and placed them on both my cheeks. He gently cradled my head in his hands. "Listen, Maggie. Your mom loves all of us—you. Me. Gam. All of us. She doesn't always know how to show it, but she does. Okay?"

I nodded, biting the inside of my cheek to keep from crying.

He kissed my forehead. "You are a special, special girl. You know that?" He pulled my head onto his chest and held me tight until I fell asleep in his arms.

"Margaret?" Gam's voice on the phone shook me to reality. "Are you still there?"

"I'm here." I sighed. "Thinking about Pops."

"Exactly, my dear. That's why you need to go. Your mother would really like to go with you."

"No way."

"I was afraid you'd say that. That's okay. I think it's good for you to go alone. I told her that too."

Gam had been playing referee between Mom and me since Mom walked out on Pops.

"Call me later to let me know how it goes. I'm going to zap you with a little energy right now. Oh, and Margaret, Sheriff Daniels stopped by again. He said he's dusting your desk for fingerprints."

"Don't worry, Gam. It's no big deal. I think someone wanted to get under my skin. I'm fine."

"Stick a rose quartz necklace in your bra. It's a heart stone. It'll help. Love ya."

Fine. If Gam wanted me to go to Pops's, I'd do it. But I wasn't going to be happy about it.

I was due to meet everyone at Beacon Rock later in the morning, so I pulled on my new hiking gear before heading out.

The road to Pops's wound past miles and miles of tulip fields. They looked like a patchwork of colorful candy fit for Willy Wonka. I kept my eyes straight ahead, hands at 10:00 and 2:00. The meandering one-lane road to our family farmhouse was where Pops had been hit. There wasn't any marker on the side of the road where he'd been run over. I wasn't sure if this made me feel relieved or more pissed off.

April rain had returned in fits. Heavy, dark clouds rolled overhead, giving way to brief glimpses of the sun and slivers of blue sky.

I spotted the top of the brick-red barn first. Pops's workshop. No way, I couldn't do this. What was Gam thinking? I wasn't ready.

Her voice sounded in my head. *You've come this far.*

The gravel road that led past the barn and the farmhouse hadn't seen traffic lately. No muddy tracks from Pops's truck. The red flag on the black mailbox at the driveway entrance was down. No mail coming or going these days.

Usually this quarter-mile stretch of gravelly road filled me with joy and anticipation. Whether I'd been gone for hours or months, I always felt like a kid again coming home. When I rode in Pops's truck to town, as soon as we passed the mailbox he'd let me honk the horn to let Mom know we were home. I honked my horn. It sounded lonely and echoed.

I pulled the car in front of the run-down farmhouse. The whitewashed wraparound porch housed chopped wood, stacks of bundled newspapers, and pots with dead flowers and herbs.

*You can do this*, I said as I slowly made my way to the front door. It was unlocked as usual. The space smelled like Pops—musty paper and an old fire. It also smelled rotten, like the trash hadn't been taken out in months. Upon entering the kitchen, I realized it hadn't. I had to plug my nose and race the decaying bag out to the porch.

Where to start sorting? I halfheartedly flipped through a pile of mail resting on the kitchen counter. Mainly bills and an invitation to a friend's fiftieth birthday bash.

I milled around the rest of the house, finding all kinds of familiar objects, like Pops's watch, his favorite biking jersey, and of course the familiar pile of newspapers in every room. For a fleeting moment, I shared Mom's frustration over Pops's junk. Immediately, I slapped my hand, scolding myself for siding with her.

There was nothing here for me, other than the bitter reminder that Pops was dead. Being amongst his things made it more evident. I didn't want any of it. I wanted Pops. That's probably why Gam had sent me here. She wanted me to face loss head-on.

Resolved I'd done that, albeit for five minutes, I exited through the kitchen door. A *New York Times* crossword puzzle calendar pinned next to the door hung frozen on the month of June. I slid my finger over the ink where Pops had scribbled in meetings, and in bold red Sharpie circled my graduation date.

The majority of Pops's appointments were written in blue and black ink and read, MEET JOHN FOR COFFEE or BIKE

Alliance Ride. On the day he died, in tiny letters it said, 1:00 P.D.J. bring MM file.

P.D.J. bring MM file? MM was code for Meth Madness. Was Pops still working on the story? What file? And who or what was P.D.J.? I mentally ran through Pops's friends—none of their names started with the letter P. Had Pops found a new angle on the meth investigation? He hadn't mentioned anything the last time we'd spoken over the phone. I guessed I'd been consumed with graduation and finals. Had I asked what was new with him?

Allowing the kitchen screen door to slam shut, I returned to the living room and checked each stack of newspapers and the pile of notes on the side of the couch. There was no reference to P.D.J. As I was about to fling the entire collection of old news into the kindling box next to the fireplace, a headline caught my eye.

OREGON ENVIRONMENTAL ACTIVIST LINKED TO OIL MONEY.

I was sure I'd printed this article when pulling research on Leaf, but I hadn't had a chance to read it yet.

A grainy picture of Leaf Green appeared above the fold on the front page of the paper. The photo showed him perched in a high branch of an evergreen tree. It reminded me of one of my favorite films from childhood, *Swiss Family Robinson*.

Leaf held camp forty feet high in a makeshift tree house. The caption below the photo explained that in protest over deforestation in the area, Leaf lived in the tree for twenty-three days, receiving food and water from fellow protesters on the ground using a pulley system, where he'd hoist a basket of supplies with a rope.

I quickly read the article, which had been written last year by an environmental reporter for *The O*. I learned that while

Leaf professed a deep commitment to all things green, his family's background was rooted in big oil. Originally from Texas, Leaf's father had procured tremendous wealth mining the oil fields of Texas—to the tune of millions. I whistled out loud. Leaf was loaded. And Leaf's christened name was Jonathan Walker. The article didn't mention when Leaf changed his name.

Reading on, I learned after the Walker family transplanted to Oregon a little over a decade ago, Leaf's father opted to try his hand at logging. Apparently that venture rivaled his success in Texas, quickly making him one of the most prominent loggers in Southern Oregon.

Turning to the two-page spread inside the paper, I discovered photos of Leaf as a young child, with tightly cropped hair and tennis shoes on his feet, standing by his father's side. His father held a chainsaw as tall as young Leaf. In the photo I could see that Leaf disdained his family's legacy. His father's free hand clamped Leaf's shoulder, which pulled in the opposite direction. His innocent eyes pleaded to the camera, as if to say, *I'm not one of them*.

The last few paragraphs in the feature detailed Leaf's estrangement from his family. It formally began when he turned twenty-five and gained access to the trust fund his father established for him. On his twenty-fifth birthday, Leaf held a press conference in the Shakespearean town of Ashland, Oregon. He announced that from that day on he intended to spend his entire trust on environmental projects. Leaf's father, through his PR team, made a one-sentence statement of his own. "Leaf Green is not my son."

Wow. I'd missed this entire storyline while consumed by my collegiate studies. Eugene, Oregon, where I went to school, served as a hub for environmental activists, hosting a variety of protests and sit-ins throughout the year. Leaf's name was notorious on campus. He was the stuff of legend—touted as a modern-day Robin Hood, working to protect the forest.

Did this change anything? Leaf had a wad of cash to burn and most likely an equal amount of pent-up family drama to hash out. He had also mentioned looking into other options. Was he trying to buy out the show too?

What was his connection to Lenny? They fought at the summit. Maybe Leaf learned Lenny wanted to invest in the show and killed him before he could?

I rolled the newspaper and tucked it into my backpack.

Back to my search for the mysterious appointment on Pops's calendar. I moved to his office. I found four discarded coffee mugs all with an inch of molding coffee remains. Reference books collected dust on shelves cluttered with news clippings, half-finished crossword puzzles, and flowers pressed into the covers of hardbound books.

I dug through his desk drawers. They were filled with Silly Putty, plastic teeth, postcards from all over the globe, dental floss, short poems written on restaurant receipts, and junk mail.

It was evident that it had been years since Mom spent time in Pops's office. His filing system (or lack thereof) was a total mess. Half of his files weren't labeled. Most were crammed together and stained with coffee mug rings. My need for order made me wish I'd brought along a box of those lovely color-coded files from my office. This would take forever. I'd have to go through them one at a time.

The antique grandfather clock on the wall chimed nine. I was due at Beacon Rock in an hour. Krissy's updated schedule had the contestants posing for a photo shoot at Beacon Rock before continuing the next leg of the race at nearby Table Mountain. Alicia and Leaf would race an eight-mile loop to the summit of Table Mountain. The hike would lead them over 3,400 feet in elevation change and to one of the most stunning views of the Columbia River Gorge.

Tomorrow, the final leg of the race would culminate with a zip-line off the Bridge of the Gods into the Columbia River below. The schedule noted Krissy wouldn't be at the Beacon Rock photo shoot as she was working with state and wildlife officials on setting up the zip-line and closing the bridge for a chunk of the morning. She would, however, meet us at Table Mountain, where she'd arranged a press conference before Alicia and Leaf headed out on their last climb.

I decided the files should come with me. I could go through them with Jill. finding a wide rubber band in the top desk drawer, I secured it around the messy files. At the last minute I grabbed the Silly Putty and shoved it in my pocket. Pops's hands had molded it while he worked; maybe mine would too. I wasn't sure whether Gam had tapped into me needing to find Pops's cryptic appointment or Leaf's surprising family background, but either way, I'd accomplished something. That was a pleasant and totally unexpected surprise.

# TWENTY-SIX

I stuck the story about Leaf in the backseat and drove to Beacon Rock to meet everyone for the photo shoot.

Beacon Rock sat on the Washington side of the Columbia River. Originally named by Lewis and Clark, who called it "a remarkably tall detached rock," the monolith stood at eight hundred feet. There'd been constant chatter in the Northwest over whether the freestanding rock ranked second in the world (behind the Rock of Gibraltar). The three-quarter-mile hike to the top was paved, with handrails and bridges, but there was no way I had any intention of climbing it with the crew—photo shoot or not.

Once, in high school, I tried to make my way up the rock. A bunch of friends and I drove out to the Gorge for a day hike. Our plan was to hike to the top and then continue to the quaint town of Stevenson for a picnic on the river. The only problem was I could only make it a quarter of the way up.

The 360-degree views stretched out in all directions on the dizzying path. I couldn't find my bearings on the skyline as I raced to keep up with my agile friends along the interlocking walkways and continuous switchbacks. The world spun. I collapsed. Then I lied, hollering for them to go on, that I had stomach flu. They raced ahead while I clawed my way to the parking lot. No one commented later when I scarfed down watermelon and burgers next to the river.

I couldn't think of any reason Greg would need me at the summit for the photo shoot, but just in case, I'd worked out an excuse so I wouldn't have to climb it. In order to write from a new lens (total journalism-school speak and the current lingo in today's media), I wanted to observe Alicia and Leaf from the vantage point of the base. That way, I could track their individual styles as they ascended and descended.

I really hoped Greg wouldn't ask, because as I practiced the speech in my head, even I called bullshit. Although, as far as my story went, it wasn't exactly a lie. Greg had returned the draft I sent him with a variety of notes and suggestions that I needed to work through. It was time for me to show him my skills. This was my chance to shine, and I wasn't going to mess it up.

Rain momentarily subsided as I snagged a parking space in the small lot next to a log cabin.

No sign of Greg's car. *Thank God.*

I paid the day-use fee, grabbed my gear, and staked a claim on a lone picnic table, hugging the side of the craggy rock.

The table sat on a small patch of grass on the east side of the rock. Cars and semi-trucks rumbled along Highway 14 behind me. Setting my phone and notebook on the table, I craned my neck, following the slimy rock all the way to its summit. It was high—like straight up. *Uh, no thanks.*

Moss and grass spotted the rock face like freckles. A sign pointing to the northwest face of the trail lay ahead. Everyone would have to walk a quarter of a mile into the tree-covered base before the trail curved and began its circular ascent.

Though I had a view of the entire monolith, it was highly unlikely I'd able to see anyone on the other side of the trail. They'd be climbing next to the river. I was stuck next to the highway. How could I explain to Greg that I'd have a better angle from here?

*You can deal with that later, Meg—it's time to write.*

I read through Greg's feedback and scribbled some new thoughts before a horn blared, pulling my attention away from my story.

I turned to see Dave hopping out of the driver's seat and intentionally looking away from me. His Australian bush hat rested on his head. How had he managed to get it back from Sheriff Daniels so quickly?

Watching the contestants and gear pour out of the van reminded me of clown cars in the circus. I couldn't believe how much camera equipment they managed to pack in.

No Greg. Maybe that would be my excuse to skip the climb. I needed to wait for him.

After four trips in and out of the van, Andrew piled sound booms, cables, and cameras on the ground next to the picnic table.

"Ready for the view up there? It's breathtaking." I didn't exactly lie. My friends, who'd actually made the climb, agreed it was a stunning view of the carved-out waterway.

Andrew grunted as he fumbled with cameras.

Dave glared at me from under the brim of his hat. "That's what they say, Meggie. You joining us?" The way he said "joining" made me shudder.

"Uh, no." I stretched my words out and tried to ignore Alicia as she rolled her eyes at me. "I'm hoping to get a fresh lens—as we like to say in the business—today. Kind of catch you at all angles. I'm going to camp out over there." I pointed behind me as Alicia faked a cough, not bothering to hide her disbelief.

"Good plan," she said through raised eyebrows and a smirk.

I needed to get her alone to ask her about my stolen files and why she was always irritated with me.

"Andrew, are you ready?" Dave asked, his tone light again,

as Andrew finished fastening the camera on Leaf. "Head on and we'll be right behind you. Okay, mate?"

Andrew muttered something indistinguishable and loped to the start of the trailhead without looking back.

Alicia's camera twisted to the side when she hunched her pack over her shoulders. She wore her usual race attire, black athletic shorts, a neon-pink sports bra, and a baseball hat in the same color scheme. Proof that eighties fashions were making a comeback.

Dave busied himself fixing Alicia's camera. I took the opportunity to pull Leaf aside.

"Hey, can I talk to you for a minute?"

"Sure," he replied in his lackadaisical tone. "What's up?"

I sidestepped away from Dave and Alicia. "I read an article about your family today. Learned you come from serious oil money. Why didn't you say anything?"

Leaf stared at one of the trees. After a long moment in a daze, I wondered if he'd smoked too much pot last night and wasn't tracking my questions.

I mimicked his craned neck and stretched my head to the sky.

He turned his attention to me. "She's beautiful, isn't she? Truly spiritual." Gam would have found him a fast friend (aside from his pot-smoking habit).

"Uh-huh," I agreed, averting my eyes to the ground.

A hint of anger flashed across his face, tightening his jawline and narrowing his eyes. "It's my job to protect her and the rest of this," he said, waving his hand upward toward the rock and sweeping it in a half circle. Recovering, he continued in his monotone. "What about my family?"

"Why haven't you mentioned them? It sounds like it was a pretty big story for months."

Leaf laughed. I'd never heard him laugh. It wasn't pleasant. It was laced with bitterness. "What? You're going to use that in your story? Go for it. You think I'm hiding something? Give it up. You're not a reporter. You're part of the corporate machine." He turned on his shoeless feet, narrowed his bloodshot eyes and said, "Yeah, and that story was front-page news all over Oregon months ago."

Dave motioned for Leaf to follow Alicia into the woods. How was I going to get her alone?

With a parting snarl, he said, "You're in over your head. I'd suggest you get back to writing about the big money machine cutting your paycheck each month."

*What was that all about?* That was the most riled I'd seen him.

Checking the ground next to the picnic table for spiders or other small critters, I spread out my blanket. The patchy grass was damp and bumpy. This really was a terrible spot to see much. Mainly I zoned out, immersing myself in the flow of my re-writes as packs of tourists and families with babies in back-packs trekked around the volcanic face.

Day hikers skipping past me with light packs and neoprene water bottles distracted me from tracking where Leaf or Alicia was on the rock. Every ten minutes, I'd glimpse toward the exposed sections of the path. I caught a flash of Alicia's neon-pink sports bra and matching hat a couple of times, but otherwise, I had no idea where they were. The climb to the top wasn't more than a mile. They shouldn't be gone long. Thirty minutes, unless Dave had big plans for the photo shoot.

Calmed by the bustle around me, I slipped into a dreamlike state, allowing my mind to wander as the words flowed effortlessly. Pops often talked about how writing was a form of meditation. I lost myself, blending Greg's suggestions for strengthening my first draft with new ideas as my hand flew over the page.

I needed to treat this like a true investigative journalist.

What had I learned so far about Lenny's murder and who might have the motivation to kill him?

Dave and his funding issues were high on my list. finding his hat on the deer trail only made me more suspicious of him, but if it was true that Lenny planned to fund *Race the States*, that didn't add up.

Andrew had been avoiding me since our altercation. I was sure he followed me out to Multnomah Falls and tried to run me off the road, but why? Other than a strong dislike of Lenny's personality, he didn't have a motive for murder. Or at least not one I'd found.

Then there was Leaf. The news of his family's history and money definitely made him a suspect. Maybe he wanted the show and really did plan to make it green. If he learned Lenny was about to beat him to it, could he have murdered him?

I still hadn't had a chance to confront Alicia about my missing files and the deleted photos. What had I done to make her dislike me? How had she really gotten the scratches on her arms? And what were she and Andrew always whispering about?

Plus there was Krissy. She seemed determined to make the production a success. But why did that matter so much? It wasn't her show.

If anything, I was more confused than ever. Each clue led to another unanswered question. I was running out of time. Tomorrow was the finale. After filming wrapped, everyone would scatter around the country.

Greg's voice disturbed my train of thought. "What are you doing here, Meg?" He stood towering over me, blending in with the sturdy, ancient trees behind him. My stomach flip-flopped. I put my hand over it.

"Working on a new vantage point," I said, pointing to my unopened backpack resting on the blanket. "And waiting for you."

Greg's eyes lingered on them, too. He grinned and plopped down next to me. Craning his eyes in the direction of Beacon Rock, he leaned his neck to the left and right. "New vantage point?"

I could feel my throat tighten.

Patting my knee, Greg said, "It's okay, Meg. I didn't want to climb with that motley crew either."

The spot where his hand touched my knee burned in rhythm with my cheeks. I couldn't get a read on him. Was he patronizing me? I wished I had Gam's skills.

"Sorry," I said, fiddling with my hands. "It's been kind of bananas the past four days, and I thought I'd take this chance to sit and let my thoughts settle. Thanks for your suggestions on my story. I'm taking another stab at it."

Stretching his taut legs and leaning his head on his elbows, Greg focused his piercing russet eyes on the sky above. His running shirt revealed his tight pectoral muscles.

I could feel warmth emitting from his body, or maybe it was mine? He smelled of musky cologne and the slightest hint of sweat. I didn't peg him as a cologne-wearing kind of guy. Maybe deodorant? I leaned on my elbows, worried if I positioned myself next to him my rapidly beating heart would betray me. Avoiding Beacon Rock, I followed his gaze to the sky directly above, where a formation of clouds rolled overhead, pushed along by the light east wind funneling down the river. The bank of clouds momentarily blocked the sun.

I flashed to a memory of Pops. On Sunday afternoons in the summer we'd eat lunch outside on a blanket and play "name that cloud." A silly game Pops made up, where one of us would try to shout out what shape we saw in a cloud first.

Without thinking, I said to Greg, "Did you ever look for shapes in clouds when you were young?"

He ruffled the top of my hair. Definitely a big brother move, not a romantic one. "Meg, you kill me. I wish I could bottle the way you look at the world." He sighed and leaned back again. "No one would buy it. World's too cynical."

The week's frustration, fear, and Pops's sweet memory flooded my system, erupting with unexpected force. "You think I'm a kid. Don't you?" I held back the hot sting of tears.

Greg sat up and chuckled. "Not at all. I think you're a budding young journalist. I liked your draft. It needs work, but it's a solid start."

Salty tears welled in my eyes. He liked my work? He thought I was a budding journalist? "I'm sorry." I sniffed. "I... I should be more professional. You're my boss." This day couldn't get any worse. I definitely shouldn't be crying in front of my boss.

Greg cracked his knuckles and said, "Sure, I'm your boss, but I hope I'm your friend too. How many times have I told you we don't run that kind of office?"

His phone rang. A look of irritation washed over his face when he looked at the screen and answered it. "What's going on?"

I wiped my eyes and tried to ignore his conversation. His voice sounded hard.

"Listen, I keep telling you I don't want to do this on the phone. We'll talk later."

He stuffed his phone in his pocket.

Who kept calling him? He obviously didn't want to talk while I was around.

"Sorry about that. What were you saying?"

"Nothing." I brushed a tear from my cheek. "It's this week, the whole thing with Lenny—it's gotten under my skin. Hey, speaking of that, what do you know about Leaf? I read an interesting article about his family money."

Greg patted my back and chuckled. "There's our budding journalist looking for dirt again. You're right. He comes from deep pockets. I know his father." He let out a whistle. "Whew—

tough one. Nothing like Leaf. Nothing like anyone you'd meet in the Northwest. He's big-oil Texas all the way."

"How so?"

"Let's just say he's not someone I'd want to cross, that's for sure."

He checked Beacon Rock for any sign of Leaf and Alicia. "Hey, Krissy and I went out for a cocktail last night."

This news made my heart sink. Krissy had her eye on Greg, and not only was she more worldly than me, but she was the kind of woman who would not take no for an answer. I could picture her with a bottle of wine in hand and her pencil skirt intentionally pulled above her knee, inviting Greg to her hotel room. Yuck.

I tried to appear casual with my response. "That's nice."

Raising his eyebrows slightly, Greg continued. "Krissy said Leaf's dad was on fire about him participating in the race. He tried to bribe her to get him off the show."

"Really?" That was new information. Leaf's father intentionally tried to sabotage him. Leaf made it sound like they didn't have any contact. But either he lied, or his father was keeping careful tabs on Leaf's activities.

"Did she tell you anything about his trust fund?" I asked. "It sounds like he came into a gob of money."

Greg shook his head. "No, it gets better. His father's been trying to freeze his assets for years. Threatened to sue *Race the States*. Krissy said Leaf is frantically trying to spend all the money that's left before his father's legal team can shut him out."

"How terrible would that be? I can't imagine."

"I know. Krissy said Leaf and Dave have been talking about him investing in the show. He wants to turn it into an eco-challenge."

A flock of geese flew above us, squawking in harmony.

"Did Dave agree?"

"I'm not sure. She didn't know. She overheard them at dinner one night. Sounds like Dave keeps the finances under a tight lip. Shocker, huh?"

I laughed. "Yeah, tight lips and Dave don't go hand in hand."

We sat in silence.

A hawk circled overhead. The hawk was Gam's power animal. They showed up whenever she was around. I wouldn't have been surprised if she could tame the wild bird by simply calling out its name and stretching her arm to the sky.

"Speaking of Dave, what's your investment in the show? How does it work to be a sponsor? Are you fronting the prize money?" I asked, breaking the moment and offering a nod for Gam to the hawk above.

"Can't let it rest, can you?" Greg said as he bent over and touched his hands to his toes. I could barely force my hands to meet my knees in a stretch like that. Greg repeated his skillful stretch again and rose to his feet.

Offering me his hand, he pulled me up in one seamless move. "I'm not fronting that kind of cash. Don't worry about it." He gave me a hard look. The kind of look I'd expect to receive from a boss. "How's your feature coming along? Any questions on my suggestions?"

I shook my head. "No, everything was clear. I think it's starting to come together. I should have another draft for you later today."

"Good. Come on, I see Dave. They're down."

My phone buzzed with a text from Matt.

What's up?

I typed back:

Working.

Snooping.

Shut it.

Did you talk to the sheriff?

Yes.

Where you at?

Beacon Rock. Heading to Table Mountain.

I could see the three dots blinking as he typed back:

How long will you be there?

Not sure. A couple hours?

Maybe I'll head out. You want company?

Sure, but you don't need to.

I'll try. Beers later?

YES!

While Greg coordinated travel to Table Mountain with Dave, Alicia, and Leaf, I hung back and took my time to shake out the blanket and carefully fold it.

This latest news from Greg threw another round of questions swirling in my brain. If Leaf had to spend his inheritance quickly, why *Race the States*? And what would that mean for Dave? If Leaf purchased the show, he'd definitely change its format. He'd made it abundantly clear that he didn't approve of how the show was being produced. For as casual as Dave liked to appear, the show was his baby. I couldn't imagine him giving it up easily. Unless the lure of money was too compelling.

How did this tie in with Lenny? If Lenny really was willing

to fund the show, that made Dave a less likely suspect. And why did Greg blow me off about sponsoring the show?

Every time I got closer to the truth, I hit another wall.

Greg waved me over as Dave addressed the group. "All right, this is the last little jog before tomorrow's big finale. Have fun. Let's be safe. I'm timing this one, but only for you. Don't know if today's climb will make the final cut, but you never know. Andrew will be filming all the way to the top." Dave turned to Greg. "What's this next hike like, mate?"

"We're heading out to Table Mountain," Greg began. "It's about eight miles, some 3,500 feet in elevation. The route we're taking today is through abandoned logging and access roads. Should help to shave a little time off." He gave me a knowing look. "Don't let Angel's Rest fool you. This is a difficult climb, especially if you're running. Be careful out there. The first part of this trail is one of the steepest climbs in the entire Gorge."

"I second that," Dave chimed in. "Krissy's got news people waiting for us there, but I don't want a repeat of what happened to Lenny. Stay safe. Don't do anything stupid."

Should I fake an injury or claim to be feeling under the weather? If I didn't bow out now, the possibility loomed that once we arrived at Table Mountain, they'd try to convince me to make the climb with them.

Thankfully, Greg saved me before I had time to sketch out a new lie. "Meg's sticking at the finish." He pulled his right elbow over his head with his left hand, revealing sculpted arms rivaling most Greek statues. Nodding to Alicia, he continued, "I could use a little cardio today. If you don't mind, I'll tag along with you."

That was easy. Greg could fill me in on anything that happened on the mountain and I wouldn't have to trudge up 3,000-plus feet. A mixture of relief and self-loathing churned through me. Obviously, Greg didn't think I could make it to the summit, and, certainly, he knew I couldn't hang with Alicia or

Leaf. Did this mean he was on to my secret? A lack of confidence in your field reporter would not lead to new assignments. Just when I thought I was ready to strike out on my own and leave Jill's couch, I'd be fired. I knew it. Greg was trying to save face in front of Dave and the contestants. He'd made a mistake in hiring me. Once this competition was over, so was I.

Alicia cozied up to Greg. She placed a lean arm on his shoulder to steady herself as she reached for her ankle and pulled it behind her knee. As one of the most limber women I'd ever seen, she didn't need Greg's support to steady herself.

"We'd love to have you along, Greg. It'll be nice to have someone who can keep up with me." She glowered at Leaf, who paid no notice.

"It's good for me too," Greg replied as Alicia twisted her body around and stretched the opposite leg, still resting her arm on his shoulder. "I strongly encourage my employees to exercise. If we can't walk the walk, we can't talk the talk, you know?"

"I can see you set a fine example for the rest of your"—Alicia paused and eyed me skeptically—"staff."

"Well, mates, that settles it. Greg, come along with us," Dave said.

Alicia glared as she pulled Greg along with her. What did she have against me? I certainly wasn't competition.

A bank of clouds closed in the view of the Oregon peaks across the river.

The sky looked as if it might unleash.

That settled my fate. I'd hang out at the base of Table Mountain and try to get used to the fact my days with *Northwest Extreme* were numbered. Maybe if I wrote a kick-ass feature, Greg wouldn't fire me.

Yes, that's what I'd have to do. Focus on the writing. Writing was my superpower, my version of cardio. I'd spend the next three hours while they were sweating it out on the exposed slope to formulate the most amazing story *Northwest Extreme* had ever seen.

I imagined Greg calling me into his office. Stacks and stacks of reader mail would pile on his desk, all raving about my incredible talent. He'd tell me it was a new record. The most reader feedback the magazine had ever received for a single story. That'd show them.

If I couldn't join them, I'd have to find a way to beat them.

# TWENTY-SEVEN

From Beacon Rock, I followed Highway 14 farther east along the river. Mist hung above the Oregon peaks on the other side. Shocks of lime-green trees intermixed with black evergreens.

After ten miles, I turned off the highway and wound under railroad tracks onto a country road. Passing a rock quarry, a crow flew overhead. Its call unnerved me. Gam said a single crow was a bad omen. Crows in pairs were a blessing. Hopefully this crow had a friend nearby.

The road stopped and turned into a gravelly, narrow trail with deep ruts and tire tracks. *This must be the forest access road*, I thought as my car bumped along.

The morning's rain had filled deep ruts in the road with mud. Water streamed down the middle, swarming in potholes. I stopped the car. There was no way I could pass. The water was too deep, at least ten inches. I'd likely get my tires stuck in the mud-filled ruts. I wished I had Matt's truck. I'd have to hike on foot from here.

I steered my car to the side, checking the rearview mirror so as not to block either of the access roads or drive it into a ditch. Locking the doors, I pulled on my backpack and slogged through the mud. Unlike Beacon Rock, which attracted tourists and day adventurers, Table Mountain was off the beaten path. Way off the beaten path. I had to dig deep into the message boards to find firsthand hiker accounts of the trek.

To access Table Mountain, hikers began their climb from the Aldrich Butte Trail, which doubled as a maintenance route for the power company. To call it a trail was misleading. It consisted of a gravel road with a grassy strip down the middle, worn from the tire tracks of Forest Service vehicles and power company workers.

Patches of wild grasses paralleled both sides of the gravelly access road. I trudged along for the length of two football fields until I caught sight of a swarm of media vans with shiny primary-colored logos and satellite beams high-centered on a swatch of weedy grass to the left.

Power lines buzzed overhead. There wasn't a marker or trailhead of any sort. Thankfully I'd done my research. This was the correct spot. I'd learned that the Aldrich Butte Trail was originally built in the 1940s for the military. They used the butte as a lookout and gunnery. Today hikers trekked from the left fork up the road, which quickly led them deep into the forest.

The hiking guides that I read to prepare for the climb at Table Mountain reinforced that I would not be climbing it.

One in particular warned that one wrong step on the 1,500-foot ledge would lead to a guaranteed death.

Uh, no. No way was I climbing a 1,500-foot-high drop-off where one misstep could mean sure death. The spectacular landmark wasn't worth death, especially after this week.

According to my research, scientists believed about a thousand years ago the south side of Table Mountain sheared off, damming the Columbia River and creating a land bridge that Indigenous Americans named the Bridge of the Gods. Over time, water washed the bridge away, but the legend continued to be passed down through the Native nations. Tomorrow's zip-line would take place at the cantilevered Bridge of the Gods built in the 1920s.

I shuffled to the *Race the States* van and busied myself taking photos of Alicia and Leaf, who were being interviewed by the news crews. Greg knew most of the reporters, who clapped him on the back and nudged their elbows into his side, telling him to make *Northwest Extreme* look good by beating everyone to the top. I hung back, feeling like the kid on the playground who doesn't get picked for the team.

Krissy looked the part of a Hollywood executive in a tailored shirt and a slim black skirt. She flirted with a reporter. How had she managed to keep her heels mud-free?

Andrew's face dripped with sweat. His cargo shorts were stained with dirt or coffee. I couldn't be sure which. He moved at the speed of a snail, securing a camera on Leaf's backpack and testing the sound boom. He moved on to Alicia, carefully checking and repositioning her cameras.

Before the media were allowed to ask questions, Krissy ran through introductions and handed out glossy press packets and *Race the States* T-shirts.

"Our contestants will be answering your questions before they embark on this final hike, with one exception." She narrowed her eyes at the team of reporters and turned to all of us with the same look of intent. "No one, and I repeat NO ONE, will be answering questions about the tragedy that occurred earlier in the week."

A reporter's hand flew into the air. "What about the confirmation the sheriff's office is treating this as a homicide?"

Krissy's voice dropped an octave. She took her glasses off as she said, "Listen, you're all getting an exclusive today. How often do you have a nationally televised show coming to film in Oregon, and not just film, but film one of the most elaborate stunts in TV history? The zip-line I'm working on for tomorrow is going to put Oregon on the map. If you want to be part of this story, please stay. If you have questions about the death of Lenny Ray, I suggest you contact the sheriff's office."

Impressive. She shut down the media in a few sentences.

Once they finished answering all the reporters' questions, Dave, Greg, Alicia, Leaf, and Andrew (lagging behind) took off on the left fork and disappeared into the thick tree cover. I grabbed my notebook and sketched notes about the scenery. Like the high-voltage transmission lines that ran along the right fork. The bases stood like giant metallic paper dolls, connected by a string of wire. Pops believed you shouldn't stand under or near these for long. He was convinced electromotive fields caused cancer, among other things.

Krissy, meanwhile, chatted with the media. I overheard her claiming tomorrow's zip-line finale would be the largest ever constructed in Oregon. I wasn't a fan of driving over the Bridge of the Gods where the zip-line would be secured. The thought of anyone intentionally zip-lining from it was impossible to grasp.

The press packed their gear and bounced along the road they'd driven in on, kicking dirt and mud onto the sides of their white vans. Krissy gathered extra press packets together and stepped carefully on her heels to me.

"You're not joining the others?" she asked. Her glasses rested on the bridge of her nose. She must have transition lenses. They were tinted a clear shade of lavender, dark enough not to be able to make out the color of her eyes.

"Nah, I'm good. I need to polish my story." I shifted my weight. "And let's face it. I couldn't keep up with them anyway."

Krissy broke out in a wide smile. She leaned on the van's bumper. "Me neither. You're half their size." Looking me up and down, she continued. "What, do you come to Alicia's waist?"

"Pretty much. She's lucky to have legs like that." I looked at my own legs. No hint of a bulging muscle or definition showed through my hiking capris. Mainly what I noticed was the skin showing between my knee and ankle was so white it reflected the sun like a mirror.

"I wouldn't call her lucky," Krissy said in a conspiratorial tone. "She's had some trouble lately."

"Why? What kind of trouble?"

She looked around the parking lot to make sure we were alone. "Well, money trouble for one. She's desperate to win the million." Krissy fiddled with the ivory buttons on her shirt and stopped. "Never mind, I shouldn't have said anything."

"Come on, you can tell me," I pleaded. "It will be off the record."

"Can't." She stood and brushed the dust off her skirt. "You'll have to ask her yourself. I'm heading into town. I need to finalize last-minute details for tomorrow. You have no idea how hard it is to pull off a stunt like the one we're setting up. This is going to solidify my career. You want to come along?" She looked off in the direction everyone else left. "They're going to be a while."

She was right; they'd probably be gone at least an hour. I did the math in my head—eight miles, four of which were uphill. I could probably walk a four-mile-an-hour pace on flat ground. Everyone else was an über-athlete. They'd probably be able to cover at least a couple more miles than me, uphill.

I was tempted to join Krissy. first, I wanted to learn what she knew about Alicia, and secondly, I really didn't want to be stuck here by myself. But what if Greg came back? I couldn't run the risk of leaving. If he discovered I'd left, he'd fire me on the spot. It was bad enough that my short legs wouldn't let me keep up with the group, but I needed this time to polish my story.

"Sorry." I shook my head. "I'd love to tag along, but I promised Greg I'd wait here and cover whoever wins."

Krissy shrugged and tiptoed to the driver's side door. "Suit yourself." She slid the van open and pulled out a roll of rope and bright red caution tape (without the word CAUTION printed on the sides). "If you're sticking around, would you put up a finish line?"

Taking the tape and rope from her, I asked, "Sure. How do I do it?"

She shrugged. "However you want. Dave's idea. Not mine. It's only for show." She climbed into the driver's seat and waved. "See ya."

The van splattered dirt and debris as Krissy accelerated in a half circle and peeled off down the gravel road.

Now what?

The empty gravel lot and buzzing wires overhead sounded ominous. While the trails on the Oregon side of the river would be packed on a Sunday like this, the Washington side was much more sparsely populated. Plus, this climb was rated the highest difficulty level. Definitely not an option for families with children. Only serious hikers made this trek.

I contemplated hoofing it to my car, but I had to catch whoever finished first.

*Stop stalling, Meg, and get writing.* I found a spot of drier grass near the edge of the road, pulled out my picnic blanket, and dropped on it.

After twenty minutes of working and re-working my introduction and hook, I was thirsty. My throat was dry. Hopefully, I'd brought a water bottle along.

As I searched my pack for a drink, I heard a muffled scream. At least, I thought it was a scream.

I froze. Was it a scream? Maybe I'd heard a bird.

Keeping my body rigid, I intently listened for any sound.

The humming of the power lines reverberated through my ears. Nothing. Must have been a bird.

I moved. Again, a scream. This time I was sure it was a scream. The sound pierced through the air.

It came from above and behind me—on the trail. Without thinking, I sprinted in the direction of the scream, through long wild grasses and over uneven rocky terrain. The route from the access road quickly wound to the east and disappeared into a dense forest. Sunlight disappeared.

The road was surprisingly steep. Within five minutes I was gasping for breath. I jogged along it for about a quarter of a mile, stopping every hundred yards to catch my breath and listen for the sound of the screaming. No more came.

The scream had sounded like a woman's voice. Alicia? Or, maybe there were other hikers out on the trail. But there weren't any other cars at the lot. It couldn't be another hiker.

I came to a fork. The gravelly road thinned to the right and turned into a dirt-packed trail. To the left, it narrowed and went straight up. It was eerily quiet. Which way should I go?

Another toe-curling scream came from the right. Yes, definitely a woman's scream. I hurried along the trail, glancing over my shoulder.

*Isn't this what characters in horror films do? Go racing after a strange noise, only to find themselves in danger?*

*Maybe I should have waited for Krissy to return. Or called the police.*

*Duh! What was I thinking? I should call the police.*

I pulled my phone out and dialed 911. I waited for it to ring. Nothing happened. I looked at the connection bars on the top. No connection.

Great. Now if anything happened to me, I was screwed.

Standing in the middle of the trail, I weighed my options. I could turn around now. I wasn't far from the parking lot. I could race to the open grassy area. Maybe I'd be able to get a connection there. Or I could trek on and see if I could find the mysterious screaming woman. With option one, I ran the risk of leaving whoever was screaming in danger if I didn't get to her in time. With option two, I ran the risk of putting myself in danger.

*One more mile,* I told myself. *Go one more mile and see if you can find anything.* That would still leave me close enough to the parking lot to find help if I needed it and maybe keep me far from the sheer ledge higher up the trail. A white moth flew in front of my vision. I shrieked and waved it away.

*Get it together, Meg.*

Table Mountain and its neighboring peaks, Greenleaf to the northeast and Hamilton Mountain to the southwest, had been called the mesas of the Northwest Cascades. In April, snow could coat the summit, making the already unnerving ascent even more dangerous. To reach the summit, the racers would have to climb the near-vertical east wall, over rock steps and a snaky exposed face. Had Alicia fallen? Was she immobile nearby? Where were Greg, Dave, Andrew, and Leaf?

I paused again. The sound of the buzzing wires muted inside the trees. A collection of birds squawked to each other, like mothers scolding young children. The screaming had stopped. I wondered if it was a bad sign.

While the steeper trail to the left must be the direction they took, I followed the sound on the flatter trail to the right. I'd go that way for a half mile. If I didn't see anything, I'd turn back and try the left trail.

Rain battered the heavy tree cover. It felt refreshing on my blazing skin. The right fork appeared flatter, but it was equally steep, snaking upward into a wet jungle. The drips changed to a sudden cloudburst. Water unleashed from the sky. It sounded as if a jet plane were roaring overhead.

My feet sank into mud as water cascaded down the trail. I slipped over rocks, trying to get my bearings. No longer able to run, I clawed my way upward. Water seeped into my boots and drizzled down my back. I hadn't bothered to grab my pack or my poncho. Soaked with rain and sweat, I continued to climb, praying for a switchback. None came.

I couldn't hear anything above the sound of the roaring water. Movement on the side of the trail caught my eye and made me jump. A squirrel scrambled for cover in the hollow of an old-growth tree. What was I doing? I should turn around.

Something icy and hard hit my cheek. I investigated the vine-twisted forest. Hail pellets smacked into my face like freezing bullets. Within minutes, ice blanketed the trail, bouncing off the trees. I ducked my head and crouched on my knees. This day couldn't get any worse. As quickly as it began, the hail receded, revealing glimmers of blue sky through the canopy of trees.

Rubbing my hands together, I blew steamy air in them and shivered.

*This is stupid, Meg. Really stupid. You need to turn around.*

Something compelled me forward. One-hundred-foot-high trees spanned around me. They dripped leftover rain and melting hail from above. The fern forest below caught the water, soaking it up with heavy leaves. The sound of another scream made me gasp. What was hiding out there behind the cover of the trees? I felt like I was playing a game of hide-and-seek gone wrong.

*Keep moving.*

*Keep moving.*

I kept moving, darting my eyes in all directions. Raindrops hitting the rocks sounded like footsteps behind me.

*Faster, Meg, faster.*

I could see light at the crest of the trail about three hundred yards straight ahead. From there the trail either switched back or curved to the right.

*Make it that far, Meg. Come on.*

My legs shook, the muscles in my thighs fatiguing with each step.

Breathless, I made it. Sunlight poured through thinning trees. The trail indeed curved to the right, revealing a meadow about thirty feet below. Steam rose from the meadow, spilling onto the trail like a dry-ice machine on Halloween. I scrambled over the slick gravelly path to the meadow.

A small trail blocked by fallen logs appeared to curve to the right, winding its way around the meadow. The main trail veered left, and up. I had an uneasy feeling I was being watched.

"Hello!" I shouted. "Is anyone out there?" A flock of birds scattered from a tree.

My voice echoed in the meadow and reverberated into the dense trees on the other side.

I tried again. "Hello!"

Only silence greeted me. *Time to turn back.*

That's when something moved.

# TWENTY-EIGHT

My body went rigid. A flash of color in the trees on the far side of the meadow caught my eye. It streaked through the heavy underbrush and darted deeper into the woods. Was it an animal? Human?

I had to get out of here—now.

Keeping my eyes focused on the spot where I'd seen movement, I slowly shuffled backward.

Sunlight blazed through the clouds. Everything smelled of baking pine needles. Water gushed down the center of the old Forest Service tracks like a waterfall. Birds squawked. No more screams.

Downhill should have been easier, but I couldn't get traction on the slick rocks and had to constantly leap over puddles that hadn't been there thirty minutes before. Water evaporated from the trail, creating a warm, gloomy mist.

How far was it to the parking lot? A half-hour? I'd been distracted by the sound of screaming and the pelting rain.

As I rounded a bend to a stretch of trail that could have rivaled the first descent off a roller coaster, I noticed something glinting on the side of the path.

I stopped and bent near delicate purple bleeding hearts stretching in the sun. Gam called these "lady in the bathtub" because you could peel back the purple leaves to reveal a white flower inside.

One of Andrew's GoPro cameras had fallen on the trail. It was wet with rain and splattered with mud. I looked at the towering evergreen tree next to the path. Sure enough, tacked into its bark was a strip of Velcro. The camera must have come loose in the storm.

I picked up the GoPro and assessed it for damage. It looked fine to me. I jammed it in my pocket and scanned the forest again. I still couldn't shake the feeling I was being watched.

Not wanting to be in the deserted forest a minute longer, I left the Velcro tacked to the tree, said a short apology on Gam's behalf, and continued my descent. I wound my way down the rough trail, sending mini-landslides of rock and gravel in my wake.

After about twenty minutes, the dense tree cover thinned. I could make out power lines two hundred feet below. A dog barked in the distance, causing me to skid to a stop. Mud splattered to my knees. My hiking capris and boots were caked in mud. It looked like I'd rolled down the trail.

Another break in the trees allowed a view of the power lines. I could see the tall grasses and tips of the lines below. Another hundred feet to go.

At that moment the sound of a gunshot reverberated through the forest. It bounced off the trees. I imagined the bullet ricocheting off a tree and slamming into me. Instinctively I ducked.

*Oh, my God, someone's shooting at me.*

Covering my head with my knees jamming into my chin, I waited for another bullet to graze past.

Where had it come from? Was hunting legal in these woods? No, it couldn't be. The trail wasn't marked, but it was maintained by the Forest Service. This couldn't be legal hunting ground. But no one was out here to stop them. Unless the power company happened to be doing maintenance on the lines, no one patrolled this area.

A new thought invaded my head as I remained folded in a tight ball on the trail. What if whoever I'd seen at the meadow had a gun? What if that's why I heard a woman screaming? Had the gunman been hunting her down? What if the screamer had been shot? Or what if the bullet was meant for me?

This thought propelled me forward in a sprint. Someone was after me. I couldn't tell where the gunshot had come from. I thought from behind, but it could have come from anywhere. The forest distorted sounds. I was a bad judge of distance.

What I wasn't a bad judge of was a gunshot. That was most definitely a gun.

I flew down the trail, not bothering to avoid puddles. I slipped and gashed my right hand on a sharp rock.

I had to keep moving. I had to get out of the forest—now.

I didn't care that I was leaving a trail of blood dripping from my hand.

Breathless, hot, and covered in my own blood, I reached the base. The buzzing power lines sounded welcoming.

Reaching the gravelly area where Krissy left me, I wasn't out of danger. She wasn't there. The makeshift parking lot was entirely empty. The only sign of human contact was the tire tracks leading out to the main road.

I pulled out my phone again. Nearly an hour had passed. I checked the bars on the top. No service. I could either hike to my car or wait in hopes that Krissy would return soon. What errands could possibly take her an hour, unless she'd gone to the city? That thought made my blood pressure spike. It was an hour's drive one way to Portland. If she had, she wouldn't return for at least another hour.

My blue and yellow striped picnic blanket was speckled with mud and damp to the touch. I fell on it anyway.

Thank God for my backpack and first-aid kit. I pulled a Band-Aid out. Not big enough. The gash in my hand was deep and wouldn't stop bleeding. I felt light-headed. Pressure, I had to put pressure on my sliced hand. I dug through my pack and found an extra pair of socks. I pressed them onto my hand with force. The white socks slowly turned pink as they soaked up the blood. I peeled them off to check if the bleeding had stopped.

It hadn't. I was going to need stitches.

Not a fan of blood, particularly my own, I threw my left hand onto the blanket to steady myself. The canyon grasses and patchy clouds spiraled together. I was going to be sick. I heard tires rumbling along the gravelly path.

*Yes! Krissy's back.*

*No, not Krissy.*

A red truck made its way up the rough road.

*Matt!*

I tried to push to my feet to wave him down, but black spots danced in front in my vision. *Better stay put.*

Matt's truck bounded over the pitted, wet tracks. His bike, secured with bungee cords, rattled in the tail bed. He parked in a patch of grass and jumped out of the driver's seat.

"Thought you might want company," he said, walking in my direction with a cloth grocery bag. As he approached the blanket, his face dropped. "What's the matter?"

The grocery bag fell to the ground as he raced to my side and knelt. I held out my shaking hand, steadying it by wrapping my left hand around my wrist.

"I fell."

Peeling off the blood-soaked sock, Matt whistled. "You did a bang-up job on that, didn't you?"

I nodded as Matt threw the sock on the grass and took off his T-shirt. His abs were surprisingly solid and well defined; the muscles in his arms flexed as he wrapped his warm shirt around my hand. I'd never seen him without a shirt on and had to resist the urge to touch his toned upper body. "You're kind of ripped," I blurted out.

Matt chuckled, and cinched the shirt tighter. "About time you noticed." He looked over his shoulder to the fork in the road. "You're alone out here? How'd you get hurt?"

Seriously, why had I never noticed how chiseled Matt's body was? His freckled skin shimmered in the cloudy sunlight. Had he recently begun working out? He rode his bike everywhere. It was one of the many things he and Pops had in common, but biking didn't chisel chest muscles, did it?

"Megs, you okay?"

"Someone shot at me!"

"What?"

"Yeah. I heard a woman scream out on the trail and went to see who it was. It sounded like she was hurt. She screamed maybe three or four times and stopped. I got about a mile to a meadow. I swear someone was watching me, but I couldn't find whoever was screaming."

"But then someone tried to shoot you? Did you see anyone?"

"Nope."

"No one?" He shook his head.

"I got kind of spooked. Something or someone moved in the meadow. I freaked out and sprinted down the trail. I would have made it fine, but I heard a gunshot. I slipped and cut my hand."

Matt cradled my hand in his and squeezed my fingertips one at a time. "Can you feel this?"

I nodded.

"Okay, we've got to get you to a doctor. Can you stand?"

"No, I have to wait here. I promised Greg I'd be here for the finish. I'm supposed to cover it."

"You can't write about anything with that hand," Matt said, pointing to where blood spread on his shirt. "You need stitches. That's a deep cut. It's not up for debate. I'm taking you now. It's just a matter of whether or not you walk over to my truck, or I carry you."

"Please, Matt, can we wait until the race is done? I swear you can take me to the doctor, but Greg will kill me if I miss this. I need to be here for the finish. My job depends on it."

Matt dropped my hand. "What does this guy have over you?"

"What do you mean? It's my job. I'm supposed to film them coming over the finish line. Oh, shit! The finish line. I'm also supposed to put the finish line up." I pointed to the rope and tape Krissy had left with me.

"Right," Matt said under his breath. "It's about the job. Not the guy."

"Matt, what's going on with you? It is about the job. You know how much I need this job. I need to get this on film. Greg wants to use it as a video teasers online and I have to finish my story. It's the only way I'm keeping this job."

"Gimme that." Matt grabbed the tape and rope. "I'll put the finish line up for you. You keep pressure on your hand."

As Matt headed off to construct a finish line, I squeezed my hand until it burned. Matt and I never fought. We rarely disagreed on anything. What was his problem?

"Now what?" Matt said, returning to the blanket. He threw the leftover tape and rope next to my soggy sock and stood staring at me.

"Listen, I'm sorry, Matt. I really can't lose this job."

"Forget it. We're cool. You want me to film them coming down? I can probably get a good angle from that patch of grass over there." He pointed directly under a power line.

"I don't think you should stand too close to those lines."

A small smile tugged at the corners of his lips. "You worried about my brain cells?"

"No, Pops always said..." I trailed off as his smile turned into a full grin. This sent us both into a fit of giggles. The tension deflated.

Matt gently brushed a strand of hair from my eye, leaning in so close that for a second I thought he might kiss me. My stomach flopped as my heart thudded against my chest, but at the last second, he pulled away. "You hang here. Keep pressure on. I'll shoot the video for you."

He turned in the direction of the vibrating power line. I checked my hand. The blood had slowed a little, but my fingertips looked like grapes ready to pop off the vine. Matt had fashioned his T-shirt into a tourniquet. Oh, well, better than gushing blood.

I heard movement in the forest to my left. Feet were pounding down the trail.

"It's a guy," Matt hollered.

How had they made it back so fast? They shouldn't be here for at least another hour.

To my surprise, Greg appeared through the weedy grasses in perfect sprinting form. He looked like he should grace the cover of the magazine, his arms bent at 90-degree angles, lanky legs stretched, with a fine misting of sweat but no grimace of exertion on his face. My heart thumped.

He stopped quickly next to Matt, dragging his right foot into a skid. "Who are you?"

Matt reached out a hand to Greg. "Matt, Meg's friend. You must be the winner?"

Greg stretched his neck in my direction. Meeting his eyes, I gave him a wave with my left hand, keeping my right hand secured to my stomach.

"What's wrong with Meg?" Greg ignored Matt's stretched hand and sprinted over to me.

I shrugged my shoulder and held out my injured hand.

"Meg, what am I going to do with you? I leave you alone and you hurt yourself again. What happened?"

Grimacing, I kept my eyes focused on the ground. "I slipped on a rock."

"Is it bad?"

"I'm not sure. Matt thinks I might need stitches. He's going to take me into town, but I wanted to make sure I got the shot of the finish line."

Greg knelt beside me on the blanket. "Let me take a look." He unwrapped Matt's bandage. "This is too tight. We've got to loosen the pressure a little."

My fingers wouldn't move as he unrolled Matt's T-shirt. I tried to wiggle them, but they stood frozen, swollen, and a deep shade of purple. The bleeding had subsided to a trickle.

"Yep, you need stitches," Greg said, peering at the cut. "Let me rewrap this and I'll take you into Stevenson. It's only a ten-minute drive down the highway. We'll get you all stitched up."

Matt stood poised under the power lines with his phone in hand.

"What about the finish? I'm supposed to catch it," I said, pointing to Matt. "Hey, wait a minute." I paused. "How are you the first one back?"

Securing Matt's shirt around my hand, Greg glanced over at Matt. "I'm not. I turned around. I thought I heard a gunshot. I was worried about you."

Warmth spread through my body. I could feel my cheeks betray me. "I heard it too. That's when I fell. I ducked."

"Was it this far? I thought it sounded higher on the trail."

"No, it was." My cheeks were beginning to burn. "I heard a woman screaming. I went up a ways to check it out, but I never found her. I was on my way down when the gun went off. Did you see Alicia? Could she have been screaming?"

Greg shook his head. "I don't think so. I lost sight of her. She was about a half mile ahead of me on the trail. I never heard her scream. Listen, we've got to get you to a doctor." He extended his hand and lifted me to my feet. The spinning feeling returned. My body rocked from side to side. Greg pulled me into his chest. "I've got you. Careful now. Let's get you to the doc."

His shirt was damp with sweat. I could feel his steady heartbeat through his chest. *Maybe I should get hurt more often.* He kept his firm arm wrapped around my shoulder as he helped me navigate over the uneven road.

My car. How was I going to get it back? "Wait," I said, stopping in midstride. "What about the finish? Matt was going to record it for me. And what about my car?"

"Don't worry; I'll take you to the hospital." Greg waved his hand in the air. "The others won't be back for hours. Someone can drive your car back when they're done."

"Well, my friend can take me to the doctor. You don't need to." I stood on my tiptoes and called over Greg's shoulder to Matt, "Come on over." I prayed internally Greg wouldn't loosen his grip on me. I wasn't sure I was steady enough to stand on my own.

Matt slunk over with his arms wrapped around his bare chest.

"Greg, this is my friend Matt," I said, nodding to Matt. "Matt, this is my boss, Greg."

"Yep we met." The grin on Matt's face vanished. He twisted the extra caution tape around his wrist. "How's it going?" he said to Greg. Catching my eye, he gave me a quick but noticeable eye roll—as if to say, *This is the guy?*

"Nice to meet you." Greg took his arm off my shoulder and reached to shake Matt's hand.

A strange look passed between them, but both recovered quickly. Greg returned his arm to my shoulder. "I'm going to take Meg into town. Can you follow us to bring her back?"

He looked at his watch. "It's only a ten- or fifteen-minute drive."

Matt folded his arms around his chest again. "Nope, I don't mind. I can take her too."

Greg surveyed Matt's truck. "Thanks, but I need to make sure we get her all squared away and paid for."

Greg moved me in the direction of his convertible sports car. "Meet you there."

"Fine," Matt said, not making eye contact with me. "Whatever's better for Megs." He turned on his heels to his truck.

"Matt," I called. He paused and glanced over his shoulder. I caught a look of longing in his eyes. "You want your shirt?"

"Nah, keep it. I'll be fine."

I should have been happy to have Greg in close proximity and all to myself, but I couldn't shake the feeling Matt was upset.

The ride into the small riverside town of Stevenson was pleasant and too short. We made our way east with breathtaking views of the carved-out Gorge miles below. Greg turned on the radio. A lulling, romantic Perry Como melody played.

"You like crooners?"

"Not at all." Greg turned the station. "I'm a Nirvana guy. That's earlier than your time. I'm guessing you're a Taylor Swift fan?"

"Yeah, sure." I could barely concentrate on anything other than Matt. Something had shifted with us, but had I ruined it by leaving with Greg?

"Something on your mind?" Greg asked as I watched the lush, green Northwest jungle fly by my window. "Your hand hurting?"

"Nope, it's okay," I said, keeping pressure on Matt's bloodstained shirt. Greg turned the music down and stretched his right arm over my armrest, leaving him with one hand to navigate the hairpin turns. The man liked to live on the edge.

"Is Matt your boyfriend?" he asked, keeping his eyes on the road ahead.

"What? No, no, not at all. He's like a brother to me."

"A brother?"

"Seriously, we're friends. Nothing more," I lied.

"I don't think Matt would agree. He's into you." Greg turned his head in my direction, but I couldn't make out his expression from behind his sunglasses.

"Matt? No. Trust me. He thinks of me as a sister. Usually an annoying sister."

"That's not the way I look at my sister." Greg laughed and accelerated around a curve. I resisted the urge to brake with my right foot.

"Trust me." I plunged my foot into the mat as Greg whipped the car through a zigzag in the road. "There's nothing between me and Matt."

Changing the subject, Greg launched into a series of questions about what I was doing on the trail. I gave him a condensed recap of Krissy leaving, hearing screams, and discovering the meadow.

"Tell me more about the scream," he said, slowing briefly and hugging the right shoulder as a semi-truck sailed past us, inching over the center line.

"It's hard to describe. I thought it sounded like a woman, but now I'm not sure."

Greg jerked the wheel. The motion pushed me into the passenger side door. Instinctively I reached for the handle above my head. Pain seared in my hand. I brought it to my lap.

"Sorry about that. Did you see that squirrel? They're brazen. You'd think they'd learn to avoid the road. Anyway, this scream, was it high-pitched?"

"Yeah." I nodded, trying to recall the bloodcurdling sound I'd heard on the trail.

"Did it sound like a shriek?"

I thought about the guttural, piercing sound. "Uh-huh." I shivered.

"Meg, I think you heard a cougar." He skimmed around a curve. The sun drifted behind the cliffs. Pulling his sunglasses to the top of his head, he gave me a hard look.

"What? No—no, it sounded like a person, not an animal." I stared at him with disbelief as he maneuvered the sports car around another bend.

"That's exactly what people report with cougar sightings—a piercing scream. Didn't you read about the hiker who was attacked last week? He got away, but just barely."

A cougar. Is that what I'd heard? I could have sworn it was a woman screaming, but with the rain, wind, and dense forest, maybe it had been a mountain lion. They were prolific in these parts, but known to keep a low profile. Occasional attacks on hikers had been reported, but I'd never considered them a danger to me. Panic welled in my throat, tightening it and making it hard to swallow. What would I have done if I'd met with a cougar alone on the trail?

We made it to the doctor in no time. Greg knew his way around town and the emergency room doctor. In less than thirty minutes I was in and out of the hospital, with eight stitches horizontally crisscrossing my hand.

Greg handed me off to Matt, talking to him like I wasn't even there. "She's all stitched up. The numbing in her hand will wear off in a while. Make sure she takes a couple of these. I'll get someone to bring her car back." He handed Matt a bottle of pills.

Turning to me, he said, "You don't have to come to the finale tomorrow. I can cover it. You should rest your hand."

"No way. I'll be there."

"It's up to you, but if you change your mind, text me." He gave Matt a wink and sauntered off.

On the ride back to Portland, Matt was strangely silent. He dropped me off at Jill's with barely more than a goodbye.

# TWENTY-NINE

I stumbled up the stairs to Jill's loft.

What had I done to make Matt so angry?

Jill was still at the beach. She texted to check in and tell me she'd be home late or maybe not at all.

The space was mine. What to do?

I had to make it right with Matt. I'd invite him over, order in pizza, and promise to watch whatever geek or gory movie he wanted.

First, a shower. I peeled off my filthy clothes and piled them on the bathroom floor. Steam filled the bathroom while I let the water run, momentarily not caring about being environmentally conscious. I climbed in the fog-like shower, carefully keeping my injured hand on the other side of the curtain.

Scalding water streamed down, burning away the dirt, grime, and worry. Was Matt jealous of Greg? Jill was convinced Matt had been crushing on me since our junior year of college. I thought she said it to appease me and distract me from the fact that wherever we went together, men drooled over her and ignored me. The way Matt behaved earlier made me wonder if Jill might be right.

Then there was Greg. Ah, Greg. I needed to stop crushing on him. He'd been concerned about my hand, demanding to drive me in for medical attention. Probably he was worried I'd open a workers' compensation claim. It was super flattering to have him pay attention to me. I had to remind myself he flirted with every woman he met and he was my boss.

Thirty minutes later, with red, wrinkling skin, I removed myself from the shower, threw on sweats and a tattered college sweatshirt, and texted Matt.

Pizza, movies (your choice), my place in an hour?

I held my phone in my left hand, watching the screen and waiting for the little green text window to pop up. Nothing. Five minutes, ten minutes, fifteen minutes.

*Uh-oh. He must be madder than I thought. I should have gone with him.*

I texted:

You there? Sorry about today. Come over, I'll make it up to you.

Another five minutes passed before my phone made the sound of a typewriter returning.

Be there in a few.

I punched in the number to the pizza spot around the corner and ordered Matt's favorite—the Rat Pack Special. It came loaded with pepperoni, beef, mushrooms, olives, and extra cheese.

With pizza on its way, I checked Jill's beer supply. Bummer, nothing but a lame can of lite beer. Her wine collection decorated the space above the cabinets. Bottles imported from Italy and Spain. They were completely lost on my unrefined palate. If only the pizza place delivered beer to go.

The doorbell rang. Matt held two growlers in his hands. "I stopped by Deschutes on my way."

"You're the best." I leaned onto my tiptoes and kissed his cheek. It was smooth to the touch. He must have shaved. "Come on in."

Matt poured two glasses of amber-colored beer and stuck the growlers in the fridge.

"Pizza should be here any minute," I said, checking my watch. "Do you want to watch a movie?"

Bringing me a frosty glass of beer, he moved to my side. I caught a whiff of his fresh sandalwood cologne. It smelled super sexy. What was wrong with me? I couldn't stop daydreaming about my boss; now I was obsessing about my best friend.

"Anything look good?" I asked as Matt scrolled through the new releases.

"What are you in the mood for?" he asked, slowly sipping his beer. I wondered what his lips would feel like on mine.

*Stop it, Meg*, I told myself. *You're setting yourself up for trouble.*

To Matt, I said, "I'm cool with anything. It's your call. I wanted to thank you for helping me out this afternoon. I'm sorry it ended so... so weird."

Matt started to respond, just as the doorbell rang. "Pizza's here."

I paid the delivery guy while Matt took our beers and the steaming pie to Jill's coffee table.

"Let's eat," he said, pulling a slice oozing with cheese from the box. "We can watch a movie later if you're up for it."

The smell of savory meat and garlicky tomato sauce filled the room. In the mess of hiking and an impromptu trip to the ER for stitches, I'd forgotten to eat. I was famished. I inhaled three slices of the wood-fired pizza before pausing to breathe. I'd never eat like that in front of Greg.

Washing the pizza down with the beer Matt brought relaxed me and made my head feel slightly fuzzy. The numbing in my hand had begun to wear off. It throbbed. I could feel it pulsating like the beat of a drum.

"You weren't hungry or anything," Matt teased as he refilled our beers and crammed the half-empty pizza box into Jill's fridge. He kicked off his shoes and lounged beside me on the couch. "How's the hand feeling?"

"It's starting to hurt, kind of throbbing a little."

Matt gently peeled my fingertips apart. His touch sent a wave of heat through my body. *Probably the beer*, I told myself. "They look good. No swelling. It's a good sign it's hurting. Means it's starting to heal."

"You think?" I asked, not wanting him to let go of my hand.

"I'm sure of it." He nodded and dropped his hand.

He pretended to read the description of a new thriller. "Your boss, Greg, he's older than I expected."

"Is he? I don't think he's old. Maybe thirty?"

"Exactly. That's almost a decade older than us."

"He doesn't act it, though. I don't really think of him being that much older."

Matt studied the screen. "You've got it bad, Megs."

I twisted a napkin in my left hand. It was stained with pizza grease. "What do you mean?"

He met my eyes. "Come on, Megs. I know you better than that. You've got a major crush." He looked away again. "Be careful. It's always the guys like him who break hearts."

The napkin shredded into tiny pieces in my hand. I tucked it under my leg. "It's not like that, Matt. He's my boss. He happens to be attractive. That's all."

"Sure, that's all." Matt landed on an action movie. "You want to watch this?"

"Always." I laughed, trying to lighten the mood. "You know me. Sign me up for an end-of-the-world disaster flick any day."

"Want a refill?" Matt asked, standing and grabbing my empty glass.

"Nah, I'm good. I'm feeling it tonight."

Matt took both our glasses to the sink. "I'm sure it's the stress of the day." He fiddled with a remote and sank onto the couch again. "By the way, that reminds me we never finished our conversation. You said you heard a woman scream. Did anything more come of that? Did your"—he cleared his throat—"boss hear anything? I asked all the others when they returned. No one else heard a thing."

Opening credits rolled on the screen. "Pause it for a sec," I demanded, trying to grab the remote out of Matt's hand. He hit Pause and the movie froze. "You're not going to believe this. Greg thinks I heard a cougar, not a woman."

I noticed Matt gripped the remote, his knuckles cracking. "Shit, he's got a point. That's cougar country. You never should have gone out there on your own." His tone turned harsh.

"I didn't do it on purpose. I freaked out."

"Stupid move, really stupid. You know a guy was mauled on a trail a week ago. A cougar's not going to attack a group, but one small woman? You could have been an afternoon snack." He loosened his grip on the remote, his fingertips white.

"What is this? Pick on Meg day?"

Matt's tone softened. "No, sorry. I can't stand the thought of you alone out there. Promise me you won't try a stunt like that again? No job is worth it."

My stomach fluttered. Matt leaned in. I thought he was going to kiss me, but at the last minute he brushed a stray hair from my eye and pulled away.

We sat in an uncomfortable silence for a minute. I racked my brain for something witty or funny to say. Nothing came, other than the sound of my heart beating in my head.

The camera! I'd forgotten all about the camera I found on the trail.

I jumped to my feet. "Hold on!" I rushed to the table where I'd dropped my backpack and grabbed it. "Here." I thrust it in Matt's hands. "I totally spaced. I found a camera on the trail. It must have fallen off in the hailstorm."

Matt unzipped my pack and found the camera. "Oh, yeah, a GoPro. I love these." He twisted it in his hands and held it to the light. "Doesn't look damaged, but a Mack truck could run over one of these and not leave a scratch."

"Really?"

"I'm exaggerating, but not much. There was an article a while ago about a kid who built a model of the space shuttle out of LEGOs. He strapped one of these to it and launched it into space. The camera survived. Completely intact. It makes sense they'd use them on the trail."

"Is there a way to watch whatever's on this one?" I asked. "I know Andrew has a mount he pops on to view the video. What if we could see the trail? Maybe we'd be able to tell if someone else was out there with me."

"Sure, no problem." Matt twisted open the waterproof casing around the camera and pulled out an SD card. He held the tiny card in his hand. "Where's your laptop?"

"On the table." I pointed to Jill's dining room set.

As Matt booted up my laptop, my heart flopped. This time not from the anticipation of a kiss, but from the possibility the film might lead to another clue into whoever was behind Lenny's murder.

Static, crystal images of the trail appeared on my screen. The film showed Andrew testing it on screen. He waved, jumped up and down, and said, "Testing, testing, testing." The next ten minutes of footage was a still shot of the forest. The rain hadn't hit, but dark clouds must have been rolling past. Shadows danced between the trees. Matt sped the film up.

After another ten minutes, Leaf, Greg, and Dave sprinted past. Where was Alicia? Hadn't she been out in front?

There was no sign of her as Matt continued to fast-forward the film. "Stop," I shouted. Something blurred in front of the camera. "Go back."

Matt rewound the frame. Andrew's bulky figure came into view. What was he doing? I thought he'd gone ahead to mount cameras all along the trail?

Minutes and minutes of footage showed him pacing. He fiddled with his fanny pack and kept looking ahead and behind him. He was waiting for someone. But who?

"Fast-forward," I told Matt. He sped the film up again. It looked like Andrew was rushing along a ten-foot stretch of trail.

"There, look!" Matt stopped the film as Alicia appeared on screen, but from the other direction—as if she was coming from the summit.

"How did she get there?" I asked Matt. "Did we miss her going past?"

"I don't think so," Matt said.

Andrew raced over to Alicia. Her model-like body looked like a toothpick in contrast to his huge frame. "Well?" she asked in her typical sullen tone.

Wind from the approaching storm whipped through the forest, making it hard to hear.

"Can you turn it up?" I asked Matt.

He slid the volume dial on my laptop and enhanced the sound.

Alicia bounced lightly on her feet—probably trying to keep herself warm. But how was she going to catch Leaf and the rest of them? They'd passed by her at least five minutes before.

Matt and I both leaned closer to the laptop screen to make out what Alicia and Andrew were discussing. I'd never noticed how Andrew looked at her like a puppy dog following its master. His eyes never left hers. Was he into her? I thought back to the other hikes and times I'd seen them together. He was always fiddling with her camera, but I'd never thought much about that. Now, images of him doting on her came flooding to mind. Why hadn't I realized this before?

"He's in love with her, isn't he?"

"You think?" Matt bantered. "Yeah. I'll say."

"Shh, listen."

Andrew looked around and motioned Alicia off the trail and closer to the tree. This made it much easier to hear what they were saying and I silently thanked him.

"What do you want?" Alicia asked, her thin arms wrapped angrily around her waist.

"I know about Lenny," he said.

Alicia gave him a look of pure hatred. "I have no idea what you're talking about."

Andrew's back was to the camera, but I could tell from the way he shifted his weight and motioned his arms in the air, he was scrambling. "Don't worry. No one else does. I'll keep your secret."

Matt and I looked at each other wide-eyed. "What secret?" Matt whispered.

I hushed him and held my breath, waiting for Alicia's response. The look she threw Andrew made me shudder.

"Tough cookie," Matt muttered.

"Shush." I kicked him with my foot.

Through clenched teeth, Alicia hissed, "Listen, what happened between me and that dirtbag is nobody's business."

Andrew nodded frantically.

Alicia held a finger and pushed it onto his chest. "You tell one person, I mean one person about this, and you're as good as dead to me. Got it?"

"You know I'd, I'd"—Andrew fumbled over his words—"I'd never betray you."

A fake, serene smile washed over Alicia's face. She moved closer to Andrew and massaged his shoulder.

Matt made a face like he was going to gag.

"That's right, sweetie. I know you won't," Alicia said in a syrupy voice. "I didn't mean to snap. I want to get the hell out of this place and get started on our life together."

The next thing that happened made me cover my eyes and scream in disgust. Alicia and Andrew made out, complete with tongue action.

"Gross. Fast-forward," I said with one hand covering my eyes.

"No way," Matt replied. "We might miss something good. This is better than any movie we were going to watch."

"Alicia and Andrew? I would NOT have pegged them as a couple." My face stuck in a permanent grimace.

Matt paused the video. "What do you know about them? I mean, I'm with you completely based on looks alone, but I'm assuming they haven't been public?"

I tried to think of any sign that might have betrayed Alicia. None. "Nothing," I said, biting my bottom lip. "She's awful to everyone."

"What about him?"

"Well, it did seem like he always spent extra time fitting her camera and stuff—more in an annoying kind of way. Like offering to get her drinks and carry her backpack. I guess it should have dawned on me he liked her. But never would I have thought Alicia reciprocated his feelings. Shocker."

"Should we keep going?" Matt asked, his hand poised to hit Play.

"Uh, totally."

The video rolled on. Alicia pulled away from Andrew's embrace, mumbled something I couldn't understand and took off, cutting through the forest, directly up the cliff face. Andrew made a minor adjustment to the height of the camera and ambled up the trail.

"You realize what this means?" I asked Matt, watching the wind rustle the bushes on the empty path.

"No idea." Matt shook his head, that damn boyish smile on his lips.

"Alicia is the killer!" I threw my left hand at the screen. "We have proof.

Right here."

"That's a bit of a stretch."

"No, listen, it all makes sense now. Think about it. Andrew figured it out too. He knows Alicia pushed Lenny off the cliff. He's covering for her. That's the secret he's talking about. She's playing him. She has to be. There's no way a girl like her goes for a guy like him."

"Tell me about it." Matt rolled his eyes. "Nice guys finish last."

"Stop it." I elbowed him with my right arm, momentarily forgetting about my stitches. Pain surged through the veins in my arm. "Ouch."

"Easy there, tiger." Matt nudged me in the ribs.

"I can't believe I didn't see it before. That's why Andrew's been such a jerk to me. That has to be why he followed me out to Multnomah Falls—he thinks I know too. He's trying to protect Alicia."

Matt fiddled with the zipper on his hoodie. "But why would Andrew choose that spot to meet her? He knew there was a camera running."

"Maybe that's why. He wanted proof just in case things don't work out for them?"

"That could be." Matt nodded. "You need to call Sheriff Daniels."

A piercing scream came over the laptop's built-in speakers, making both Matt and me flinch on the couch.

"Oh, my God." Matt leaned forward, peering at the screen and then at me. "Was that the sound you heard?"

"Uh-huh." I nodded, feeling bile rise in my throat. The sound was more high-pitched and guttural than I remembered.

Matt hunched over the laptop, clicking on the video. He zoomed in on a small patch of trees to the right of the trail. "Look on that branch."

My eyes followed his finger where he'd zoomed in. The image became grainy and pixelated. I squinted. "I don't see anything."

"Right here." Matt tapped the screen. "Perched in this tree."

For a brief moment I considered not looking. I had a sinking feeling that whatever was perched in the tree would visit my dreams in the coming nights, and not in a Gam guide kind of way.

Is that a...?" I hesitated. "A cougar. It's a cougar."

We exchanged a look of disbelief. Matt clicked Play, keeping his eyes glued to the tree. The cougar blended into the tree cover, perfectly positioned to pounce on any hiker who happened upon the trail.

Another shrill, wild scream came from the cougar. Ten minutes later, I appeared on the screen. Huffing my way up the incline, red-faced and stumbling.

Matt put his hand on my knee, but said nothing. We both watched in stunned silence as I scrambled past the camera. The cougar remained statue-like in its lookout. Rain streamed in front of the camera's lens. Wind made the video shake. Matt focused on the cougar, which had yet to move. A gust of wind or a barrage of hail must have knocked the camera off the tree because it flipped, landing facedown on the dirt. The last twenty minutes of film consisted of a black screen.

Matt released my knee. "Megs, that was close. Way too close."

"Is there more beer?" I asked, my voice shaky.

"Beer?" Matt couldn't keep the irritation out of his voice. "We witnessed you escaping death by cougar by inches and all you can think about is beer?" He stopped and stared at me. "You're shaking all over."

I blinked, trying desperately to hold back the tears pooling behind my eyes. "I could really use a beer." I quivered.

Jumping up, Matt raced to the kitchen, rinsed out our pint glasses, and poured two new ones. He handed me one and raised another in a mock toast. "Me, too."

The carbonation tickled my throat as I took a long sip. It had a refreshing bite. What else could go wrong this week? So far I'd witnessed a murder, been run off the road, threatened, and now stalked by a cougar.

"You okay?" Matt slugged half his glass.

"Um, yeah." The pint glass shook in my hand.

"Sorry, I didn't mean to snap at you." Matt took the glass from my hand and rested it on the coffee table. "You got lucky. Promise me you won't go off on an unpopulated trail like that again."

"Are you kidding me? I don't know how I'm going to get myself out to the Bridge of the Gods for the finale tomorrow. I think I need a nature sabbatical."

Matt knocked back another quarter of his beer and laughed. "Yeah, a stint stuck in here for a week is probably a good idea." He panned to the moonlight reflecting off Jill's patio doors.

"One more day. If I can get through tomorrow I'll be done with this story and hopefully Greg will put me back on write-ups for gel packs and hiking boots. Otherwise, I'm pretty sure he's going to fire me."

"Don't do anything stupid tomorrow, all right?"

"Me? Never."

Swirling the beer on the bottom of his glass, Matt said, "You're not going to sit around and do nothing. What are you scheming?"

"Tomorrow's my last chance to confront Alicia. It'll be fine. There'll be people around. Krissy explained what a production it is to shut down bridge traffic and rig a zip-line. In fact, Sheriff Daniels is going to be there to help direct traffic. I'll call him tonight."

"Great idea. I'm down with you looping the police in, but I don't want you confronting Alicia on your own. Who knows? She could have a perfectly reasonable explanation, but if she doesn't and it turns out she did kill Lenny, I don't want you anywhere near her. Got it?"

"Got it." I nodded. "I'll make you a deal; I'll text Krissy tonight and find out if the police will be there. If they are, I'll fill Sheriff Daniels in before I talk to Alicia. Cool?"

"Cool."

Matt offered to stay and sleep on the floor, but I talked him out of it. I wanted to get an early start tomorrow. I couldn't believe I'd been so shortsighted.

Had Alicia killed Lenny in a fit of rage? Was it an accident or had she hiked to the top of Angel's Rest intending to shove him off the ledge?

Tomorrow. Tomorrow I'd have answers to all my questions. I took a couple Advil, hoping they'd ease the throbbing in my hand, and texted Krissy.

She responded within minutes.

> Police will be directing traffic. Briefing at 5:00.
> Come early.

Perfect. I could talk to Sheriff Daniels first thing in the morning. I sent Matt a text letting him know my plan and set the alarm on my phone for 4:00. Ouch. It would take me an hour to get out to the Bridge of the Gods. I had to get there before Alicia.

# THIRTY

Sleep evaded me most of the night. I tossed and turned on Jill's couch, trying not to squish my hand as I ran through every interaction I'd had with Alicia. When the alarm buzzed at 4:00 A.M., I was already half awake.

As promised, Greg had returned my car, which was waiting for me in the garage.

Heading out in darkness in the direction of the rising sun, I sped along the highway toward the Bridge of the Gods. The once-sacred site where Indigenous Americans believed you could cross the river without your feet getting wet now featured a silver bridge spanning the mighty Columbia River.

I pulled off the freeway and into the town of Cascade Locks. A coffee would hit the spot. The clock on my dashboard flashed 4:50. I'd made good time. Slowing to 25 mph, I peered into shuttered shop windows. Nothing was open at this ungodly hour. Coffee would have to wait.

There was no sign of Krissy, Dave, or any police presence at the base of the historic bridge. I'd have to make my way onto the steel structure. The overriding urge to finally get to the bottom of Lenny's murder helped propel me onward. I hung a U-turn in the middle of the barren street and headed under the freeway and onto the bridge.

I cringed as I looked at the towering bridge. It sloped upward toward a tollbooth, and climbed to a peak in the middle before descending into Washington.

"Morning." A tollbooth operator greeted me from her window.

"I'm a reporter. I'm here for the *Race the States* finale. Has anyone else come this way?"

The gray-haired woman thumbed through a stack of paperwork. "Oh, yeah, that's happening later this morning. Uh, haven't seen anyone myself, but my shift started five minutes ago."

"Do you know where I'm supposed to go?"

"Hmm, well, I'd suggest you drive over to the Washington side." She leaned farther out the tollbooth and pointed across the river. "As soon as you come off the bridge, take a sharp right. You can park there. You'll have to walk."

"Thanks, I appreciate it."

"You still owe me the toll."

"Oh, right," I said, rummaging through my purse to find change. Who had cash anymore? Handing her the cash, I gave her a quick wave and rolled my window up.

She held a wrinkled finger in the air. "Be careful, dear. There's no sidewalk. Cars won't be looking for walkers this early."

I thanked her again, took a deep breath. Midway across the span at the bridge's highest point, I noticed wires and riggings attached to the silver beams. *This must be the spot.*

I forced myself to look to my right. Downriver sat Thunder Island—the landing spot for the zip-line. The lines stretched from the steep bridge, over the river, and to the island. *Why would anyone in their right mind opt to do this? Oh, that's right. None of these people are in their right minds.* That thought comforted me as I returned my eyes to the front windshield and crossed into Washington.

The tollbooth operator's directions led me to an empty lot. I parked the car and looked around. Where was everyone? *Krissy said 5:00 A.M., right? She must be on the Oregon side.* I grabbed my pack, which contained a notebook, the GoPro (Matt made me promise I'd give it to Sheriff Daniels), and the first-aid kit. I wouldn't leave home without it now.

Walking across the bridge, alone in the dusky morning light, was not in my plan. The Pacific Crest Trail crossed the bridge and I remembered years ago Pops telling me they had to blindfold horses to get them to cross, otherwise they were too spooked.

*Whatever you do, don't look down,* I told myself as I started across.

The open steel grating on the bridge's surface gave an excellent view of the river rushing hundreds of feet below. The slow-rising morning sun cast shadows on the Oregon mountains. Sheer terror pulsed through my body as I stepped onto the grate. I tried to keep my gaze focused ahead and ignore the sound of the forceful river below. A semi flew past on the opposite side. The bridge buckled and shook.

In the distance I thought I could make out an orange and yellow vest. The crew must have arrived. I quickened my pace, stepping lightly so as not to get my feet stuck in the grating. Nearing the halfway point of the bridge, Krissy's silhouette came into view. She was ahead about fifty feet, fiddling with the zip-line rigging. How had she made it across the grating in heels and flared black pants? She wore a construction-style orange vest over her professionally tailored shirt.

Otherwise, the bridge was devoid of movement or traffic. I hoped Sheriff Daniels would hurry up. If Alicia arrived before him, it would be hard to get him alone and fill him in on what I'd learned.

"Where is everyone?" I called to Krissy, coming within earshot.

She looked around and shrugged. "Should be here soon. Come give me a hand, would you?" She held a handful of shiny carabiners and what looked like a climbing harness.

I shuffled my feet to the left side of the bridge, grabbed on to a steel trellis, and accidentally looked down. Big mistake. The Columbia River raged below—a long, long way below.

What was I thinking? I had to get off this bridge and fast. My heart pounded. I desperately had to pee. My entire mind went blank. I was losing it.

"You okay?" Krissy asked. "You look pretty pale."

Digging my left hand into the metal bridge, I thought I might vomit. Heights were bad enough, but heights with one of the largest rivers west of the Mississippi flowing underneath my feet made my stomach churn. Probably a good thing I hadn't found an open coffee shop.

"I'm feeling a tiny bit dizzy this morning." I held up my bandaged hand. "I think it's from the medication they gave me for this."

She glanced at my hand and continued untangling the harness. "How high are we anyway?" I asked, biting the inside of my cheek.

"About 2,000 feet. At least that's the distance from here to Thunder Island," Krissy replied, pointing with the carabiners to the island far off in the middle of the river.

"Did I hear you say this is the largest zip-line ever constructed in Oregon?"

"That's right. We're going to say that on the show anyway. Too bad no one else will have a chance to try it. It has to come down by noon today. All that work for a fifteen-minute shoot. That's showbiz."

She appraised me and dropped the carabiners in a pile at her feet. They clinked on the bridge. One dropped through.

Holding the harness, she said, "Can you try this on for me? It's too hard to make adjustments without anyone in it."

I gulped. "The harness?"

"Yeah, why?" She looked confused.

"My hand," I lied. "I thought you meant adjust the zip-line. I don't think I can do it with one hand."

Krissy ignored my protest and helped me into the harness. I pulled one foot through at a time, holding on to her shoulder with my free hand. After I clumsily stuffed my body into the harness, Krissy cinched straps and added carabiners, walking around my back to secure the other side.

"When did you say Sheriff Daniels and the police were going to arrive?" I asked as she hoisted the straps from behind. She was surprisingly strong.

"I didn't."

The hard edge in her voice sent a shiver up my spine. Something about her tone made me begin to panic. Gam believed I had the gift of immediate intuition. Slowly I turned around.

A gun pointed directly at my forehead. Krissy's piercing eyes stared at me from behind the gun and her librarian glasses. Her body was perfectly poised, as if she were about to perform a Pilates move.

"What are you doing?" I asked, trying to remain casual and locking my knees to keep them from shaking. I'd never been this close to a gun.

"I'm done with your stupid little innocent act." She pushed the barrel of the gun closer to my face. "Get moving. You're going for a ride this morning."

My head screamed, *Run!* But instead I took a tiny step backward. What was going on? Krissy was involved in this? Had she partnered with Alicia? But why? None of this made sense.

"Krissy, I don't understand. What have I done?"

"Shut up, you stupid bitch." Spit sprayed from her mouth as she motioned me backward with the gun. "Stop playing games with me. You have no idea who you're playing with here."

*Keep her talking.* I heard Pops's voice in my head.

"I'm not playing any game," I said, holding both hands in the air. "I swear."

"Enough," she commanded. "I'm not letting an idiot wannabe reporter ruin all my hard work. Now let's get you hooked to the zip-line. Won't it be a shame, when we learn the harness failed? Such a tragedy."

"Wait," I pleaded. "What about Alicia?"

A wave of surprise crossed over Krissy's otherwise stoic face. "Alicia? What the hell does she have to do with this?"

"She killed Lenny."

What was I saying? Of course Alicia wasn't the killer since Krissy was pointing a gun at my face. But why?

Krissy laughed, keeping her eyes and the gun focused on me.

"Please. You've got to be kidding me. Drop the act anytime."

"I'm not acting. I thought Alicia killed Lenny. That's why I sent you the text. I was planning to tell Sheriff Daniels this morning before she got here."

For a brief moment I noticed the gun waver in Krissy's hand. It took her less than a second to regain her composure and her grasp on the gun. "Joke's on you. Isn't it? No one's coming for hours." She motioned to the cathedral sky. "We can't shoot in this light."

The shock of having a gun pointed at me and Krissy's rage wore off, replaced by an intense internal fight for a solution.

I could run, but the tollbooth was at least a half mile away. Crying for help was futile.

*What's the worst that could happen if she sent me sailing down the zip-line?* A 2,000 foot descent into the water. I couldn't survive that. And if I did, the water temperature couldn't be much higher than forty degrees. I wouldn't survive long. Not to mention the fact the river was running high with spring runoff. The current would probably swallow me before I'd have a chance to kick myself up to the surface. And I'd have to contend with debris—floating logs eighty to ninety feet long. No, I was going to have to find another way out of this.

"Krissy." I tried to keep my voice calm, holding my injured hand across my diaphragm to steady my breathing. "You don't have to do this."

"Yes, I do," she hissed. "Lenny's out of my life for good and now I clean up this one loose end and everything I've worked hard for will happen."

"I don't understand. You weren't there. How could you have killed Lenny? Or did you and Alicia team up?"

"Ha! What's your obsession with Alicia? I do my own dirty work, thank you." She looked at her pointed black heels. "I'm pretty fast when I'm not wearing these babies."

Something clicked in my brain. "The deer trail! That was you?"

"Ah, now you're catching on. There are definite advantages to scouting out locations. Like finding hiding spots."

"But Dave's hat? I found it on the trail."

"You found it there because I put it there. If you would have left this whole thing alone from the beginning, we wouldn't be in this position now, would we? But no, you couldn't let it go. Come on, I want to get you hooked up. Let's go." She pushed me three steps farther back.

Keeping the gun aimed steadily at me, she motioned to the pile of carabiners on the ground. "Grab those."

As I bent over to grab the carabiners, I noticed a faint light coming from the far end of the bridge on the Oregon side. Krissy's back was to the light. I had to keep her facing me. The glimmer of light might be my only chance for escape.

"Clip that one to this cable," she said, pointing to a two-inch cable fastened to the bridge.

My hand shook as I tried to attach the cable.

"Use both your hands."

I could feel the stitches ripping apart as I tried to secure my harness to the cable with both my hands. Fresh red blood seeped through the bandage.

*Keep her talking, keep her talking.* Now I could hear both Pops's and Gam's voices ringing in my ears.

"How did you do it? Lenny was a huge guy. How'd you push him off the cliff?"

"Please. It was so easy." She reached her head around the pointed gun and looked out into the water. "I found the perfect hideout, waited until everyone ran past, and threw a camera at Lenny's feet. When he looked down to check it out, I snuck up and pushed him off. He never saw it coming."

"I still don't understand. What did Lenny do to you?"

An even more severe look flashed across Krissy's face. I wished whatever or whoever was generating the light would hurry up. There was no way she was letting me go.

"What didn't he do to me? He ruined my life once and was about to do it all over again. As soon as he took over the show, he'd cut me out. I couldn't let that happen. I've devoted my life to this project. This is my meal ticket. So I worked my own deal with the network. The show's mine. Dave's out. He just doesn't know it yet."

The light was getting closer; my heart sank a bit. It wasn't from a police car (as I'd been wishing), but a bike. Someone was biking over the bridge. Maybe I could flag them down.

"Get moving," Krissy demanded. "Put one foot over the guardrail."

I swallowed bile. "Listen, Krissy, it doesn't have to be like this. I swear I won't tell a soul. We can end it now. You walk away. No one else gets hurt."

"Is that right, little Miss Reporter? You'll let me walk away. Yeah, right. Get your leg over." She waved the gun again.

My entire body trembled as I hoisted my left leg and placed it on the six-inch grating on the far side of the guardrail. The bike was gaining speed. It climbed the hill. How could I get the rider's attention without alerting Krissy to its presence?

Blood saturated the bandage on my right hand and hemorrhaged down my wrist.

"Other leg," Krissy hollered.

"Please," I begged. "You don't want to do this. You'll never get away with it either."

"If there's one thing I know, it's that I'll most definitely get away with it. Accidents like this happen all the time. You were eager to test the lines; you forgot to clip the harness in correctly. I'll turn on the waterworks and be on a plane to L.A. first thing tomorrow."

The bike was within ten feet. Its rider's helmet was flashing white. Now was my chance. I prayed the rider wasn't wearing headphones.

"NO!" I screamed. "You're not going to get away with this. Put the gun down!"

Krissy shot me a look of disdain. She threw her head from side to side. "Why are you yelling?"

Clinging to the jagged side of the bridge with one leg straddling the guardrail, I watched the cyclist put a finger to his lips and steer his bike directly at Krissy's back.

It all happened so fast. The bicycle rammed into Krissy, knocking the gun out of her hand and her off her feet. In the distance, I could hear a police siren and make out flashing red and blue lights.

I remained frozen, saddled between the bridge and rail, my knees shaking so hard I thought they might give way. The cyclist hopped off his bike, letting it crash onto the steel grating.

"Matt?"

# THIRTY-ONE

Matt ran to where Krissy's body lay flat. He bent over and checked her pulse. "She's fine. Knocked out, but fine."

"What are you doing here?" I asked, my fingers numb from digging into the cold steel. My entire right arm dripped with blood, like melting ice cream on the side of a waffle cone.

"We've got to get you out of this contraption," Matt said, leaping over Krissy and grabbing my waist. He hoisted me over to safety and unbuckled the harness.

"How did you know it was Krissy?" I wondered where the gun had landed. It didn't appear to be anywhere next to her body. What if she came to and went after it?

The wail of sirens came closer. Strobe lights danced off the bridge like a disco ball. Matt pointed to the approaching police car. He shouted something unintelligible over the sound of the siren.

"Huh?"

A police car lurched to a stop in front of us. Sheriff Daniels exited the driver's side and strode to the passenger door. He opened it to reveal Gam sitting in the front seat.

"Gam?"

"Oh, honey, I wasn't sure Matt would get here in time," she said as Sheriff Daniels took her hand and helped her out of the police car.

While the sheriff attended to Krissy and called for an ambulance, Gam wrapped Matt and me in a hug.

"Good on you," she said, patting Matt's arm. "You must have pedaled your heart out."

For the first time I took notice of Matt. His green and yellow bike jersey, soaked with sweat, clung to his chest. He removed his neon helmet. His hair was plastered and damp, his face red and streaked with sweat.

"I don't understand. How did you both know to come?" My hand throbbed. Gam noticed as I cradled it next to my waist.

"Here, honey, let me give you a zap." She took both her hands and placed one on the top of my palm and the other on my wrist. Closing her eyes, she slowly rocked back and forth.

Heat spread from the tips of my fingers to my shoulder. Blood continued to trickle from my freshly opened wound, but it slowed and the pain subsided.

"Better?" Gam asked, her face serene.

"Much. Thanks. Now, will one of you fill me in? What's going on?"

"Matt, let's get her in the car and sitting, shall we?" Gam directed Matt to Sheriff Daniels's car.

He led me to the backseat of the police car. Gam sat in the front seat and spun around to face us. Matt's arm rested on my shoulder and I leaned in to his salty, warm chest.

"Okay, okay, I'm sitting. I'm fine. Will you please fill me in? It's driving me bananas."

Gam raised her well-outlined eyebrows and nodded to Matt.

"I couldn't sleep after I left you last night," Matt started. His breathing was fast. "Something didn't add up. Anyway, I tossed and turned. finally I gave up. Don't ask why, but I decided I needed to burn off energy. I went for a ride."

Gam gave me a knowing look.

"I ride this route a bunch. You know, down the old highway, over the bridge and on the Washington side. It's a great loop—" He paused to catch his breath.

Gam interrupted him in midsentence. "You're very intuitive."

Matt grinned and waved her off. "Anyway, I knew you'd be out this way later in the morning and figured I could check in on you. About an hour into my ride, your grandmother texted me. She said Sheriff Daniels called looking for you and you were in danger. I rode until I thought my quads were on fire."

Nothing Gam did should surprise me, but I gave her an incredulous look.

She reached and patted my knee.

"It was Krissy," I said, still partially in disbelief. "She said Lenny ruined her life once and if he took over control of the show, he'd fire her and she'd be completely ruined. I can't wrap my head around it. She was on the trail the whole time. It was her I saw on the deer trail."

Matt nodded vigorously. He pulled his arm off my shoulder and grabbed his phone out of the pocket of his shorts. "I know. Look what I found when I couldn't sleep last night. I didn't think much of it, but the girl can run. She easily could have caught up with everyone."

An article from three years ago highlighted the racing talents of Krissy Ray, a competitive adventure racer, who placed in the top five women in *Racing the World*, set in New Zealand.

"Krissy Ray?" I said aloud. "Her last name is Miles... oh, my God!

Krissy Ray, as in Lenny Ray's wife?"

Matt and Gam both bounced in their seats like kids waiting for a roller-coaster ride to start.

"Exactly!" Matt yelled.

"She was married to Lenny?" My mind made frantic connections. She and Lenny must have participated in the adventure race together. That's where she met Dave. But why the secrecy about her athletic skills? Unless she'd planned Lenny's murder. I let out an involuntary shudder. Gam held my knee.

"Sheriff Daniels found her prints all over your desk and phone," she said as heat pulsed from her hand. "When I couldn't reach you, I called Matt. He told me you planned to meet Krissy here. We raced here as fast as we could."

"Krissy must have been the one following me up Angel's Rest. I could have sworn someone was behind me. She snuck off the deer trail and found a way to the summit off the main path. She killed Lenny and took the same route back. We were there for at least an hour with the Crag Rats. That would have given her plenty of time to get to the van and change."

"Yep. Sheriff Daniels found footage of her on the trail. Andrew rigged the entire path with cameras. She must have not realized she was in view of one of them. That broken camera you found had her prints all over it. She must have ripped it down on the summit. Stupid mistake."

An ambulance siren sounded. The back of the car lit up. Sheriff Daniels showed the paramedics to Krissy. We watched as they placed her on a stretcher. She'd regained consciousness. As they loaded her into the ambulance, she gave me a death stare.

"Thank you," I whispered to Matt. He returned his arm to my shoulder.

Sheriff Daniels sent the ambulance on its way. He strolled to the cruiser's passenger door, which Gam had left open. Closing it, he made sure her legs were tucked safely inside. Why was he treating her like they were on a date?

"Okay, folks, here's the plan," he said as he sat in the driver's seat and pointed to me in the rearview mirror. "We're going to get you to a doctor to stitch up that hand. I'll take your statement and bring you to your car." He paused and caught Gam's eye. Did I notice a look pass between them or was I delirious from my latest brush with death?

Matt raised a finger as Sheriff Daniels turned the key in the ignition. "Uh, one problem. My bike. I can't leave it on the bridge."

"Already took care of it." Sheriff Daniels eased the car into a sharp U-turn. "I'm sending out my deputy in the truck. He'll bring it to town for you."

"What about Krissy?" I asked, buckling my seat belt.

"She'll be fine. Looks to be a slight concussion. Nice work on that one." He nodded in the mirror to Matt. "She'll have plenty of time to heal where she's going. I'm booking her on murder and attempted. Not bad work yourself." He turned his head slightly in my direction and snapped it forward as he sped past the tollbooth.

# THIRTY-TWO

I sat in *Northwest Extreme*'s conference room a few hours later with a new set of stitches and a creamy latte.

Sheriff Daniels briefed the *Race the States* team and Greg on the morning's events and the fact that Krissy had offered a full confession.

It turns out she and Lenny were married for less than a year. They'd met at a race. She fell for his macho personality, which soon turned into a wandering eye. He cheated on her numerous times before she finally called it off.

Then it got ugly. She'd filed for a restraining order, dropped out of adventure racing, and started a new life in Hollywood. For all her talk of hobnobbing with movie stars and producers, she'd really been slinging coffee. This was her first big break.

Lenny followed her onto the show and planned to buy Dave out. As soon as he had control of the show, he planned to kick Krissy to the curb. Something snapped. She decided the only chance she had was to kill him. I couldn't help but feel a little sorry for her.

When Sheriff Daniels finished, Dave let out a low whistle. "Crikey. Didn't see that one coming."

Greg explained in light of the morning's detour, the authorities had agreed to postpone filming of the zip-line finale until tomorrow. He suggested we all take the day off.

Dave walked out of the bright conference room with his arm wrapped around Sheriff Daniels, asking about whether he could shoot footage of Krissy in jail. Imagine the ratings.

A call came in for Greg. He excused himself, hurrying to take it in his office. On his way out the door, he stopped and whispered in my ear, "Be sure to come see me before you leave. I need to talk to you about something."

Great. What did he want to see me for? Did he hate my piece? That would likely solidify my firing because he'd obviously already figured out that I was terrified of heights and pretty much everything else in nature. I could hear him now. "Sorry, Meg, but you're not cut out for this job."

Leaf ambled his way out of the conference room behind Greg. "No hard feelings, you know?" He paused and twisted his long, unruly dreads around a finger. "I thought you were trying to stir things up. Didn't want me to buy into the show or something."

"So you were going to invest in the show?"

"Yeah. I've got some cash to spend. Still might. Andrew and me have been talking about how to make it more green. We'll see. I wouldn't have pegged Krissy as a killer. That's deep. Really deep." He flashed two fingers in the air. "Peace."

That left Alicia, Andrew, and me alone. They sat with their backs to the wall of windows, their chairs touching. The camera!

I reached into my purse and retrieved the GoPro camera I'd found at Table Mountain. "Hey, I think this is yours." I slid the camera across the table to Andrew.

He held it toward the lights and examined it. "Where'd you find this?

I've been looking for it everywhere."

"Table Mountain."

I waited to see how they would respond. Andrew flipped the camera in his hand. Alicia darted her eyes from the camera to Andrew. They shared a look I couldn't decipher. She shrugged at Andrew and said to me, "Did you watch what was on there?"

"Yeah, but I don't get it. What was the big secret? I thought for sure you killed Lenny."

Andrew cleared his throat and looked at his feet. Alicia slugged him. "So did he."

"What do you mean?"

"Lenny and I had a brief—very brief—fling. Believe me, I'm not condoning what Krissy did, but that guy was such an ass. When I broke it off with him, he totally flipped. That's when I met Andy." She batted her eyes and reached for his hand. "He's been my rock. Wouldn't back down when Lenny tried to threaten me."

"Threaten you with what?"

Alicia inspected her nails as she continued. "Lenny and I met in Vegas on the same day I learned I didn't make the Olympic team. I wanted to blow off some steam and ended up drinking way too much. We got married. I had it annulled the next week. That's when he got nasty."

"That's the secret you were talking about."

"Yep. With the media swarming, I didn't want them to get wind of the fact Lenny was my ex. I knew it would blow up and I don't want that kind of attention. Of course, Andy here"—she slugged him again—"thought I had something to do with knocking him off. Got all worked up for nothing."

"So you did follow me out to Multnomah Falls?" I asked, trying to make eye contact with Andrew.

He refused to meet my eyes. Alicia slugged him a third time. He sat up and mumbled, "Yeah, sorry about that. I made a mistake. I didn't think she could really kill him, but I thought maybe they got in a fight and it was an accident..." He trailed off. "I really didn't mean to hurt you or anything. I wanted to scare you off so you'd drop it. I'd do anything for this woman." Leaning in, he kissed Alicia on the lips.

It was a sweet sentiment, if it weren't for the fact he'd run me off the road.

"What about my files?" I asked Alicia. "Did you steal my notes and delete everything from my machine?"

She pulled her ponytail loose. Her hair fell to her shoulders. She shook it free. It softened her face. "Sorry about that. I thought maybe you found out about the marriage, so I grabbed the notes you'd gathered on me before Sheriff Daniels took my statement. I didn't touch your computer, though; that must have been Krissy. Are we cool?" Alicia asked, standing and grabbing Andrew's hand.

"We're cool. Good luck tomorrow."

"Thanks." She smiled. "Doesn't matter anyway. I've already won." Looping her arm through Andrew's, they left.

*Time to face the music.* I wondered if I should save myself the embarrassment and clean out my desk before I talked to Greg.

Unfortunately, en route to my desk, Greg spotted me and waved me into his office.

"Meg, listen, I'm sorry to do this to you..." He tapped a pencil on his desk, looking like he was searching for the perfect word before he continued.

I put my head in my left hand and leaned forward on his desk. "Oh, no."

Greg looked at me in surprise. "Oh, no—what?"

"You're firing me, aren't you?" I tried to hold back tears.

He flicked my forehead with the pencil. "What?"

"I'm sorry. I know I haven't done a great job. I'm really trying. I swear I am."

"Meg. Stop. I'm not firing you. Come on, I'm not an idiot." He pulled a box of tissues from his desk and handed me one.

I wiped my nose. "Huh?"

"Look, I knew you were an outdoor novice when I hired you, but I trusted my instincts." Pulling a stack of paper from a pile on his desk, he held up a copy of my feature. "My instincts weren't wrong. This is great, Meg. Really great stuff."

"You knew? The whole time?" I twisted the tissue around my finger.

"Please, no extreme sportsperson wears that much pink. Also not breaking in your hiking boots was a dead giveaway."

I threw my head on my hand, feeling heat spreading through my cheeks. "Okay, I know. I'm sorry. I might have fudged my experience a little, but I swear I love this job and I'm going to sign up for some outdoor training. One of the Crag Rats invited me to come to one of their sessions."

"That's a good idea because you're going to be taking on even more responsibility."

My eyes must have been the size of baseballs. "What do you mean?"

"Mitch isn't coming back. During his recovery he finally finished a novel he's been working on for years. He pitched and sold it, all in a week."

"Wow. That's amazing."

"Yeah, well, that means you'll be covering more of his stuff. I'm going to divide projects throughout the team. I don't really have much more to offer you in terms of salary right now. Ad sales continue to be slow."

"That's okay," I blurted out. "I'd love to cover more features." Actually, I could really use a salary bump, too, but the fact that he wasn't throwing me out the door was enough for the moment.

"I have some"—he struggled over his words—"some business to

take care of out of the country." He tapped the desk with his pencil again, this time so hard it snapped in half. I watched the top half roll on the desk and fall to the ground. Greg made no move to pick it up.

"I don't want to go, but I don't have a choice. In any event, I had originally planned on writing a second piece for the next issue about what happened with Lenny. It's not our normal gig, but what an opportunity. Not to sound like Dave, but I think we could see our biggest single-issue sales ever with this one."

"Better ad sales maybe?"

He laughed. "Keep your fingers crossed. We're closing in on deadline, and I'm not going to make it. I was hoping you'd be willing to finish my piece. I know it'll be extra work, but you've been right in the thick of it. Plus it'll give you two bylines. What do you think?"

Before I could stop myself, I leaped to my feet and ran around the desk. I threw my arms around him and screamed, "Thank you! Yes! Of course I'll write the piece. This is all so much better than getting fired."

Realizing I'd hugged my boss, I clapped my hand over my mouth and stood back. "I'm soooo sorry. I didn't mean to hug you."

Greg threw his head back and laughed. "Oh, Meg, you're really something. Not to worry. Glad I can count on you. The final piece is due tomorrow—2,000 words."

"I'm on it."

"Great, I'll look forward to reading it. See you in a couple weeks."

"Weeks? What about the zip-line tomorrow?"

A slight frown turned at Greg's lips. He shook his head. "Don't think I'm going to make it." He didn't offer any more information. I waved goodbye and returned to my desk.

What a week. I'd solved a murder and secured my first two bylines in an international magazine. Now I'd better get writing.

# THIRTY-THREE

Three weeks later, with an editorial copy of the next issue tucked under my arm, I trotted down the sidewalk to meet Matt, Jill, and Will at Deschutes. We'd hit a stretch of summer weather in late May. Patio tables cluttered the sidewalks with happy diners basking in the warmth and lingering light.

At 7:00 P.M., the sun remained above the horizon. It would be two hours before it set. The sound of laughter and clinking cocktail glasses filled the air. A block from the pub, I could smell the hickory scent of grilled meat.

"Over here, Meg!" Jill called from one of the wooden outdoor picnic tables on the far side of the restaurant. Her satin scoop-necked tank top shimmered in the sun. A collection of silver bracelets dangled on her delicate wrists as she waved me over.

She and Will sat facing the sun on one side of the picnic table. Matt scooted next to the open-windowed wall. I squeezed the magazine tighter under my arm as I squished beside him.

"What do you have there?" Matt asked, eyeing the roll of paper sticking out from under my arm.

I threw my hand in the air to stop him from grabbing it. "Wait, I need a beer first."

"I've got a pitcher coming," Jill said, squinting in the sunlight. She reached into her purse and pulled out a pair of purple-rimmed sunglasses.

Will made a sound of disgust under his breath. "Beer. Really?"

"Don't worry. I ordered you a martini," she said, putting her sunglasses on.

Adjusting his tie, Will slid his hand way too high on her thigh and let it rest there. "That's my girl."

*Gag*. But I refused to let Will Barrington ruin my moment.

Our drinks arrived a minute later. The waitress sloshed the pitcher of beer and three glasses on the middle of the table. She held a martini in her hand and glanced at Will. "I'm guessing this is for the suit?"

Matt poured pints for Jill and me. I unrolled the magazine and sat on it to flatten the edges out.

Holding his beer in the air, Matt turned to me. "We all have our drinks. Are you going to spill now?"

"Everyone hold up your glasses," I said, grabbing my beer. "A toast to you! I can't believe how lucky I am to have friends like you. We helped solve a murder."

We all clinked glasses.

"Yay for us!" cheered Jill.

Taking a swig, I set my glass down and slammed the magazine on the table. "My first—wait for it—not one, but two bylines! I couldn't have done it without you all."

"That's awesome, Meg!" Jill reached over and kissed my cheek across the table.

Matt scanned the masthead. "Here it is! Margaret Reed, pages 32 and 48.

Congrats!"

Will loosened his tie when Matt passed the magazine around. He leafed through my articles and said, "Not bad."

"Look at your cute photo," Jill said, pointing to a one-inch square headshot of me grinning at the bottom of the story. "And it says you're the newest addition to *Northwest Extreme* and an intrepid adventurer. Nice!"

The story on page 32 was a one-page synopsis of the murder of Lenny Ray and subsequent arrest of Krissy Miles. She was arraigned on one count of first-degree murder and one count of attempted murder. Her case was due to go before a jury next month. My second story was a much longer and detailed account of the entire *Race the States* crew and experience. In my humble opinion, seeing the photos running alongside it showcased the majestic, untamed beauty of this historic part of the world I called home. I was pleased with the end result and ecstatic to see my work in print for the first time.

After finishing their drinks, Jill and Will excused themselves. They were due to make an appearance at a cocktail party hosted by their law firm. Matt ordered us another celebratory round.

He toasted me again, holding his glass frozen in midair; he grabbed my right hand and gently massaged the scar etched in it like a lifeline. "Your hand's all healed."

"I know. When I got the stitches removed the doctor couldn't believe how quickly it had healed. Gam, of course, is convinced it's all the Reiki she's been doing on it." I fingered the scar. "The doctor says this will improve over time but will always be there. Kind of how I feel about Pops, you know?"

Matt circled the scar with his finger. The lightness of his touch gave me goose bumps. "I think it's a mark of how resilient you are. You're one tough cookie, Megs."

We drank our beers, watching the theater crowd across the street, in an eclectic assortment of outfits from cutoff jeans to floor-length dresses, pour outside for a hit of the evening sun at intermission. Matt became quiet, with a far-off look in his eyes.

"What are you thinking about?"

He sighed and brought his attention to the present. "So many things, Megs. I have something I need to talk to you about, but I'm not sure you're going to want to hear it."

*Oh, no! Why now? Why ruin my perfect night?* I knew what Matt wanted to say to me, but I wasn't ready to hear it. Why couldn't our relationship stay the same for a while? We were young. Too young. I had way more to figure out and I wasn't ready to change our relationship yet.

"Matt, listen... I—I'm in such a great space tonight. Can we enjoy it for one night?"

I thought he might cry; his eyes welled and he looked away. "Of course, Megs. Believe me. There's nothing I want more than to see you happy. But what I've learned—well, we're going to have to address it soon."

"Learned?"

"Forget it. You're right. Let's enjoy this amazing night." He grabbed his pint glass.

"Wait. Now I have to know. What do you mean 'learned'? What did you learn?"

"Are you sure?"

"Yes. Tell me."

"It's about your dad."

My heart thumped in my chest. "What about him?"

"I have proof his death wasn't an accident."

# A LETTER FROM THE AUTHOR

Huge thanks for reading Meg's story! I hope you felt like you were off on an adventure with her. If you want to hear about my new books and bonus content, you can sign up for my newsletter!

www.stormpublishing.co/ellie-alexander

If you've enjoyed Meg's adventures—or perhaps misadventures—I'd love it if you would take a minute to share your review so other readers can grab a mocha and hang with Meg and her friends!

I am so grateful you picked up this book. I know there are so many distractions these days, and the fact that you spend your time in the pages of a book makes my heart happy. Here's to more armchair adventures from the comfort of your couch!

Ellie Alexander

www.elliealexander.co

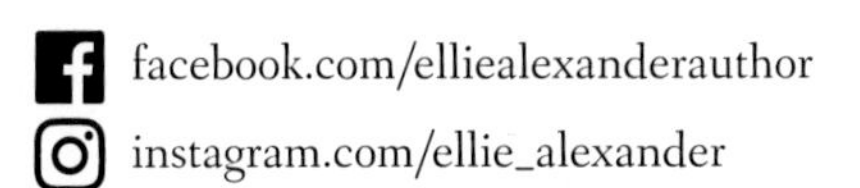

## MEG'S ADVENTURE TIPS

**Rule One—Function before fashion.** Sure, those pink-laced boots Meg scored were cute, but when it comes to choosing a hiking boot, think fit and function before fashion. New boots should feel stiff at first, but will soften as you break them in. Greg recommends wearing your boots indoors with socks before venturing outside. Once you've worn your boots around the house, try short trips to the grocery store or a walk around the neighborhood. Be sure the boots aren't rubbing or pinching. If you notice any hot spots, take them back to the store. Most outdoor stores and shoe repair shops have stretching equipment that can fix the problem. If the fit feels good, slowly extend the time you spend in them. After a few weeks you should be ready to hit the trail. Meg learned the hard way that not breaking in boots can be murder on your feet. Take the time to do it right.

**Rule Two—Pack light.** Regardless of whether you plan on a short two-mile jaunt or an eight-mile trek, it's imperative to be prepared. Meg learned the balance of packing just the essentials. Leave hiking guides and bulky clothing behind. A day pack should be comfortable to wear—shoot for between ten and twelve pounds. Your pack should contain: a map, compass (or GPS unit), matches, a safety whistle, an emergency blanket, a first-aid kit, a flashlight, a pocketknife, snacks, and plenty of water. Plan to drink two full water bottles for every hour of exercise. If you're hiking in the elements, be sure to bring raingear and a change of clothing. Most importantly, always inform a friend or neighbor where you're going and the anticipated time you expect to return home.

**Rule Three—Friends in high places.** Meg's lucky to have friends around to help her out of tight spots. Maybe she should have listened to Jill's advice and steered clear of cliff faces. But now that she's had a taste of the great outdoors, she's committed to learning all she can and being prepared for her next pursuit. Meg's gearing up for her newest *Northwest Extreme* assignment by training with the Crag Rats—talk about having friends in high places. She'll be taking a wilderness survival class with the Crag Rats, where she'll learn skills that just may save her life. From basic hiking safety tips to how to build an emergency shelter, the Crag Rats will help Meg get up to speed and ready to hit the slopes. Outdoor survival classes are an excellent option whether you're a novice or seasoned climber. You never know when a storm might hit, or if you'll have to face off with a cougar. Most outdoor stores, hiking clubs, and even the Forest Service offer inexpensive training courses that will give you a bag of tricks for the next time you hit the trail.

# MEG'S A MURDER ON THE MOUNTAIN SCENIC LOOP

Just outside the city limits of Portland, Oregon, a world of adventure awaits. You can follow Meg's scenic loop and challenge yourself by trekking to the top of one of the Columbia River Gorge's stunning peaks, or simply drive along the meandering historic highway and soak in the breathtaking views.

**Stop One—Angel's Rest.** Head east on I-84 from Portland, Oregon, to Troutdale. Take Exit 17 and follow the signs for the Historic Columbia River Gorge Highway. This meandering, scenic route will take you along the banks of the Sandy River, up to Crown Point Vista for jaw-dropping views of the Gorge, and eventually wind its way through old-growth forests and waterfalls to the trailhead. Angel's Rest is located just after Bridal Veil Falls. There are no fees required for day use, but parking can be tricky on busy summer weekends.

This moderate, 4.8-mile, up-and-back hike climbs 1,450 feet in elevation. Be sure to bring water. While this trail is a relatively easy climb (even for families with children), there are some steep switchbacks that might have less-seasoned hikers catching their breath. The payoff is an incredible view from the summit. A 270-degree view of the Columbia River, Washington mountains, and Beacon Rock await you.

**Stop Two—Multnomah Falls.** From Angel's Rest, continue east on the Historic Columbia River Gorge Highway for approximately two miles. Multnomah Falls is a must-see for any trip to the Pacific Northwest. As one of the region's most popular tourist destinations, you'll find locals, families, and international travelers regardless of the time of year. The Multnomah Falls Lodge at the base of the falls is a great stopping point to grab a snack or souvenir in the gift shop, stop for a bathroom break, or stay for a leisurely meal in the dining room.

Then take the short, paved quarter-mile hike to the Benson Bridge, where you'll be treated with views of the 542-foot upper falls and a dramatic 69-foot drop to the lower falls. Fair warning: You might get wet. The mighty falls kicks out a spray as you enter the mist zone around it. Or if you're feeling more energetic, lace up your hiking boots and trek another 1.1 miles along a steep, narrow trail to the head of the falls. It's well worth the climb.

**Stop Three—Bridge of the Gods.** After cooling off at Multnomah Falls, jump back in the car and follow the historic highway east until it connects with I-84. After approximately eight miles you'll see signs for the Bridge of the Gods and Cascade Locks. This steel cantilever bridge connects Oregon and Washington. Be sure to bring some change. The bridge is tolled. If you're not a fan of heights, like Meg, don't look down. But really, the bridge isn't all that high and it offers a close-up view of the Columbia River and Washington foothills.

**Stop Four—Table Mountain.** Table Mountain is a stop for serious hikers. At 3,417 feet in elevation, it's one of the tallest peaks on the Washington side of the Gorge, and one of the most difficult climbs. Meg took a wrong turn here and never made it to the heart-stopping, sheer cliff face that climbers must ascend on the way to the summit. An eight-mile round-trip hike, Table Mountain greets hikers with a 360-degree view from the top. If you're up for the challenge, bring a day pack and plenty of water. The trail is accessible from the Aldrich Butte power line road, which is 4.5 miles from the Bridge of the Gods. Note: This is not a hike for families and small children.

**Stop Five—Beacon Rock.** A relatively easy and extremely rewarding hike, Beacon Rock is a short distance from the Bridge of the Gods. Follow Highway 14 west for 7.4 miles and Beacon Rock State Park will be on your left. There's a parking lot (fees required), which, like its counterparts across the river, can be busy on weekends. The 848-foot freestanding rock is carved with paths that switch back and forth to the top. Guardrails and handrails line the path, making it a popular destination for tourists and families. Be sure to watch any small children, as they could potentially sneak through or under the railings. It's just a little under a mile to the top of the monolith and literally at every turn you'll be greeted with gorgeous views of the Columbia River.

**Stop Six—Deschutes Brewery.** Meg and her friends like to toast to a successful day out in the wild with a pint from Deschutes. Located in the swanky Pearl District, stop by this neighborhood pub for a cold one. The pub is open daily for drinks and dining. It's a great spot to linger with friends. Meg's favorite year-round brew is Hop Henge IPA. Pints up!

# ACKNOWLEDGMENTS

This book was the first mystery I ever wrote—the book that launched dozens more. This story has held a special place in my heart for many years, and I've wanted to come back to Meg's journey for quite a while. It feels like reconnecting with old friends to be in Meg's world again. I had no idea what I was doing when I wrote this book. So much so that when I got to the murder, I naively called the Hood River County Sheriff's office to ask who would show up at the scene of the crime. They were incredibly helpful and connected me with the Crag Rats. I feel like I got a crash course in mountain rescue and crime scene dos and don'ts! It was a huge gift at a very early stage in my mystery writing career.

A special shoutout to my dad, who hiked Angel's Rest with me multiple times, stopping often to let me take copious notes and photos to use in the book.

And a huge thank you to the team at Storm for re-releasing the entire series! I hope you enjoy this Meg refresh!

Made in United States
North Haven, CT
19 September 2025

73049733R00178